HIS WILD SEDUCTION

A WILD BILLIONAIRE ROMANCE

WILD BILLIONAIRE ROMANCE
BOOK 3

C.D. GORRI

C.D. GORRI

HIS WILD SEDUCTION

A Billionaire Romance Novel
Wild Billionaire Romance Book 3
By
C.D. Gorri

Before you begin sign up for my newsletter here:
SUBSCRIBE HERE

DEDICATION

To everyone who's ever carried a torch. Sometimes it's worth the wait and the heartache. Hang in there.

Xoxo,

C.D. Gorri

These wild billionaire playboys are used to getting their way...

There isn't much money can't buy, especially when it comes to pleasure. But can these curvy women tame these billionaire beasts and win their love? Or will their souls be sucked into oblivion by the wanton bliss their bodies crave more and more with every surrender?

Each of our heroes wears a mask on the outside to face the world, but his disguise comes off when he runs into the one female who makes his blood run hot. Need and possessive passion abound in these books, but our heroes know only one way to control their desires.

Will they f*ck the feeling they see as weakness out of

their systems, or will their needs only grow more wild with every touch, kiss, and plunge into ecstasy with the object of his affections?

Our Billionaire Heroes

Adrik Volkov
Marat Volkov
Josef Aziz
Andres Ramirez

Content Warnings
(3rd try…)

This series has profanity, graphic, steamy scenes, violence, homicide, talk of deceased relatives, references to sexual assault and abuse (not by the MCs), mention of domestic violence (not perpetrated by MCs), mention of suicide, alcohol consumption, misogyny (not the MCs), questionable morals, hurtful past, manipulations, fake relationships, lies, revenge, forced marriages, very bad decisions, and romantic obsessions that may be unhealthy. The FMC works at a shelter for abused women and children.

This is a fictional story with fictional characters. This is not real life.

Always take care of your mental, emotional, and physical self because you are important.

P.S.

For those who asked Adrik is pronounced Ade-drick and Marat is Meh-Rut. Happy reading!

HIS WILD SEDUCTION

Some debts demand hefty payment.
Some loves are too wild to set free.

Meredith Gray had no choice but to meet with the last man on earth she ever wanted to see again. He ruined her once, and now he was threatening the livelihood of the thousands of people employed at her stepfather's company.

The last time she saw him, he'd lied to her face and broke her heart. Would she remain unscathed this time around? Meredith could only hope.

Josef Aziz had a reputation for stealth and lethality. After he was dishonorably discharged from the military, he found himself in the employ of the Dark Wolf. Nowadays, Josef had his own security firm, with Volkov Industries as his only client. Worth billions, he could have retired already, but with no family and no wife, there was no reason to.

Once upon a time, he thought he'd have all of that and more. But betrayal was a hard lesson he learned at the hands of the woman who was now at his mercy. He never thought he would see her again, but now he had her right where he wanted her.

She needed help only he could deliver, but seeing her beg was not enough. He needed her so addicted she could not survive without his touch.

There were no lengths he wouldn't go to secure his seduction of her.

PREFACE: JOSEF

When Meredith reached out to Volkov Industries with a request to meet to discuss terms regarding the default on the loan her father had taken out with his business as collateral, I was the one who received the message.

After all, I was the one who approved the loan. Backing it with my own personal money as collateral.

It wasn't because I believed Gray Corps was a good investment, or that they could afford to repay the loan. And it wasn't because I thought the company could improve any of my own, or the Volkov brother's holdings.

I had one reason to set up such a guaranteed disaster.

Meredith Gray.

She was the reason. She was the only woman who'd ever brought me to my knees, and it wasn't a past I liked to remember.

But this time, our positions were reversed.

This time, I held all the cards.

I knew the second I walked into the boardroom I'd do anything to keep Little Red from getting the upper hand again.

Fuck.

I didn't mean to call her by the nickname I gave her all those years ago, but I couldn't actually help myself.

That gorgeous mane of red was fastened at her nape, making me fight a losing battle with a smirk. The style should have looked severe. She'd always hated her hair, but it was the thing I first noticed about her.

She'd been years too young for me. A senior in high school, but one with an old soul. Meredith wasn't like other girls. I could see it in her eyes.

And that hair. That fucking glorious mane of red was something she could never tame. It was as wild and stunning then as it was now.

I swallowed hard, tamping down on my cursed reaction to this woman. This siren. This breaker of men.

Her emerald eyes sparked surprise as I entered the space. Surprise turned to anger as I took my seat across from her.

"Josef," she said my name, and I had to close my eyes at the emotions roiling through me.

"What are you doing here?" she asked.

"I represent Volkov Industries and I am calling in your loan *in full*, Miss Gray."

"What? You can't!"

"I can. And I am," I replied, fury feeding my desire to see her squirm.

My gaze roamed her face, absorbing the shock, taking in the changes time had made. It had been fifteen years since I'd seen her. She was little more than a child then. But Goddamnit, how I'd loved her.

The curve of her lips was the same. But there were fine lines around her mouth.

Not smile lines.

These were different.

Sadder.

The dead organ inside my chest squeezed, and I nearly grunted at the pain of it.

Why was she sad? Did someone hurt her?

Fuck. I shouldn't be having thoughts like that. Besides, I was the one hurting her. That was the whole fucking plan, wasn't it?

Squeeze her father by tearing apart the thing he loved most, his company, and squeeze her in the process.

So yeah, Meredith was supposed to be upset. But I wasn't supposed to care.

"Where is your father? I should be discussing this with him."

"He's in the hospital. Heart attack."

I paused.

Heart attack? Why the fuck wasn't I notified?

"I am sorry, I hadn't heard."

"Why would you?" she spat the question.

My phone beeped, and I looked down to see a message from Adrik.

Oh shit. Marat's daughter was just born.

A mixture of disbelief, happiness and envy filled me, but happiness won out, outweighing the others. I had no family of my own, and the Volkov brothers were the closest thing to it.

Adrik and Marat were the family I chose, who chose me. I was sorry I'd missed the part where Marat had gone rogue wolf and hunted the motherfuckers who'd sabotaged one of the Volkov mines.

But since I'd trained the man myself, I believed every single rumor of the Devil Wolf I'd heard since then.

Well done, brother.

It was a good thing Marat was younger than Adrik, or he'd have given his brother's rep a run for his money.

I smirked.

It was about fucking time Marat realized what he was capable of. And how very interesting that a woman had shown him the way.

"Is that a smile for another life you ruined?"

I flicked my gaze to Meredith, schooling my face to show no emotions.

She looked hostile, angry.

And I was confused.

"You can't mean you think *I* ruined *your* life, Little Red."

What the fuck was she talking about? I was there all those years ago, rooted to the spot we'd promised to meet.

I'd waited hours only to have her father come with some shitty little note from her saying she didn't mean any of it.

Not the declarations of love.

Not the giving of herself to me in the moonlit garden behind her bedroom.

Not the promise to leave with me.

Franklin Gray promised not to press charges against me if I left that night, so I did. I'd been young. Stupid. Not the powerful man I was today.

But none of that explained why she was staring daggers at me, pissed as all hell.

Goddamnit.

She was still so damn pretty when she was angry. Her emerald eyes spat green fire at me, and that red hair seemed to glow like flames.

My cock stirred and only through extraordinary self-control did I manage to sit there seemingly unaffected.

"Ha! You're the one who walked out, and I was left to pick up the pieces," she said, stunning the fucking shit out of me.

I frowned.

I had a feeling maybe neither of us had the full story. Something was not right in the way things had gone down all those years ago.

True, it had taken me some time to find a weakness in Gray Corp.

Years, actually.

But once I'd fooled her father into taking out a loan at a bank I happened to have a controlling interest in, the rest was easy.

It just took patience. Eight months to be precise. But that was nothing after I'd spent the past fifteen years in torment, waiting for the chance to pay back the woman who almost broke me.

Goddamn her for still looking so beautiful.

Once upon a time, I was mad for her. But she threw me away.

I'd been a fun distraction. Just something she'd used to scratch an itch. She'd wanted a bad boy between her legs to piss Daddy off, and I stupidly ran to fill the position.

Once upon a time, Meredith Gray used me.

Now it was my turn.

PROLOGUE: MEREDITH

"Ha! You're the one who walked out, and I was left to pick up the pieces."

I regretted my outburst immediately.

I shouldn't have said all that. But I just couldn't believe my eyes.

After all this time, I was sitting in the same room with him.

Josef Aziz.

The man who broke my heart. Only, he wasn't the same man I knew.

This Josef looked harder, older, a little scary, to be honest.

His thick hair was the same rich mahogany color I remembered. He wore it shaved on the sides and long on top, carefully combed away from his chiseled face. The full beard was new.

Meticulously trimmed and combed, it did nothing to detract from his appearance. No other man affected me the way he did.

I wonder if it is as soft as it looks. I wonder if he'll let me touch it.

Oh my god! Stop it.

Fifteen years ago, Josef Aziz was the most mesmerizing man I'd ever met. Larger than life, he'd exuded a confidence I could only have ever dreamed of possessing.

Unfortunately, all of that still held true today.

Josef was every bit as intriguing now as he'd been before. The suit he wore was tailored to fit his muscular body. They didn't make jackets with shoulders that wide off the rack. A man his size, with the obvious wealth he now had, would definitely have a private tailor see to his needs.

He looked good. Rich. Handsome. Fool that I was, I imagined what his wife or girlfriend looked like.

She would have to have been equally stunning. A man like that did not have to settle. Someone tall, thin, well-dressed—*the total opposite of me.*

Why that thought should send sharp slices of pain shooting through me was something I didn't want to look closely at. Hurt and jealousy had no business at this meeting.

But the past was a tricky thing to let go of. I clasped my hands together beneath the table, trying for a calm I didn't feel.

Once upon a time, I'd been in love with Josef Aziz.

Foolish girl that I was, I thought he loved me, too. But that had been a lie.

Fifteen years hadn't dulled the pain of his rejection and abandonment.

God, he'd walked away so easily. I wanted to hate him for that. Maybe I did.

I wished I had a better story about how I spent my life after he left. I wish I could just brush it off and say it was all forgotten now. Bygones and all that.

But the hurt was as fresh now as it was then.

How did a woman get over the first and only man to break her heart?

Was there a secret society? A book of how to instructions?

Goddamnit.

I wanted to slap his face. I wanted to kiss his lips. I wished I could close my eyes and count to ten, but I couldn't break eye contact.

He was staring at me. Looking for something. I wasn't sure what.

The night I'd learned of his betrayal was ingrained in my brain for eternity and each horrifying image was replaying itself like one of those little tourist flip books you bought at a museum or gift store.

Yes, I'd thought about him over the years. But I never expected to see him again.

What am I doing here?

I inhaled a deep breath and squeezed my hands on my lap beneath the wide boardroom table. I couldn't afford to show weakness. Not where he was concerned.

But tell that to my heart.

It seemed that useless muscle was doomed to repeat past mistakes.

Oh, it quickened the second I recognized him. Stuttering in my chest like it had a mind of its own.

Why should he still affect me after all this time?

Squeezing my hands again, to the point of pain, I gritted my teeth, betraying no emotion.

Josef's dark gaze zeroed in on me. He was every bit as intense as I remembered.

The only difference was I could no longer tell what he was thinking. And the not knowing was driving me mad.

My gut twisted, every instinct I had screamed at me to get the hell out of there. To run while I could. To get away from his maddening presence and the pain of our past that kept slapping me in the face every second that ticked by.

And yet, despite my natural instincts for self-preservation, I couldn't move. It all seemed surreal.

I'd just been notified Franklin, the man I'd once thought was my father, had just gotten out of surgery.

He'd been moved to the Intensive Care Unit after a heart attack sent him to the hospital late last night.

But Franklin Gray was not my father by birth.

Yes, it was his name on the birth certificate. And yes, I suppose he'd raised me after my mother's death.

Well, not really him, more like the nannies and bodyguards he'd hired to watch over me.

Including Josef.

I had a rather complicated history.

My mother was already pregnant when she conned Franklin, a well-known tycoon, into marrying her.

But anyone with eyes in their head would know I wasn't his. Both my mother and stepfather were thin, tall, with dark hair and brown eyes.

I was barely five foot three, curvy as fuck, with bright red hair—*the bane of my existence*—and green eyes surrounded by copper eyelashes. I had a smattering of pale freckles across my nose and shoulders and on my stomach. I absolutely abhorred them when I was a child.

The point was it was obvious he was my stepfather, not my bio dad whose name I still didn't know. But the embarrassing truth of it was I didn't know he wasn't my father until the day I turned eighteen.

I closed my eyes tightly, pushing away that terrible memory.

Franklin Gray might not have donated any biological matter to my birth, but he was all the father I'd known at the time. I had no idea who my real father was. His identity was a total mystery.

The trick my mother played, hoping to pass me off as his daughter backfired. He found out and treated her differently afterwards. It proved too much for her to handle.

Goddamnit. I hated it when those thoughts consumed me. Grief over my parentage was something I'd spent years in counseling sessions to come to terms with, and I was in a good place now.

Really, I was.

But sometimes I wondered if I wouldn't have been better left in a firehouse.

Yeah, it was unkind, and I probably sounded like a spoiled little brat, but I had my reasons.

No one knew what happened the night I turned eighteen. No one but me and the old man currently in the ICU.

Josef had already abandoned me when my father

drunkenly tore my shirt and slapped my face, calling me a whore and threatening to take what I'd already given to another man.

I'd wanted to hit him back. But I was afraid. So, I ran outside into the night blindly.

Not far, of course. How could I?

I wound up in one of the guesthouses on our property, and that was where I'd stayed.

The funny thing about traumatic events, like your stepfather slapping you and touching you inappropriately, was that sometimes you doubted yourself.

Sometimes your mind played tricks on you, and you wondered if all that really happened. It was like an out-of-body experience.

Did Dad really say I was a whore? Just like my mother.

Did he slap me across the face?

Did he really tear my shirt and grab me?

And even after all that, did I really just not say anything back?

Self-loathing had me swallowing, but I managed not to puke all over the pristine boardroom.

A man walked in, handing Josef a folder, and placing one in front of me as well.

"Take a moment to look over the numbers, Meredith," Josef said, his voice grave.

I pretended to read over the papers Josef's team of

lawyer sharks had prepared, but I was stuck back in time.

I'd had to wait until early the morning after that scene with Franklin before I could bribe a maid, Gretchen was her name, to pack a small bag with my clothes, my license and passport.

I also asked her to get the few pieces of my mother's jewelry I had on my dresser, the small picture I had of her by my nightstand, and my wallet, which held a couple of hundred bucks and a few credit cards.

She did it and I handed her a stack of twenties after she met me on the edge of the property where another member of the house staff waited with a car to drive me to the airport.

I flew to Europe on my eighteenth birthday. I spent the first few months frugally backpacking across the continent.

Yeah, I supposed I went a little wild. I started using my mother's maiden name as my own. Meredith Blake, not Gray.

And I didn't return to the states. Not for years.

When I did come back, I went to a small suburb outside of Washington, D.C., I found a cheap apartment and I got a job. I started working at a women's shelter, which had only just recently expanded, bringing me back to New Jersey a few months ago.

I should have known better than to come back to

my home state. Franklin found me weeks after I'd returned and sent a private investigator to request a meeting.

I'd refused, and my father, *er,* stepfather left me alone. I thought that was that.

And it was.

Until last night.

CHAPTER ONE
MEREDITH

S pring was unpredictable in the Northeast.
Always had been.
The trip to Manhattan to meet Josef Aziz in a boardroom in the imposing building that was Volkov Towers had been long.

Morristown, New Jersey, was not terribly far, but traffic sucked.

The room itself was comfortable enough. Masculine furniture made of dark stained wood, wrought iron, and leather with neutral beige walls that were softened somehow by the lighting comprised the interior.

There'd been tall, fresh floral arrangements in the hallway. The scent they gave off was light and pleasant. But there were no flowers or plants inside the room. No sign of life at all.

The temperature had to be set at seventy degrees. Maybe slightly higher. But the hum of the vent told me they were filtering the air, which made me relax.

I hated the idea of breathing stale air.

Still, I was glad I'd decided against wearing a bulky sweater over my outfit. The dress was the most formal thing I had back in my Jersey City apartment.

My current wardrobe consisted of mostly jeans and cotton shirts on my off days, and plain blouses and slacks bought on sale at Marshall's or TJ Maxx, or at a consignment shop.

God, I loved those.

It had been a long time since I could afford anything really worthy of Volkov Towers. Longer still since I'd bought anything not red tagged for clearance.

But I knew quality and I could bargain hunt with the best of them. When you had curves like I did, cheaply made clothes were easy to spot. They hung wrong and brought attention to problem areas like my thick waist and soft belly.

Josef wouldn't know that, though. He didn't know anything about me.

But that didn't matter. I wasn't there for me.

I was still having a difficult time accepting this was all really happening. That I was sitting there. At a conference table. With him.

Josef Aziz. Blast from my past. Taker of my virginity.

Breaker of my heart. Reminder of times I'd much rather forget.

Suddenly, Pat Benatar's *Heartbreaker* played in my head at full volume.

Once upon a time, Josef Aziz destroyed me.

But I was still standing.

Different. Changed. But still here.

He probably thought I was the same vapid girl with too much money, and not enough scruples to know when a man was toying with her.

But I was not that teenaged girl anymore. No longer bright-eyed and naïve.

The world was a rough place.

Cruel at times. Brilliant at others.

But there was one constant truth I'd learned over the past fifteen years.

No one left the table without paying their bill.

I'd seen that very thing on a sign in a restaurant in Naples, Italy.

It was a shitty metaphor for life, and my translation was probably bad, but the meaning still held.

Fifteen years ago, I thought Josef had left my table without paying the bill. But time catches up with everyone.

Judging from the hard glint in his once whiskey warm irises, I'd have to say he paid for something, alright.

I hardened my heart against the sudden concern that welled inside of me. He didn't deserve my compassion. And I couldn't afford to feel it.

Not there. Not when he was about to takeover Gray Corps and send thousands of people home without jobs by the end of the business day.

"So, let's begin. Did your father discuss the terms of the loan with you? Do you understand what is at stake?" Josef asked.

"Does it matter? We can't pay it back. I checked with his accountants this morning."

"Then Sigma International will seize control of all the assets, properties, and holdings of Gray Corps, under Volkov Industries, starting when the clock strikes twelve. You best prepare yourself, Miss Gray," Josef said coolly.

I glanced at the clock. It was already ten AM. Anger filled me.

How could he be so damn uncaring?

"Prepare? What about the employees? We have thousands of people working for us! You can't just—"

My chest heaved, I could hardly breathe. I was so mad. I was damn near spitting.

"All employee contracts will be terminated within the first twenty-four hours of the takeover. Those were the terms of the loan. Your father should have read them more carefully," he said.

So much time had passed, but this was the moment I realized I had no idea who Josef was anymore.

That realization hurt.

"What happened to you, Josef?"

His dark eyes flashed, and I knew I'd made a mistake, referencing our turbulent past.

But I couldn't help it.

The man I knew and fell in love with could never just hurt thousands of people with no sign of conscience.

"Of all people, *you* are asking me that?"

Like it was preposterous. Like I was the one who'd left him standing, waiting for hours in the dark.

"Look, I only became aware of this situation last night, if you could just give me some time—"

"There is no time, Meredith. Your father—"

"Stepfather," I corrected him.

"Stepfather? Since when?"

Josef's silence had me meeting his gaze boldly. Seemed like Mr. Know-It-All didn't know everything.

"Since always. I thought you knew," I replied and shrugged. "It doesn't matter. Whatever our past, the fact is Franklin's situation is precarious. His immediate future is uncertain. To answer your question, I learned of all this just last night. Franklin and I have been estranged for years. He sent for me after a long day of work, so I am sorry if I am not up to speed, but he barely told me about this loan, asking for my help, before he had a heart attack," I said, shouting the last.

Pressure. So much pressure, and all of it sitting on my chest.

When I thought about all the employees. Fired with no notice. Fuck, there had to be another way!

"Are you trying to tell me you are not involved with Gray Corp? Your name is on the employee list," Josef said, and I could tell he did not believe me.

I gritted my teeth.

Of course, my name was there. Franklin never took it off. He just kept paying me a check every week, depositing it into my account.

To date, I had over a million dollars in untouched money sitting in the bank.

Well, mostly untouched.

Occasionally, I withdrew funds to use in my line of work, but that was my business.

I owed neither Franklin nor Josef any explanation.

"That's correct. He's had me on payroll for years. I was not aware of him taking a loan. Last night was the first time I'd seen him in almost fifteen years. He contacted me, claiming it was a life or death situation. Shortly after I arrived, he had a heart attack. That's all I know. But you can't just put all those people out of work!"

Josef showed no reaction, and I had no idea if he believed me.

"In his absence, you have power of attorney?" Josef asked.

"According to what the lawyers told me, yes. I do."

"And his condition?"

"It's volatile. The doctors have assured me they would notify me if there was a change."

For the good of my own soul, I hoped for the best. Franklin Gray was not a good man. But I was a good woman. And I was working on forgiving him before it was too late.

"If you aren't involved in the business, why are you here now? Why do you even care, Meredith?"

I paused.

It was true, I had no love for my stepfather, though Josef apparently was unaware of that.

I'd already come to the conclusion that along with years of poor habits, the notice Franklin had received from the bank calling in his loan had proven too much for his stony heart. I was already at his home when it just gave out on him.

So yeah, I'd made calls to the lawyers and to Volkov Industries. Of course, I'd dialed 911 first and waited till after the subsequent trip to the hospital to contact everyone.

Franklin had needed emergency surgery, but the

doctors had given me no sign one way or another if he would survive.

Guilt, shame, and regret threatened to strangle me.

Whatever it was I felt over the past, I could not help but shoulder some of the blame for the strained relationship between my stepfather and me.

I didn't owe him anything, but I had the dire urge to make this right. Gray Corps employed thousands of people, and from what I'd read, Volkov Industries had a ruthless reputation for gutting businesses they took over.

What would happen to all those people?

Damn my stepfather for putting me in this situation. And damn Josef for being involved.

Fuck. Why, Franklin? Why did you have to do this to me?

"I want you to tell me what happened step by step," Josef said, breaking the silence.

I didn't see any other option. So, I started telling him.

"Franklin sent a private investigator to my apartment asking me to come to his office last night—"

"He sent a strange man?" Josef asked, jaw clenched so tight it was a wonder the vein at his temple didn't pop right out of his skin.

"Well, no," I replied, suddenly wary. "I mean, I'd met him before. He was the detective who found me when I came back to the states."

"No," Josef said, shaking his head and once again I was struck by how handsome he was. "Go back. Farther back."

I gritted my teeth harder. The past was not some place I visited much. It was too dark. Too painful.

He wanted me to relive it, did he? Well, he could go right to hell.

"Meredith, I am trying to offer you an out of all this. But unless you are honest with me, I will follow through with my plans to gut Gray Corps and lay off all its employees."

"You wouldn't," I gasped.

But he would.

The look in his eyes said as much.

"What do you want?" I asked.

"The truth about everything. We need to talk, Meredith."

"About what? Why do you even care about this? What do you want from me?"

"You seem to be concerned with your stepfather's employees. Start by telling me what you have to offer," he said.

My mouth opened and closed, eyebrows raised, and anger warred with total shock inside of me.

This fucker.

"I can't imagine I have anything you want, Mr. Aziz," I replied, trying for a formality I did not feel.

"Agree to disagree, Little Red. But, to streamline things, why don't you start by telling me what happened to you? Where have you been?"

"That has nothing to do with this," I began, but he interrupted me.

"It has everything to do with this," he growled.

"We're here to talk about Gray Corp."

"We are here to talk about whatever the fuck I want to talk about, Meredith," he replied. "And I want the truth. Now."

He wanted the truth. Well, so did I.

CHAPTER TWO
JOSEF

Being in close proximity to Meredith was wreaking havoc with my entire being.

No, I wasn't a virgin.

I wasn't a kid.

And I hadn't been chaste over the last fifteen fucking years.

But desire coursed through me like molten lava, melting my reserve and hardening my cock.

Fuck, I hadn't felt that goddamn hard in years. If I didn't calm down, I was likely to bust the seam of my too tight pants.

Why did she have to look so good?

Goddamn.

I craved this woman like I craved no other.

Hungered for her even when she looked at me like she hated me.

That was okay. I could deal with her hatred. It would have been so much worse if she'd been indifferent.

Fact was, Meredith looked good.

Too damn good in her sedate dress with her hair wildfire pulled back from her face.

The dress was a little too big on her, bagging around her waist and arms where it should have been taken in by the dressmaker or seamstress. Her purse was scuffed, and her shoes were a different shade of gray.

The Meredith I knew had a keen fashion sense and dressed to enhance her full figure. She'd always had piles of money and an individuality I'd admired.

This Meredith was every bit as beautiful. Even more so.

I'd come there with a purpose. To bring her to heel.

But looking at her, I realized there was so much I didn't know. Trying to remain aloof was a fighting battle.

My interest was piqued.

There was a storm brewing behind her eyes and whether it was made of the same stuff as the hurricane wild winds billowing inside of me, I didn't know for sure yet.

But I wanted to find out.

I wouldn't lie to myself. Not when it came to her. My blood burned when I looked at Meredith.

They said where there was smoke, there was fire. Well, I smelled smoke, alright.

Maybe it was time to check for fire.

CHAPTER THREE
MEREDITH

Anger hummed through my veins, and once again, I was really glad I wasn't wearing a sweater.

The room felt very warm all of a sudden.

Sticky. Uncomfortable.

I shifted in my seat, aware of the stiff backed chair in a way I wished I wasn't. I'd grown up with money and I was aware of corporate tactics.

Rooms like this were set up to make the opposing party feel nervous and ill at ease.

I felt downright fucking annoyed. I had no business being there. No dog in this fight, except that I cared about all those people who would suffer if I didn't agree to sit there with a man I considered my sworn enemy.

A man who sat and glared at me like I was a blight

on his pristine suit. Or something grotesque beneath a microscope.

This was not the man I knew fifteen years ago. That man wouldn't be caught dead in a business meeting wearing a fucking tie.

This Josef was a stranger, and I needed to keep reminding myself of that fact.

Cold. Hard. Calculating.

But I wasn't the same whimpering little miss anymore. If he thought he could bully me into saying or doing what he wanted, he was wrong. So wrong.

Fuck this man so much.

"Fine. The truth. After my eighteenth birthday," I said, refusing to acknowledge Josef's part in that fiasco. "I went to Europe. I made friends. Got a job. And I stayed there for almost nine years."

"And then?" he prompted.

"And then, I came back to the states. To Washington D.C. first, then to Jersey City. My job had a new location and sent me there to do what I do, and I found a small apartment that suits me."

"You stayed undiscovered for so long, how did he find you now?" Josef asked, and it was a good question.

"I don't know that he looked. But I was using my mother's maiden name in Europe. To return, I had to use my real passport, of course. Franklin must have had his detectives monitoring it."

"Is that when he sent the investigator?"

"Yes. He sent his PI with a request, asking me to meet with him. I said no. The end."

It wasn't the end.

Not really.

But for all intents and purposes, it was as far as Josef was concerned.

He didn't deserve my secrets.

But even as I acknowledged that to myself, I couldn't help but replay the incident in my head.

He'd been clutching a notice from the bank in one hand, a glass of scotch in the other. The house was empty, except for the two of us.

The staff must have left around seven. Like they used to every night. The sprawling mansion in Morristown was exactly the same as I remembered.

Pompous and badly decorated, showing off Franklin's wealth, and the fact he had no taste.

He'd earned his wealth over the years through wheeling and dealing, and other schemes I wanted nothing to do with. But the bulk of it had been inherited.

Money was such a fucked up thing.

We needed it to live, sure. It was a necessary part of life. But I wished it wasn't.

Growing up rich was one of the banes of my existence. It had cost me the man I loved. Cost me my mother, too.

Greedy fragile thing.

She couldn't stand her loveless marriage. She wasn't cruel in the normal sense, but she never cared for me.

Not like a mother should.

Of course, I knew all about it now. Franklin had blamed her for the lie she told to get him to marry her, as was his right.

My stepfather didn't like being tricked any more than my mother could stand not being adored.

I was just collateral damage.

I didn't know when he'd decided to *gift me* to one of his business associates, to use my virginal status to seal a deal, but it was sometime during the summer he'd hired Josef Aziz for extra security.

That was the summer I turned eighteen.

The summer I fell in love and gave myself to a man for the first and only time.

I had no idea what my stepfather's plans were, or that Josef was just using me. Unwise and too green to understand, I didn't know that men had different motivations and intentions than women did.

But we really were fundamentally different.

I thought Josef loved me. I thought my stepfather was my father, and that he, too, loved me.

I'd been horribly wrong on both accounts.

The dark, nefarious plans Franklin Gray had for me still turned my stomach.

Oh, but I ruined those plans without even knowing about them. And even though it ended badly, I would not change a thing.

Josef might have broken my heart, but he'd saved me from a fate I believed to this day would have been much worse than death.

Josef didn't know about that. I could tell by looking at him. And I wasn't going to tell him now.

He doesn't get my secrets. Good or bad.

I gave my virginity, my heart, my everything to Josef freely that summer, and he ruined me. But my stepfather's plan to give me to one of his oily business partners was so much worse than my heartbreak.

At least, I'd always thought so.

But looking at him now, I had to wonder. Was it?

Pain lanced my heart at the memory. I gave Josef everything. But it wasn't enough.

I wasn't enough.

The sound of Franklin's cruel laughter as he showed me proof of the payoff he'd given to my lover. A copy of the check he'd cashed that same day in the amount of twenty-five thousand dollars made out to Josef Aziz.

At least, I learned what I was worth.

Money really was the root of all evil. I was certain of it. I'd witnessed it firsthand.

Besides, if that old saying wasn't true, why did so many people stitch it on pillows?

Money could turn people you thought you knew, people you loved, into absolute strangers.

I fucking hated my stepfather's money.

But I was a hypocrite. Because his money had paid for my life for so long.

Even after I ran away, he put money in my account, and I did my best to not use it. I hated his money.

But maybe Franklin owed it to me after what he did. After his brutality had caused me to run. After he'd cost me the only thing I'd ever really wanted. After bribing Josef.

"It's all over. Merry, I lost it all. The house. The cars. Everything, I lost everything, but worse, I lost you. Please forgive me. Your mother wouldn't have wanted this. Forgive me," he'd blurted when I walked into his office last night.

God, I always hated my stepfather's office.

It was cold and unforgiving, all wood panels and black furniture. Like a coffin.

There'd always been something soul-destroying about that space. But I had no idea at the time that it would be the last place I'd see him alive.

"What are you talking about?"

I was confused and shocked by his haggard appearance. I hadn't seen him in years and time hadn't treated him well.

My modest living conditions over the past decade and a half made it so I wasn't used to the opulence of my childhood home. I hardly even thought of that place.

So, I certainly wasn't prepared at all for the pity I'd felt when I saw all the *nothing* his wealth and grandiose home had given Franklin.

He used to seem so big to me, the man I'd called father. But not since the summer I turned eighteen.

"I expect you to fulfill the terms of the loan by the close of business today," Josef said finally, and I knew I'd lost.

He slid a copy of the contract my father had signed across the table to me, bumping it against the other documents his man had already given me.

But I made no move to touch it.

I didn't have to read the letter to know he was telling the truth. My stepfather had taken an enormous risk, using the business, the house, everything really, as collateral to fund his latest scheme.

He lost, and the people who worked for Gray Corps would suffer because of it.

"Shit," I said, lowering my gaze.

"There is another way, Meredith," Josef said, calling my name, but I was too distraught for words.

"Really, What would that be, Josef? I'd give you everything I have in the bank, but it wouldn't make a dent. God, all those people without jobs," I muttered, putting my elbows on the table, and holding my head.

I couldn't bear to think about it.

Desperate people did desperate things, and I'd spent much of my adult life trying to help those who found themselves in desperate situations.

I stood to leave, holding on to the back of the chair while I looked at the man I once knew for any sign of recognition.

But the old Josef was gone. I didn't know whether to be glad for him or remorseful.

Just then, my cell phone chirped, and I took it out of my bag. It was the hospital.

"Hello?"

"Miss Gray, this is Dr. Montgomery, I am sorry to inform you, your father has expired."

I closed my eyes, the weight of expectations sinking me to my knees.

My stepfather was dead. And now, the company would die, too. All those people would be fired. Countless lives ruined.

I failed.

CHAPTER FOUR
JOSEF

I vaulted over the table the second I saw Meredith falter.

"Meredith!" I roared, my pulse racing as I cradled her close to my chest.

My ass landed hard on the unforgiving floor with a dull thud. But I caught her before she came into contact with the hardwood.

Thank fuck.

"Boss?" Mario, one of my personal guards, called me.

But I wasn't focused on him. My attention was on her.

Meredith always had the uncanny ability to capture every bit of my focus.

For a guy, whose primary job was protecting people and being aware of my surroundings, that sure as fuck was not good.

Sure, I'd stepped back from personal security. Adrik was married now, and so was Marat. I had excellent men and women working for me, and they did their jobs well.

Besides, I was starting to feel like a goddamn third wheel. I was the president of my own company and had enough stock in theirs that I did not need to play bodyguard any longer.

I only did it for so long because I had nothing else to do. The cold, dark shadows I lived in were just so empty. Guarding Adrik and Marat myself was simply a way to remind myself I was still human.

After all the years of committing God knew how many sins, I was at my core a man.

Not just the Big Bad Wolf. But a real flesh and blood man.

Being near Meredith was a sore reminder of how much I'd cut myself off over the years.

Starving my humanity. Hardening my heart. Bleeding my soul.

It seemed the only way to survive at the time. But now, fuck, now I was beginning to suspect there was another way.

Maybe the Big Bad Wolf didn't have to end up starving, cold, and alone, after all.

Goddamn.

She smelled good. Really good. Mouthwatering.

Her skin bore the same rich cocoa butter fragrance I remembered from our time together before.

I'd never seen a woman faint, so this was a first. But watching her beloved face go pale as her eyes rolled in the back of her head was more than I could stand.

"Get me a fucking doctor!" I shouted at Mario, who was hovering close by.

I shuffled her in my arms and rose to my feet carefully.

She was so damn beautiful up close, and I was a goddamn lecher for thinking so when she was clearly suffering from stress and fuck knew what else.

Fifteen years of self-loathing and anger.

Fifteen years of wanting vengeance.

It was right in front of me, within my grasp. I finally had Meredith Gray right where I wanted her.

But it seemed I still hadn't learned my lesson when it came to this woman.

Needing to make sure Meredith was safe was as deeply ingrained in me now as it had been then. As if protecting her was simply a fact of life.

Fuck me.

I'd searched for her over the years. Frustrated myself to no end when I couldn't find her.

Tried to forget her with other women. With booze. With violence.

Nothing worked.

I thought I'd die without the satisfaction of bringing her to her knees.

But all that changed a little over eight months ago when her old man started trolling banks for loans. Gray Corps was in trouble, and I finally had an in.

I wasn't a good man.

Hell. That was an understatement.

No one who was *good* would have earned the nickname Big Bad Wolf.

But when you worked for the Volkov Brothers, it sort of came with the territory. Adrik once explained that his surname, Volkov, meant wolf. So, that was what we were.

Adrik, Marat, and me.

The Dark Wolf. The Devil Wolf. And the Big Bad Wolf.

Though technically, I had earned my nickname and my reputation in the military, and that was before I knew them both. At forty years old, I was older than Adrik by one year and Marat by over ten years.

Fucker.

But they were my brothers by choice, and I owed

them everything. They were the closest thing to family that I had.

That I would ever have.

Meredith had destroyed whatever good there might have been after the military threw me away. I was twenty-five when I met her. And she'd barely been legal.

It was stupid, putting all my faith in someone so young. But she seemed older than her years. She was one of those rare old souls.

Her brilliance, her wit, her confidence were things of beauty. She had an appreciation for life I'd never seen in anyone else.

Meredith was like the sun coming out after what had been a long time in the shadows for this jaded ex-soldier.

She flirted. She teased. She chased. I evaded every attempt she made to waylay me and dismissed her feelings as hero worship or a childish crush.

But eventually, we became friends. We talked. Confided in each other. And yeah, I fucking fell for her. Head over goddamn heels.

But I didn't fucking touch her until the clock chimed midnight on her eighteenth birthday.

I was going to marry her. We were supposed to leave the following night after she had a birthday dinner with her father where she was going to tell him everything.

Only Meredith didn't meet me at our planned rendezvous. Her father, or stepfather as I'd just learned Franklin Gray to be, had shown up instead.

Fucking smarmy prick had apologetic crocodile tears in his eyes when he handed me her note. He'd added a check, of course, to shut me up and soften the blow.

"She's too young for a commitment. Too young to know she shouldn't play with men's hearts."

That was his half-assed explanation. A pitiful excuse for his failure to educate her in matters of the heart.

But I still accepted it and his check.

I took that bastard's money and gave it to Adrik and Marat for their fledgling company, buying myself a nice piece of stock.

It took a few years, but I made enough money from that initial investment to start my own company. Later, I diversified my assets and now I qualified as a bonafide billionaire myself.

Not bad for a ward of the state who never knew his own parents.

But that didn't assuage my thirst for revenge.

It took years for the opportunity to arise. But it had. It finally fucking had.

I'd kept tabs on Gray Corps and waited for the Franklin motherfucking Gray to fuck up.

Like a viper hiding in the grass.

So, when the opportunity arose, I struck. I went for his fucking jugular.

I knew taking his company would hurt the old prick. I'd hoped the cutoff of her funds would sting the woman who broke my heart.

But I never wanted to see Meredith physically injured. I wasn't that much of a monster.

I did not physically hurt women. I hired female staff, mercenaries, and experts in the security field to do that. Sure, I was all for equal opportunity.

But I knew my physical strength and I would never unleash that kind of fury on a female. Nor would I allow any of the men who worked for me to do so.

One fucking foot out of line, and they were gone.

My feelings for Meredith were fucking complicated. I wanted to hate her. I wished I never loved her.

Despite all that, I couldn't stand the idea of one strand of her fiery mane being hurt.

No way I could watch her crash onto the hardwood floor.

Not waiting for an ambulance, I carried Meredith to one of the several armored SUVs I had waiting in a fleet in the garage below Volkov Towers.

"Let's go," I told my driver, Edgar.

Traffic wouldn't be bad yet.

My heart hammered inside my chest, and my gut clenched with worry. I didn't realize how much I needed her to be okay until I saw her faint.

"Uh, where to, Boss?" he asked.

"Get us to the hospital," I growled, realizing I hadn't given him any direction.

I sat in the back with Meredith still unconscious in my arms. My attention was on her pale face as my driver did what he was told.

Fuck. Shit.

More of her essence filtered through to my nose, and I could hardly wrap my head around it. After all this fucking time, her scent still drove me wild.

She smells the same. So damn good.

I closed my eyes, just breathing her in, allowing the cocoa butter essence to wash over me. It was crazy how smells could affect the brain.

A thousand images of Meredith popped into my head.

Her smiling up at me.

Her pale skin glowing in the moonlight as I unwrapped her beneath the stars.

The way she looked when I took her innocence.

A plan started to form in my brain. A dark, twisted plan, far more ruthless than the one I'd put into motion all those months before.

Ruining Gray Corps had been my end goal. But I suddenly realized I didn't have to stop there. I didn't have to settle for some empty corporate victory.

My pride demanded restitution for what she'd done to me. And now that I had her in my arms again, I realized there was a way for me to have it.

The possibility left me tingling.

CHAPTER FIVE
JOSEF

Minutes ticked by like hours, and I gritted my teeth against the clinical smell of the hospital.

"We donate money to this place?" I asked Mario, one of my most trusted men.

Darius, my second in command, was currently at Volkov Towers, making sure everything was running smoothly.

After him, Mario was the one I entrusted with the things that matter. This mattered.

I fucking hated it when I was made to wait.

"Yes, Boss. Volkov Industries and Sigma International Security are listed as top donors."

"Mm," I grunted.

That was going to fucking change if I sat there one minute longer.

Smoothing my suit coat, I paced the floor, stepping outside the little waiting area where I'd just chugged an espresso. I noticed the doctor leaving Meredith's room.

He'd likely just been delivering her test results, which meant she was awake.

"Is she okay? What's going on?" I asked the doctor.

"Excuse me?"

"I am enquiring after Miss Gray. I'm a personal friend," I said.

"I, um, well, I'm not supposed to disclose—"

"Allow me to introduce myself, I'm Josef Aziz," I said, watching as understanding dawned.

My name might not be as well-known as Volkov, but like Mario just confirmed, I was a major donor of this institution. Dr. Reynolds here, *head of Emergency Medicine*, would certainly know who I was.

"Yes, yes, Mr. Aziz, nice to see you. Um, Miss Gray is fine. I imagine it was the shock of learning her father had passed that caused her to faint," Dr. Reynolds explained.

That made sense. I was told of Franklin Gray's death seconds after we entered the ER.

The old bastard had it coming, even if he was kinder to me than his daughter had been.

I admit, I was shocked when Meredith said he was her stepfather.

I hadn't known that little nugget. But I had my best guys researching it now, running down her claim. I needed facts. I needed indisputable truths.

If Franklin Gray was Meredith's stepfather, why hadn't she said so before?

I fucking hated not knowing. But at least I could busy myself taking care of her while I had my best team figuring all that out. If Meredith had secrets, I was going to learn them.

One way or another.

"Did you do the usual workup?" I asked.

"Oh yes, a full blood panel and exam."

"And?" I asked, eyebrows raised.

What the fuck was up with this guy?

"And Miss Gray is in optimal health."

"Good. And her father's remains?"

"All taken care of. He had his wishes on record since he was a donor, as well," Dr. Reynolds said, tipping his head towards me.

I really didn't like being lumped in the same category with Franklin fucking Gray and my displeasure must have shown because Dr. Asshat backed away from me.

"Yes, well, um, excuse me. I must be going," Dr. Reynolds said.

I moved past the physician and grabbed the handle to her door, ignoring the way his eyebrows shot up. If he expected me to ask permission to enter Meredith's room, he could think again.

Seeking approval for my actions was something I had not done in a lifetime, or so it seemed.

I was Josef Aziz. Former soldier. Mercenary. Bodyguard. Founder of Sigma International Security.

True, my security firm had only one client. But when you worked for Volkov Industries, you didn't need another.

I'd known Adrik and Marat Volkov for over twenty years. Longer than I'd known Meredith. But it was her father's—no, *her stepfather's* money that allowed me to invest in their company.

The idea I was missing something, something big, in Meredith's personal life sat in my stomach like a brick.

Had she purposefully neglected to tell me Franklin was her stepfather? Why? There was a time I would have sworn I knew everything about her.

Including how sweet she tasted.

Fuck.

Yeah, I'd crossed lines. I tried to resist the pull I felt towards her. God knows I did. But it was difficult.

Maybe I should have tried harder to stay away from her. But from the very first moment we met, with her stomping her feet the entire way down the spiral stair-case to the foyer in her stepfather's house, I'd been inexplicably drawn to her.

Like a moth to a flame.

I knew the fire was going to fucking hurt. That it would burn me alive. But at the time, I just didn't care.

I wanted her so badly.

I'd just taken a side job as a bodyguard for the Gray heiress after the company had received some threats.

Seeing her for the first time, all soft, pale skin and wildfire hair, was like a sucker punch to the gut.

She was beautiful then. And I hated to admit it, but she was even more beautiful now.

Meredith had been in her senior year at a private high school for stuck up millionaire brats. And she was pissed I'd been assigned to protect her.

She'd tried to make my life hell those first few weeks. And she very nearly succeeded, but not for the reasons she thought.

She had a fiery nature that matched her gorgeous flaming mane of hair.

"Are you going to lurk behind me while I study?" she snapped one afternoon when we'd arrived at the old library in town.

"Sure am, Little Red."

"Little Red? Does that make you the Big Bad Wolf?"

I remembered freezing at her correct guess at the nickname I'd earned while working as an enforcer for Adrik Volkov. But I said nothing about that.

I didn't want to mar the pretty princess in her ivory tower with any of my darkness.

"Anyway, might as well grab a book then. If you can read," she'd muttered.

"Got a recommendation?" I asked, not able to stop myself from goading the razor tongued beauty.

"Sure. How about this?" she'd said, flinging a copy of *One Hundred Years of Solitude* at me.

"I've read it. In English and Spanish. Got any other recommendations?"

"You can read in Spanish?" she asked, curiosity flaring in her green irises.

After that, we talked about everything. I fell for her like a ton of bricks, but I never crossed the line. Not until her eighteenth birthday, and no, it shouldn't have fucking mattered.

It wasn't like hours or minutes or seconds suddenly made her an adult, but Meredith was unlike anyone I'd ever met. Maybe it was that fancy school or her sheltered upbringing.

We spent weeks together. And in those weeks, I'd shared more about my personal life with her than I ever had with anyone else.

That was still true today.

And that was why I was about to do the unthinkable.

I'm going to marry my enemy.

CHAPTER SIX
MEREDITH

The sterile, unmistakable scent of hospital stung my nostrils.

Oh my God! I fainted!

I was so embarrassed. I couldn't believe I did that.

Maybe it was the shock of learning about Franklin's death.

Or maybe it was seeing Josef for the first time in years.

Or maybe it was having him threaten to fire thousands of people from their jobs because of some stupid loan Franklin had taken out all for the sake of petty revenge.

Or maybe it was the combination of all those things.

Yeah. That was it.

I wished I could lie and say I was out cold the entire

time, but that wasn't true. At some point, I started to come to, and it was soon after I realized I was being held by someone.

Someone warm and strong who smelled delicious, like spicy cologne and man.

My long dead libido came flaring to life, and it was all I could do not to moan and squeeze my thighs together to ease the sudden unbidden ache between my legs.

I knew I didn't owe anyone any explanations, but the facts were the facts. Once I ran away from home, after the whole ordeal that happened after I gave my virginity to Josef, I'd never been able to be intimate with anyone else.

I just couldn't. And that was completely my choice. My decision. And no, I didn't care what anyone else said.

The idea of a man touching me, someone I wasn't in love with, was just not something I could do. I wasn't judging anyone else.

I mean, I tried. A couple of times. But something always held me back. Something always had me putting the brakes on things.

Sure, that usually led to whatever guy I was dating to break things off with me. And that was fine.

But suffice it to say, I'd become an expert at self-pleasure. I was not ashamed of my toy drawer. In fact, my stash of rechargeable fuck buddies had gotten me through the last fifteen years,

But none of them could compare to the electric jolt I'd gotten just sitting on Josef's lap.

Holy sexual awareness, Batman!

It wasn't something I'd planned on feeling. Or something I even wanted to acknowledge.

Lucky for me, this whole thing would be over soon. I'd sign whatever papers Josef needed me to sign, and I would try to live with myself knowing I was the last word on putting thousands out of work.

Fuck. Me.

I just wished there was another way.

CHAPTER SEVEN
JOSEF

I frowned as I stepped through the doorway to Meredith's hospital room.

She'd woken up shortly after arriving and had sobbed uncontrollably until the doctor gave her a mild sedative. I wondered why she cried so hard for a stepfather she barely saw anymore by her own admission.

Nothing was making sense to me. Not her reactions. Not my feelings.

Nothing.

Awake now, but turned away from me, she looked so much like she had all those years ago. I took a moment to study her, committing this version of her to memory.

Still so petite. Too fragile for this world. So precious.

Her hair was spread out against the white pillow

behind her head, and I clenched my fists to stop myself from reaching for it.

The color was so like the fire I'd seen in her eyes those precious few moments she'd been animated in that boardroom.

It might be sick, but I loved it when she told me off.

Whatever.

I knew what I was. I was a fucking monster. A big, scary guy who intimidated most people. But Meredith was never afraid of me. Not then and not now.

I fucking loved that. Loved her confidence and her courage.

I stood there for a moment, just taking her in. Her face looked too pale. She seemed tired. She'd been running herself ragged.

I now knew what she'd been up to. What she'd been doing for work, and with her life over the past fifteen years.

My best research team was on it. They'd started sending reports on what they'd learned about her as of thirty minutes ago. The updates were still coming in as they uncovered more.

It seemed Little Red wasn't quite so spoiled these days.

She lived in a shitty little apartment and spent most of her time at St. Elizabeth's Shelter for Women and Children in downtown Jersey City.

Of course, I had them running background checks on all the employees and inhabitants.

If Meredith was going to spend time at a place like that, I needed to make sure she was safe.

Call it a biological imperative. Every instinct I had demanded she be safe and secure.

There's only one way to accomplish that, Josef. Tell her.

Closing my eyes to silence that Big Bad part of me, I exhaled softly, not wanting to interrupt her train of thought.

She looked like she was pretty deep in it, and I understood.

Hell.

I was in danger of drowning in the past myself.

I always knew the day would come when I would have my revenge. I just didn't expect to feel so fucking concerned about the woman who'd given her virginity to me so wantonly one hot summer night, only to leave me the next day like so much garbage.

It made me angry that I still cared.

It made me fucking furious at myself for feeling that way, and at her for evoking those same feelings inside me.

The sounds of the sheets moving as she turned reached my ears. Meredith must have felt my heavy stare.

Good.

She turned towards me. And I held her stare.

I didn't look away. Neither did she.

Stubborn thing. Gorgeous little firebrand.

I waited for her to blink those rust colored lashes of hers, holding my breath until her green irises flashed at me.

Meredith's gaze flicked around the room as she tried to calm herself. I allowed her the time she needed, exhaling when she settled her gaze on me once again.

I guess you could say I wanted her attention.

"I suppose I should thank you," she said, her voice hoarse.

"We've got a lot to discuss, Little Red, but I'm not sure thanks are necessary."

"Don't call me that," she muttered, but I ignored her.

"Here," I said, handing her a cup of ice water with a paper straw.

She frowned and removed the offending thing, choosing instead to drink directly from the cup.

Same as me.

I fucking hated paper straws. What was the point of them? The cup was still plastic, for fuck's sake. And it tasted like you were drinking through cardboard.

"Discuss? Like what?" she asked, interrupting my wayward thoughts.

"Like our wedding."

"What?" she gasped, choking on her second sip of water.

"Shit. Here," I said, handing her a napkin.

"Your stepfather's dying wish was for you to save his company. I'm offering you the chance to do that."

I stood in front of the bed, breathing in her cocoa butter fragrance and trying not to fucking drool at the sight of her plump, pink lips parted as she tried to come up with an answer.

She was in a hospital bed, wearing a scratchy green gown. But she was still so fucking beautiful.

"So, what you're saying is I'm supposed to what? Marry you to save the company?" Meredith asked me.

"You said it," I agreed.

"And then what?"

"Then what *what*?"

"I marry you, and then what?" Meredith asked, pursing her pretty pink lips.

The seemingly innocent action sent lightning bolts of lust right to my cock, and it was all I could do to remain passive.

"The *what* is this. You marry me, then I don't fucking sell your company off piece by piece, making thousands of your employees jobless."

What the fuck did she need? A manual on how to be married to me?

Note to self: Find out if there is a guidebook on how to be married.

"Do I have to live with you?" she asked, eyebrows disappearing into her hairline.

I barely refrained from crossing my arms over my chest and settled on simply cocking my head to the side.

Meredith stirred.

She hated it when people looked at her like that. Like she was being obtuse.

Sometimes it was good to remember things. It helped me be prepared for moments like this.

Annoying my soon to be wife was simply a fucking bonus.

"Wives generally live with their husbands," I replied.

"Fine. I suppose they do. But you don't expect me to sleep in the same bed as you?" she asked, turning bright pink, and shocking the shit out of me.

"In fact, I do," I answered, surprising myself.

Admittedly, I hadn't thought through to that part.

But my dick had been half hard from the first second I'd walked into that conference room and saw her sitting there. Now that we were exchanging words, it was at full fucking mast.

"I expect a wife, Little Red. Not a trophy."

"But why now? Why me?"

"I'm forty years old. It's time," I said.

"I can't believe you would threaten all those people just to force me to marry you," she said, but I just shrugged.

"I'm not threatening anyone. Franklin signed the contract. He knew what would happen. Now, do you want to save those jobs or not?"

The fact was, I had no real plans to fire anyone. But she didn't know any of that.

And I wasn't even considering making her share my bed as part of the agreement until she'd suggested it.

I mean, I was a bad guy, and I was definitely going to do something.

I just hadn't worked out the *what* part until I saw her. Then I knew exactly what I wanted.

Meredith Gray. Always Meredith Gray.

Marrying her seemed the perfect answer. I could satisfy my perverse obsession with seducing her and bring my Little Red to her knees. Finally.

Hey, I might be a dick. But I was fucking owed.

This woman raked me over the coals. She killed whatever heart I used to have fifteen years ago.

I was marrying her for vengeance. Not for love. I could have sex with her without falling into old habits.

I just had to keep telling myself that.

And I was man enough to admit that despite every-thing this here felt right.

It was like a light switch had flicked on in my dark

side of the world the second I decided to marry her. Even when I said it, I thought it was because I wanted her to suffer like I had.

Only as I stared at her in that hospital bed, looking so fucking lost and tired and fragile, I didn't want her to suffer anymore.

I wanted to take care of her.

In fact, I was thinking maybe I just wanted her. *Period.*

"Tick Tock, Little Red. What will it be?"

I didn't think it was possible for her to go paler, but she did.

Her mouth opened and closed, and I thought for sure she was going to tell me to go fuck myself.

Instead, she did something extraordinary.

Meredith Gray said yes.

CHAPTER EIGHT
MEREDITH

I sat beside Josef in the back of the enormous SUV, my hand clenched against the cool leather seats.

He was on the phone, making arrangements for our wedding and Franklin's funeral simultaneously. Both of which were jobs I'd gladly allowed him to handle.

"Do you have your ID with you?" he asked.

"Me? Yeah," I replied, glancing down at my scuffed handbag.

"Yes.," he said to whoever was on the phone. "Prepare the paperwork and email it to me. I'll print it on the plane. We will be at the airport in fifteen minutes."

"Plane?" I asked, my mouth going dry.

"Yes. We're flying to Las Vegas, getting married, and we'll be back by tomorrow night. Did you want a wake and a funeral or just the latter for your father—*stepfather?*" Josef asked, his voice businesslike.

The way he said it made me wonder if he still didn't believe me, but the truth was it didn't matter.

It was the truth.

"Oh, um, I know he had friends who might want to see him. Maybe the VP of Gray Corps, ugh, Richard Hamilton. He called me after Franklin had the heart attack and I spoke to the lawyers," I explained.

"But as for me, I really don't feel up to a whole circus of a funeral or anything like that where he's concerned."

Josef nodded. Relief filled me he didn't make me voice the real reason I would not be attending that man's funeral.

"Alright," Josef told me before turning his attention back to the person speaking on his cell phone.

"Tell the funeral director it will be a private affair. Yeah, he can tell the press the family will hold an exclusive service. No outsiders. Any mourners are welcome to visit the mausoleum afterwards. No, no flowers. And finish the report on Richard Hamilton for me. Yeah, I want a new contract drafted for him. Yep, him and all the managers and admins at Gray Corps. Today. I want it done today," he said.

I exhaled, closing my eyes for a moment. Everything was moving so fast. It was barely one o'clock. The deadline for the loan had passed, but I guess my agreeing to Josef's terms negated that.

He really was a sight to behold. This new Josef. But he'd always been the kind of man to step up and take over where it was needed.

Images of my stepfather ran through my head.

That time I'd disappointed him when I wouldn't continue studying dance.

The time he promised to come to my recital, but never showed up.

The time I refused anymore of his etiquette lessons.

I always wondered why he seemed irritated by my presence when I was younger. The nannies he hired never stuck around more than a year or two.

I'd felt their pitying eyes on me when we celebrated Christmases and birthdays all alone in that cold house of his. Franklin was usually off gallivanting with his latest romantic entanglement or finishing some business deal.

The truth was, he was no kind of father at all. We never talked. He didn't know me.

I had no one growing up.

When I was in my senior year, Franklin made one too many enemies. We'd received threats. The house had been broken into and my room was one of the ones ransacked.

The perpetrator had scrawled *"the princess will choke on her cake"* in red paint across my walls.

It was terrible.

A gross violation and invasion of privacy. For the first time in my sheltered life, I remembered feeling afraid.

Next thing I knew, I was told I would have a bodyguard shadowing me at school and at home.

God, I'd been so fucking mad.

It was bad enough being the only natural redhead in my entire school. I stuck out like a sore thumb as it was. I thought having some mercenary following me was going to be torture.

And it was. Just not the kind I'd expected.

My poor teenaged heart never stood a chance. Josef was this enormous man, tall, muscular, and devastating. He was so quiet at first. So serious.

I'd never wanted anyone the way I wanted him.

"Wait there," Josef said, exiting the vehicle and snapping me out of my reverie.

I jumped, startled.

"Easy, Little Red," he murmured, and I wondered if he knew he'd said it before closing his door.

I hadn't realized we'd arrived at the private airport. Before I could regulate my breathing, Josef was there, opening my door.

The spicy scent of his cologne filled my lungs with my next inhale, and I swooned.

Goddamn, why did he have to smell so good?

I cleared my throat, wishing like hell that I had the right to lean into him and just breathe. I ignored his hand and slid off the seat, pretending not to see the way he clenched his jaw.

My feet dropped to the dusty asphalt, and I landed with a slight wobble.

I was still slightly off my game after fainting, but I appreciated the hospital slippers I still had on my feet.

High heels weren't a possibility just yet, but I had mine in the small bag I'd brought from the hospital room.

"Oh, what about an overnight bag?"

"Everything you need will be waiting for you in the hotel room. I've already arranged it," he said.

"You mean clothes and toiletries?" I asked, biting my lip.

"Yes. Toiletries, clothes, shoes, and if there is anything else you want, just ask."

"But how would you know my size—"

"You removed your things in the hospital, remember? I checked your sizes, but if something doesn't fit, we'll just order something else. Okay?"

I wasn't sure whether to be pleased I didn't have to

deal with all that or pissed that he now knew my dress size.

I'd always been a curvy girl, but I was a helluva lot curvier now that I was in my thirties. Should I be embarrassed or ashamed?

I mean, it was stupid. He had eyes. Clearly, he could see me.

"What's wrong?" he asked, taking my elbow this time as we walked up the boarding stairs and entered the private airplane.

"Nothing. It's just men don't usually paw through my clothes," I muttered, feeling ornery.

"First, I'm not *men*, Little Red. I'll be your husband this time tomorrow. But you got that right," he said, his voice rough.

"What are you talking about?"

"I'm talking about the fact that men won't be *pawing* through your clothes or any part of you! Are you dating someone?" he asked.

Stunned, I had no idea how to answer. But I must have shaken my head *no* because he replied with a growly sort of hum. Like he approved.

"Good. Because even if you were, Meredith, it's all over now. No dating. No guy friends. Nothing like that. And no fucking men pawing through your goddamn drawers. Anyone who tries it will lose their fucking limbs. I'll see to it personally," he growled, dragging me down the aisle before nudging me into a seat.

I sat down. Quietly.

What could I possibly have said to whatever the heck that was?

He sounded angry. Jealous even. But that wasn't possible. And I wasn't about to ask him to clarify. I just kept my mouth closed and squirmed a little in my seat.

I expected Josef to move to another row, but of course, he didn't. And I supposed he was going to just sit there, broody, handsome as sin, and smelling exactly how you'd expect the hero of your favorite smuttiest romance novel to smell.

Spicy, Exotic. Masculine. Divine.

CHAPTER NINE
MEREDITH

*T*his *motherfucker.*

I thought I'd get a little reprieve from all his potent masculinity during the flight, but of course not.

Josef took the aisle seat beside me. He actually squeezed his big ass frame into the admittedly large seat for a normal sized person, but just a touch too small for him, right beside me.

I bit back my moan as the entire side of his hard, warm body pressed into mine.

"Seat belt."

"What?" I asked dumbly.

"Put your seat belt on, Little Red," he repeated, taking the thing from my useless hand, and clipping it in place.

"Are you sure about this?" I asked, finding my nerve.

"About your seat belt? Absolutely. Safety first," he repeated, turning his attention to his cell phone.

"No, you ass. I mean, are you sure about marrying me?"

He just stared at me until I started fidgeting.

This wasn't me. I wasn't the sort of woman who looked down when in the company of men.

I was confident. I was a badass. In my line of work, I had to be.

Never one to back down, I faced down angry husbands and boyfriends at St. Elizabeth's all the time.

My job as an intake counselor meant I had to deal with the brunt of them and really, doing that was nothing compared to having to ask this man if he was serious about this.

"Isn't there something else I could do to save those people's jobs besides marrying you?" I whispered, feeling like an idiot.

Flashes of the past scattered through my frazzled brain. I remembered the things we'd done once upon a time, and it made me want to weep.

How could he sit there so unaffected?

It had all been so new and fresh. Scary, too. He was the first man I had ever wanted physically and emotionally. Just being near him made my pulse race and my entire body tremble in my seat.

"Josef?" I said his name, but it was a question. A repeat of what I'd already asked him.

I hated how fragile I sounded. But that was what he reduced me to. A shivering shadow of myself trapped somewhere between nightmares and dreams. Our past and our future.

Josef wasn't like the men who came to St. Elizabeth's pounding on the door because their wives and girl-friends had left, refusing to be their doormats anymore. Those men I could face. Those men I could argue with.

No, Josef was not some abusive, angry ex. But I thought maybe he was worse.

He was my first love. The man who broke my heart. And I knew if I did this, if I married him, I would give him access to that part of me all over again.

This was madness. There had to be another way—but my hopes were dashed when he pressed his finger against my chin and lifted my face, so I was forced to meet his gaze.

"No."

That was all he said. That one syllable. And it was so final.

I turned my head towards the open window, taking in the evening sun as we taxied on the runway. I needed to put a name to what I was feeling, and I tried. I really did. But what I found was not exactly reassuring.

I should have been angry or outraged at Josef's

bland announcement that I would marry him if I wanted to save Gray Corps employees' jobs.

But I felt none of that.

Nope.

My traitorous heart felt something that shouldn't even be in the vicinity of my emotions when it came to this man.

Relief.

I felt relief.

CHAPTER TEN
JOSEF

Nervousness crept up my spine like the sneaky bastard it was. I cracked my neck, tugging on my suddenly too tight collar.

Where is she? Is she having second thoughts?

Before I could work myself into a lather, I heard soft footfalls in the hallway, followed by some murmuring, and I froze.

Mario opened the door. My heart stuttered. I smelled her before I saw her, and the sweet scent made me groan.

Goddamn.

It took me years to hunt down that particular brand of cocoa butter body cream.

It was made by a Swiss shop, something she must still order despite the expense and her limited funds.

Yes, I'd already looked over all her financials.

I knew about her job, which was almost volunteering with as little as she made there. She hardly touched the money Franklin had been paying her over the past fifteen years.

Well, save for a few large withdrawals. My men were still digging into that.

Did she give the money to an old boyfriend? Spend it on something frivolous?

I had no idea, and it made me curious. I was aware I didn't really know Little Red anymore.

Hell, maybe I never had.

But I trusted she wasn't doing anything diabolical with it. If she spent some money to pamper herself with expensive body cream, who was I to judge?

Fact was, I hunted for the origins of her cocoa butter scent until I finally found the closest thing to it in a Swiss chocolate shop when I'd been overseas for Volkov Industries.

It was a short jump to where she got the cream. Since I couldn't walk around smelling like a chick, I did the next best thing. I bought the chocolate. By the fucking ton.

Apparently, it was all made in the same little town where her body butter was made. Both the chocolates and the body cream used the same grade cocoa butter.

Every single fucking night I ate a piece.

No, I did not gorge myself.

I couldn't.

My position demanded I keep fit. So being a glutton was out of the question.

But I was definitely an addict.

Limiting myself to one piece with the promise of another the next day was the only way I made it through some nights.

But I was marrying Meredith now. I'd have access to her softly scented skin whenever I wanted it.

Hmmmm.

I wondered if the chocolate would still be necessary.

Breathing in her sweet flavor, I sure as fuck didn't think so.

After all, it wasn't chocolate that I was addicted to.

It was her.

My gaze raked over her from the pile of red curls pinned on top of her head in glorious disarray, down the flutter-sleeved dark pink gown she wore that hugged her curves in all the right places.

The deep v showed a scandalous amount of cleavage, and my mouth was fucking watering for a taste.

She looked like the perfect combination of innocent and wicked. She looked like a fucking goddess, promising heaven, but more likely to send me to hell with a blink of her emerald eyes.

"You look," I said, pausing when my voice sounded rougher than I wanted.

"Oh, um, I exchanged the dress," she confessed, as if I didn't know.

I'd asked for something classy in an ivory or off-white. Something that said bride or first wedding, but nothing in stark white cause I knew she hated it.

I remembered.

But this was so much better. I couldn't believe I didn't think of pink. She used to always wear one shade of pink or other. I just never considered it for a bride.

More fool me.

She was breathtaking.

"You went to the boutique?" I asked, suddenly angry that she left without me knowing.

"No. I called down. The salesperson did a video call and showed me the selections they had available. I hope you don't mind. I have money if—"

"Little Red, I don't ever want you to offer me money again. Understand?"

The idea of her paying for anything made my hackles rise. Wasn't money the reason she left me to begin with?

I didn't have any back then. But I had plenty now. More than Franklin Gray ever had.

"I understand," she repeated, her voice soft and hesitant.

Shit. I was fucking this up.

"You look beautiful, Meredith. Pink suits you," I said, trying to make up for my temper.

"Thanks. So do you," she replied instantly, a smile teasing the corner of her mouth.

"I look beautiful?" I repeated, and fuck, was I smirking?

When was the last time I did that? I hardly knew.

"You know what I mean, Josef," she replied, rolling her pretty green eyes at me.

"Boss? They're ready for you," Mario said, letting me know the officiant was all set up.

I extended my arm and waited. A pregnant pause filled the room, but Meredith finally, gingerly, slid her small hand into the crook of my elbow.

I pressed it against my side. I knew better than to enjoy the way she felt tucked close to my body.

But I couldn't help it. I did enjoy it.

A lot.

Exhaling softly, I led the way inside the small private room I booked for the ceremony.

The overhead lights were turned almost off, but the wall fixtures were on, and the effect was a soft, ethereal glow. It was nice.

The officiant was an older man. He stood between two large flower displays, and I looked down, frowning at Meredith's empty hands.

Fuck.

I should have bought her flowers. Regret slammed into me, almost making me trip. I felt her questioning gaze on my face, but I just kept walking.

There were papers to sign, and we went through the motions. First her than me. She handed me the pen when she was done, and I frowned.

Meredith didn't take time to read them. She had no way of knowing I'd arranged for ownership of her step-father's company to be transferred back to her the second the ceremony was complete.

I didn't want her beholden to me from the start. Even though I'd used Gray Corps as leverage to get her to marry me to begin with, I wanted her to know it was hers.

But how the fuck was I supposed to admit that now?

So I kept my mouth shut.

"Are you ready?" the officiant asked.

I looked at Meredith and noted with pride the way she nodded immediately.

Goddamn. She's perfect.

I was dangerously close to believing she wanted to marry me.

And that was not okay.

This woman had played me for a fool before and there was no way I could allow that to happen again.

This time, I held the reins. I decided the *when* and *how* and *what* of our relationship.

I wasn't that stupid jackass she led around by his collar anymore. I was Josef motherfucking Aziz. A man to be reckoned with. Powerful. Rich. Influential. Still lethal as fuck.

And soon, I would add husband to that list of attributes.

"Dearly beloved," the officiant began.

It was difficult to concentrate. I was aware of her on a level I hadn't quite expected.

We were quite the pair. A hunter and his prey.

Big Bad Wolf and Little Red.

The vows we recited were simple. I didn't want to futz around, so I stuck to the classics.

To have and to hold.

I couldn't fucking wait to have her in my arms.

For better, for worse.

We already had worse. I was looking forward to better.

For richer, for poorer.

Neither of us would ever have to worry about that one. I'd made sure of that.

In sickness and in health.

I was healthy as a horse, and I would always take care of her. The idea of her being sick made my heart squeeze and my stomach turn.

No, I wasn't willing to look too closely at that just yet.

To love and to cherish until death do us part.

This was a problem. I couldn't love my wife.

Oh, I had no plans to let her go.

But I couldn't allow myself to be vulnerable with her.

Not again.

Despite that, I could cherish her body with mine.

Could she love me?

The thought appealed to me in more ways than one. I never had someone who loved me. Never had someone who cared.

I thought she loved me, once upon a time, but that was just a fairytale.

Maybe I could seduce her into caring for me. I definitely wanted to try.

All I knew was if she ever tried to leave me again, well then, I'd just have to prove how ruthless I could be.

I wasn't kidding when I said *until death.* Oh, I'd never hurt her. But I'd kill anyone who tried to take her from me.

Meredith Gray was mine now.

CHAPTER ELEVEN
MEREDITH

"I do."

That was it. Two little words, then we were married.

No flowers. No rings. No personal vows.

Just a whispered *I do* from the both of us.

How could two little words have such importance in a person's life?

I sat across from Josef in the dining room of our hotel suite not paying attention to anything I was eating.

It was delicious. I'm sure it was. I just didn't taste it.

How could I?

I was a wife now. The reality of it sat squarely on my chest, suffocating me with its irrefutable truth.

I am Josef's wife.

Years ago, this was exactly what I wanted. To belong to this big, brooding man.

But I didn't know *this* Josef.

Over one day, he'd shown me a dozen different sides to him.

He was quiet, demanding, bossy, ruthless, and yet he'd been tender and kind. His behavior contradicted his words, and I felt lost.

I was his wife.

But I was not loved. Not cherished. Not half of the things our vows claimed.

"What is it? Is something wrong with your meal?" Josef asked, and I realized I'd frozen with my fork halfway to my lips.

"No. Um, it's fine," I whispered, taking the piece of perfectly cooked salmon between my lips.

"Good."

The rest of the meal was finished in silence, and servers came to take everything away while dropping off a dessert cart with coffee and the makings for cocktails.

"Would you like me to pour?" Josef asked after dismissing the staff and his men.

"Yes, please," I said.

He prepared a cup of coffee for me, lifting the bottle of Whiskey Neat in silent question.

I nodded.

I could use a little liquid courage for what was going to happen next. I accepted the cup, took a sip, and closed my eyes as I felt the whiskey spiked coffee burn as it slid down my throat.

The scent of his spicy cologne hit my nostrils a second before I felt him draw near.

I couldn't breathe.

Was it going to happen now?

How could I explain to him that I'd never done it with anyone else? What kind of pathetic woman did that, anyway?

Fifteen years, and I'd been so scarred by my past, so heartbroken, I'd never allowed another man to come near me.

I sincerely doubted Josef hadn't had sex in all that time.

But I didn't want to think of the beautiful women he'd undoubtedly taken to his bed. I just couldn't.

I supposed my hangups were about trust. How could I trust anyone ever again after I'd been betrayed by Josef?

Not in the mood for a pity party, I took another sip of whiskey spiked coffee. Weddings should be happy, but I felt like I'd just attended a funeral.

Oh, I'd mourned the girl I was years ago. The past was the past.

This version of me was older, wiser, stronger.

Sex didn't have to mean anything more than that. My heart didn't have to get involved.

I knew that. Really, I did. And I certainly wasn't judging anyone for the way they lived their lives.

"You're not wearing jewelry," he said.

Josef's gruff whisper interrupted my racing thoughts, and I was almost grateful for the distraction.

"Oh, I don't really have any, anymore," I confessed, slightly embarrassed.

It didn't skip my notice that we hadn't exchanged rings during our vows. But I guess it didn't matter. Marriages didn't require rings. I shrugged, wanting to speak, but I couldn't.

I couldn't lie and say I didn't care. I always thought I would be the type of person who wore my wedding ring with pride.

I remembered conversations we'd had about that very thing all those years ago and my heart hurt. But maybe he didn't feel the same.

"I'm sorry this wasn't ready during the ceremony," he added, and suddenly, he was there.

Josef was standing right in front of me, stealing all my attention. He took my left hand in his and I blinked hard. I lifted my chin, his gaze was locked on mine, refusing to release me.

His dark irises were smoldering as he slid something cold and hard onto my finger without looking.

"There. It fits," he grunted.

I nodded, because yeah, it did. Then I looked down. And I gasped.

"You remembered," I whispered.

On my finger was a single, solitary stone set in a thin gold band.

A pink ruby.

My absolute favorite gemstone.

Tears pricked my eyes, but I refused to let them fall. I flexed my hand in the light, noting with glee it didn't entirely cover the small tattoo encircling my finger.

He hadn't said a word about it. So, I assumed he either hadn't seen it or he didn't care.

Either way, I was glad the tiny pink ribbon tattoo was still there. The color had faded with age, and it was hardly visible anymore.

If I wasn't so fair skinned, it probably would have disappeared over the years. But I was, so the tattoo remained visible.

"It took a little while for the jeweler to find the right one," Josef said.

"It's perfect. Thank you, Josef."

My voice was barely above a whisper, but he heard me, if the tightening of his fingers around mine were anything to go by.

I looked at the box still in his hand and sucked in a

sharp breath. Inside the velvet folds of the jeweler's box was a plain gold band.

"Is that for you?" I asked, plucking the masculine version of my wedding ring from the box.

Josef's brown eyes blazed, and he nodded once. I took his left hand, sliding the ring onto his finger.

Grabbing my courage, I held his gaze, mimicking his pose as I pushed the band all the way into place.

My pulse was racing like mad, and it was difficult to breathe.

I should probably just get it over with.

"Are we going to go to bed now?" I asked, wetting my lips.

I didn't know if I was supposed to want to fuck my husband, but suddenly, *or not so suddenly*, I did.

I wanted to fuck him. Very much.

My core throbbed. That secret place inside of me that had gone with no attention from a real, live human being for so long was aching with need.

Working in a place where women sought sanctuary from the real monsters in their lives had hardened me to the careless flirtations my coworkers and every day strangers trying to get into my pants.

I had no use for casual sex.

But I wasn't strictly against fucking Josef.

I mean, we were married, and I'd neglected my needs for a very long time.

"I'd planned on walking you to the bedroom and taking the guest room tonight, but I guess that's not going to happen now, is it?"

The way he said it, it almost sounded like he was talking to himself. Head cocked to the side, chest rising as he sucked in a greedy breath, I was helpless to do anything but stare.

Josef's nostrils flared. His chest rumbled as he turned his body into mine, walking me backwards until I was against the wall. He crowded me, and I trembled.

Honest to God, I fucking trembled with need.

"I was going to be the good guy. To let you have the night to yourself," he growled and pushed his body into mine, allowing me to feel his hard length against my stomach.

We both groaned as he flexed his hips a second time.

"You want to fuck me, Wife? Is that what you want?"

My mouth was dry.

So fucking dry.

There was no way I could answer him.

"I planned to let you have tonight alone. To let you rest after the long fucking day we've both had," he growled, and it sounded like anger, but his pulsing dick against my soft stomach told me otherwise.

"You asked me if we're going to go to bed now, and now I'm hard as a rock. So, do you want me to fuck you? Huh, Wife? Cause if you do, you just have to say so," he growled.

"Oh, God," I whimpered.

Josef flexed his hips again, dragging a tortured sound from my lips. His huge hands ran up and down my sides, sending pools of arousal dripping into my panties.

"I don't know—I didn't mean," I started, not sure what I was trying to say.

"Didn't mean what? You asked if *we* were going to bed."

"Yes, yes," I said, not sure what I was saying yes to. But meaning it.

Oh, I meant it.

"Yes? Then, that's what we're going to do. No take backs, Little Red," Josef growled.

"Wait," I said, needing him to understand.

"Wait for what?" he asked, but he stopped, and that was all that mattered.

"I mean, it's not the same as before," I mumbled.

"I, um, look, Josef, I haven't done this. I mean, I'm not like your women. And I look different now," I blurted, embarrassed.

"What are you talking about?"

"I'm talking about this," I said, gesturing to my body.

"I'm having a hard time following, Little Red. Better use small words."

I rolled my eyes.

This prick.

He thought I didn't remember how fucking smart he was.

Ha! That was a laugh.

I remembered everything about him. Including how good he looked without his clothes.

"I'm not a teenager. I've gotten older, and fatter, okay? Are my words small enough for you?" I asked, angry at myself for all my stupid feelings of inadequacy.

I knew people got older.

It was natural. It was nothing to be ashamed of or apprehensive about.

But Josef was ridiculously fit and attractive. I didn't even want to imagine the kind of women he'd been with.

Svelte, sleek, physically superior women. Women who probably did not share my views on aging naturally.

Fuck.

"So, let me get this straight, Wife. You think I give a shit that you look different now as opposed to fifteen years ago?"

I nodded, arms crossed over my chest.

"Fuck, okay. Meredith, look at me," he said, gripping my chin between two fingers. "I will never lie to you.

Not ever. So, let's start with me telling you this truth. Okay?"

"Okay," I whispered.

"Eighteen-year-old you was beautiful. That's no lie, Baby. You were the prettiest thing I ever saw. A truly lovely girl," he said, his voice dropping to a deep whisper.

"But, Little Red, and this is important so pay attention," he demanded, and I nodded again. "Thirty-two year old you is fucking stunning. Every time I look at you, you just get better. Now, give me your hand," he growled.

I listened. I gave it to him. My body trembled, but I followed his command, helpless to do otherwise. Josef took my hand, forcing it down on his hard as steel cock. I swallowed.

Holy shit.

He felt even bigger than I remembered.

"It's true you're not a teenager anymore, and I'm fucking glad. Because what you are is a sexy as fuck woman whose beauty increased tenfold since I knew you last."

"Josef," I moaned, squeezing his cock, and feeling it move against my hand.

"Fuck, I want you so fucking bad, Wife. I'm willing to commit any number of crimes to get you. You believe me, Baby?" Josef asked, and I nodded.

"Yeah. I believe you."

"Good. Now, come here, Wife, because I'm taking you to bed."

I was mesmerized by his words, his scent, the feel of his hard body so close to mine.

It was intoxicating, knowing someone like him wanted me back.

His warm breath fanned my cheek before he turned slightly and slammed his lips to mine.

Fuck. I was drowning. Losing myself in him. Clinging to his shoulders just to stay upright. If I let go, I just knew I'd melt into a puddle at his feet.

His kiss was *everything*.

It was true, I was a novice when it came to sex, never taking part with anyone else.

But I'd been kissed. More than a few times.

Needless to say, Josef's kiss blew the others all away. They were nothing compared to this.

Having Josef's mouth on mine was everything I remembered and more.

His lips were firm, demanding, and hungry. It was that hunger that stoked the flames of my forbidden desire for this man.

My dress felt too tight. My nipples strained against the material, dying to have a bit of attention. My panties were soaked with my arousal. Need roared through my veins like a blazing inferno.

Josef was an addiction I'd never cured. I knew he married me out of spite or vengeance, or both. I knew he didn't really love me. He never had.

But I couldn't stop my reaction to him. It was as natural as breathing.

God help me, I want him so much. I would do anything to have him.

"Good. You're almost desperate enough for me," he growled, pulling his mouth from mine, causing me to whimper.

I froze for a moment at his words. Was he going to leave? Did he get me all worked up just to walk out? Then he pressed his mouth against mine in a biting sort of kiss before squeezing my hips and backing away.

"Now, turn around so I can undress you."

Thank God.

CHAPTER TWELVE
JOSEF

Pure, unadulterated desire roared through my veins like a pack of wild wolves. Meredith trembled beneath my fingertips as I spun her around to face the wall.

"Arms down," I commanded, dragging the zipper on the back of her wedding dress slowly down her spine.

She looked so goddamn perfect in pink. The perfect blend of innocence and sin. Novice and seductress.

Fuck.

Why did it have to be pink?

Like a fucking princess.

Beautiful.

Unattainable.

Perched in her ivory tower.

Up high and away from the unwashed masses. Far away from me.

Wasn't that the truth? Wasn't that how it always was between us?

How many times had I dreamed of this very situation? How many fantasies had I spun in my fucked up head where I had Meredith within my reach?

Once upon a time, I'd wanted to ruin her. To wreck her. To fuck with her heart the way she'd completely wrecked mine with her callous rejection.

But ruination wasn't this Big Bad Wolf's plan for his Little Red.

Not anymore.

Now, I wanted to own her. Not wreck her.

But maybe she needed to be wrecked a little bit. Just a touch before she could give in to me.

And that was what I truly desired. I needed it. Needed her total and complete submission to me.

But how to accomplish that?

I had an inkling.

Working with the Volkov brothers meant I'd had a first row seat to their mastery when it came to women for years.

Sure, Adrik was sedate when compared to his playboy brother. Then again, Marat really didn't have to try to win a woman's attention. Not with his face and body.

So maybe Adrik would know more about working for it. Fuck. What was I thinking?

Of course, both men were married and happy now. But they'd had some pointers on how to seduce my wife when I'd called from the hospital to tell them my plans.

"I thought this was vengeance, Josef," Adrik asked.

"Started that way, but I think I never really stopped wanting her," I confessed bluntly.

"I see, well then, don't trifle. Just tell her plain."

He had a point. But as I slid the dusky pink confection from her pale shoulders, revealing the naughty bit of blush colored lingerie she wore underneath it, I was lost for words.

Her sweet ass was on display in those barely there panties. The almost sheer fabric did a lousy job of covering her rounded cheeks.

I'd never felt grateful for panties before, but I wanted to send a big old thank you note to whoever made these.

Meredith gasped as I ran my hands down her sides, touching her soft flesh lightly.

She was so fucking perfect.

"Did you wear this for me, Little Red?" I asked, ghosting my fingertips down the crack of her ass, and listening to the hitch on her breath as I took a firm hold of her cheeks.

"Josef," she moaned my name.

Fucking. Moaned.

I closed my eyes at how good my name sounded, spilling from her lips. She was all panting need and breathless desire, and goddamn, I was so hard.

I couldn't wait another second. Bunching the material in my fists, I tugged on her panties, tearing them from her body.

"Hands on the wall. Bend over," I commanded, pushing her forward with my palm on the space between her shoulder blades, while tugging her hips back.

Rough. Too rough.

Last time, it was all making love beneath the moonlight and whispering promises of love and the future to one another.

This time, I wasn't making love to her.

This time, Meredith was my wife, and I was going to fuck her.

The sight of all that soft, pale skin, the scattering of freckles across her shoulders, and the dimples above her gorgeous ass were too much for me.

I needed to calm down. But I couldn't bring myself to let go.

Instead, I focused on the tasks in front of me. I unclasped her bra, tugging it forward but not letting her move her arms so it was stuck between the wall and her.

Meredith gasped as I pulled on her nipples, pressing my suit covered body into her completely naked one.

"Your bigger here," I growled, testing the weight of her heavy breasts in my palms before I went back to plucking the hardened tips.

Lower, my hands roamed down her soft belly, skating over the curls covering her sex and moving to her thighs.

"Open your legs," I growled, rubbing my hard, cloth-covered cock against her sweet ass.

"Josef," she whimpered, but obeyed, parting her thighs, allowing me access.

I cupped her pussy. The heat of her scoring my hand. Parting her lips with broad strokes of my finger, I hissed at the wetness there.

"You're fucking soaked for me, aren't you, Little Red?"

"Y-yes. I feel so wet *there*," she answered, surprising me.

I hadn't expected a response. But I also hadn't expected her heady reaction to my rough touches.

"Fuck, yeah, you are," I grunted.

Without sparing another moment, I plunged two thick fingers into her tight channel. Her walls squeezed me, and I closed my eyes at the sensation.

"Goddamn. Fuck."

She really was tight. Almost as tight as that first time.

Sudden jealousy reared its ugly head. The idea of anyone else touching her like this, feeling her wet heat surrounding them.

"How many have you had since me? How many men?"

I unbuckled my pants, pulling them down just enough so I could pull my dick free. I had one hand on her pussy and the other on my cock.

"Josef, please," she moaned.

I rubbed her needy little clit with my thumb while pumping my fingers in and out. Her pussy clenched around me. And I growled, precum leaking over my dick as I pulled my fingers free and lined myself up at her entrance.

"How many others have been inside you? Tell me and I'll make you come," I demanded.

"No one, Josef. There's been no one, please," she said.

She was sobbing and wiggling her ass, trying to get me inside her.

"Don't fucking lie to me, Baby. I'll tolerate a lot, but no lies," I growled.

"There haven't been any others. I couldn't—"

I couldn't listen to her denials. Hard as fuck, her wet entrance sucked at my tip. I was almost ready to bust just from feeling her slick cunt pulse around my fingers, and now her pussy was kissing my cock.

Goddamn. I couldn't wait. I pushed inside her.

"Ohhh fuuuuuck," she keened, tensing around me.

I cupped my hand around her throat, the other on her hip, holding her in place as I started to thrust.

The sound of my balls slapping against her ass was lewd, loud, and so fucking hot.

"Fuck, I'm fucking you bare, Little Red, because you are mine now. I'll have nothing between us. Not ever," I grunted, slamming harder inside her tight heat.

"Fuck, you're so wet. So hot. That's it, grip me with your cunt. Show me how good I make you feel," I growled, hardly recognizing my voice as I pounded her sweet pussy.

"Josef, please," she begged, her needy little slit squeezing me tight.

"What is it, Baby? Do you need to come? Is that it?"

"Please," she repeated, and the sound of her begging was like a balm to my savaged pride.

I pulled out of her, dripping with her arousal. I spun her around and picked her up with one hand on her ass, the other cupping her head.

"Wrap your legs around my waist," I said. "That's it. Now, feel."

I thrust my hips, impaling her on my dick, using the wall to prop her up.

Meredith's eyes rolled back, and her small hands clutched at my shoulders.

The silk of my shirt was too smooth for her to find any purchase, but I should have known that wouldn't stop my Little Red.

She grabbed my collar and pulled. Buttons scattered across the room, and I grunted my approval. I fucking loved how far gone she was.

For me. All for me.

Her nails scored the skin on my shoulders, and my muscles bunched in reaction.

This little vixen was going to eat me alive.

I squeezed my hand around her throat, slamming her mouth to mine, needing to taste her while I fucked her against the wall.

The feel of her big tits squashed against my chest made me wish I let her rip the shirt all the way off my body. But this was fine for now.

I'd pay better attention to those bountiful beauties later.

Just then an image of me titty-fucking Meredith popped into my head, and I groaned, ramming my cock deeper inside her tight wet heat.

I leaned back, my gaze locked on her face as her mouth dropped open.

"Reach between us, Baby, rub your clit. Make yourself come all over this cock," I instructed her.

"Good Girl," I rumbled, feeling her little hand squeeze between us.

"Oh god, J-Josef, I'm gonna," she moaned.

"Tell me, Baby. I wanna hear you," I growled.

I needed to hear her say it. Hell, the Big Bad Wolf inside me demanded it.

"I'm coming. Oh god, I'm coming!"

"Good Girl. So tight. That's it, Baby. Keep coming. Give it to me," I growled, pounding into her harder.

That was my orgasm. I fucking earned it. I wanted it.

Mine.

"Now, take it. Take it all, Wife. Take me," I grunted.

My movements turned jerky as her sweet cunt contracted, pulling the cum right from my balls.

Goddamn.

CHAPTER THIRTEEN
MEREDITH

Bliss seeped through my bones, and I was barely conscious of Josef carrying me into the bedroom of the extravagant suite he'd booked for our wedding night.

I winced as he withdrew his massive cock from my body. It was a little uncomfortable, but it was worth it.

So worth it.

He bypassed the bed, pulling a surprised squeak from me, and went straight to the ensuite bathroom.

Oh. That makes sense.

It was enormous. There was a sunken tub and a separate shower stall, twin sinks, a toilet, and a bidet.

"Slide down," he murmured, and my body obeyed.

I unlocked my legs and lowered my feet, gasping when my butt met with the cold marble of the vanity.

"Cold?" He smirked, and I wanted to hit him.

But I didn't. I just watched as he turned on the faucet to the tub and added some bath oil.

I almost interrupted, knowing my skin was sensitive.

Then, the familiar scent of cocoa butter hit me, and my gaze darted to his and to the bottle in his hand.

"That's the brand I use," I blurted.

Josef didn't reply, he just dipped his chin and started taking off his clothes.

Stunned, I did the only thing I could do.

I kept on watching.

His body was superb. He looked thicker, like he'd added more to his already impressive bulk.

Unnecessarily so if you asked me. But he didn't. And I wasn't complaining.

He'd already been the biggest, most powerfully built man I'd ever seen. But fifteen years was a long time. And he was even hotter now.

He'd added more tattoos to his collection. I remembered tracing them with shivering fingertips and had the urge to do so right now.

Swirling ink expertly crafted covered his bulging arms, his broad back, and his muscular thighs. Only his chest was bare, and I wondered why that was, but was too shy all of a sudden to ask.

Heat pooled low in my belly, and I suddenly remembered I was sitting there, slouched over, my belly rolls on full display. Clearing my throat, I straightened, but his eyes pinned me in place.

"Don't move."

My mouth gaped open, but before I could respond to his ludicrous command, he was there.

Josef's big hands gripped my waist. He dropped his head, licking across the top of my tits with a groan right before he lifted me up.

Like I weighed nothing at all.

"What are you doing?" I squeaked.

"Taking a bath," he replied.

"With me?"

"Yes. With you. My wife."

"Why?" I asked as he stepped over the small ledge onto the first of three small stairs leading into the over-sized bathtub.

The water was deliciously warm, almost hot as he lowered us down, so I was perched on his lap.

"Because I want to," Josef replied.

His husky voice sent shockwaves of awareness rioting through my body. He wanted to. That was as good a reason as any.

Really, I didn't have a response to that.

Imagine that. Me, rendered speechless?

"There are things we need to discuss. Air that needs to be cleared. But that can wait till we get home."

"It can?"

"Yeah. It can. I've got other plans for now, Little Red."

"What plans?" I asked, my breath catching in my throat.

Years of abstinence be damned, I was panting for him like a pro.

Even if my mind thought I couldn't keep up with the demands of a man like Josef, my body sure hadn't gotten the message.

My pussy ached with need, and I squeezed my thighs shut.

"Hold on, Baby," he grunted, maneuvering me in the water so I was sitting astride him.

My eyes widened. I could feel him.

There.

Josef's cock was hard and long. So fucking thick. It pulsed against my seam, and goddamn, I wanted him.

I expected him to just go in for the kill. But he didn't.

Rough hands rubbed over my shoulders and neck, my clavicle, my tits, my belly, ass, and thighs, all the way to my feet.

I moaned, his fingers massaging me felt so damn good. Closing my eyes, I felt him cup the oiled water into his palms and pour it over my skin. Warming my flesh and making me feel loose.

Then his lips were there. His kisses teased my skin. He tasted me with his tongue, made me feel good with his attentions. At the same time, I craved more.

Hell, I whimpered with need.

"Are you sore, Baby?" he asked.

"No," I replied, the warm water already doing a good job of soothing my muscles.

"Good. I'll never hurt you, Meredith. Believe me?"

I looked into his whiskey brown eyes and saw nothing but the truth there.

Our past was complicated, but when Josef said he wouldn't hurt me, I nodded. He wouldn't hurt me physically. I knew he wouldn't. I believed him.

His hands spanned my waist. He let go with one hand so he could tug my face closer to his as he rocked my pussy along his hard length, not taking him inside, just coating him with my arousal.

Sparks of pleasure spiraled through my body, and I gasped. He pulled me down, and I closed my lips over his.

It was the first time I'd initiated a kiss, and I felt empowered by it. Kissing him was just so damn good.

His beard was surprisingly soft, and his lips were hard, but tender. He was a symphony of the senses.

His scent. His touch. His sounds.

The feel of his muted strength beneath my body as I

clung to him, trusting him to take care of my needs, even if I didn't trust him with my heart.

I didn't want to go there. Not here. Not now.

This was about the physical.

Josef fucked like a god, and it had been way too long since I'd worshipped.

I wrapped myself around him like a redheaded anaconda.

He was everywhere. Everything. All at once.

Claiming my attention, I felt more attuned to him than I ever had to anyone else. His hand tightened on the back of my neck, and he started thrusting his pelvis in time with my hips.

When did I start moving on my own?

"I will never humiliate you or hurt you like this, Little Red. You're my wife now. Sex between us is natural and it will always be mutually pleasurable or not at all. Do you understand? Tell me."

"Yes. I understand." I nodded.

"Then I will ask you again. Are you sore? Will it hurt if I fuck you again?"

"No, Josef. It won't hurt," I told him, even if it was not the whole truth.

I wasn't sore now. I would be. He was so long and thick. Just sitting astride him was causing my muscles to strain. His thighs were just so big.

Everything about him was demanding and intense.

So, no, I was not sore right then. But yeah, if I was lucky, I would be sore later. After Josef fucked me like only he could.

But it was an ache I craved. A soreness I wanted. I licked my lips, my gaze locked on his smoldering whiskey colored irises.

"Good Girl. Now, lift. That's it. Grab my cock, Wife, and put it inside of you."

Holy. Fuck.

CHAPTER FOURTEEN
JOSEF

L as Vegas was a feast of carnal delights for those searching.

Most recently, I visited there with Marat. But this was the first time I'd ever felt anything like this in Sin City.

And it had everything to do with the woman bouncing up and down on my lap, her big tits jiggling in my face as water splashed over the side of the tub.

Holy. Fucking. Shit.

Fucking Meredith into submission had been the plan, but if we kept going at it like this, I would be the one caught in her thrall.

Seriously, the woman was going to kill me.

My balls tightened, and I fought against my orgasm, needing her to come first.

It was all so much. Her soft body just felt too damn good.

Meredith moved on top of me like she was born to do just that. I was a big guy, but her cunt was made for my dick. Her heated channel squeezed me so good.

Goddamn. She was gorgeous.

A wild thing with flaming hair. Acres of soft, pale skin. Smelling of cocoa butter and broken promises. And it was more than I could take.

"Need you to come on this dick, Little Red. You ready?"

She whined and panted, and fuck, I was about to blow.

But not without her.

I grabbed her to me, tightening my hold and flexed my hips, grinding her dripping slit on my pubis, while sealing my mouth over her neck.

"Come for me. Now." I commanded, holding still while she wiggled her sweet pussy on my shaft.

"Josef," she gasped my name a split second before her eyes rolled back.

"Fuck," I groaned, lifting her hips, and slamming her down once, twice, three times while I filled her with my cum.

When I was finally able to move, I carried her over to the shower stall. We washed together in silence. I wasn't sure if it was exhaustion or wariness that held our tongues, but I was grateful for the reprieve.

I held her robe open, wrapping it around her flushed body before stepping back to grab a towel for myself.

"I just need to comb my hair," she muttered, her brows furrowed, and I understood.

I needed a moment to myself, too. I reluctantly left her inside the bathroom, leaving the door ajar while I tugged on a fresh pair of boxer briefs.

When she finally exited the bathroom, Meredith's hair was in a loose braid down her back. She pulled a pair of chaste looking pajamas from a shopping bag, and I turned my head so she wouldn't see my grin.

If she'd had any idea that sleeping in some Victorian getup was going to dampen my lust for her, she had another think coming.

By the time I turned back to look at her, she was already dressed.

"Um, did you want me to sleep somewhere else?" she asked.

But I was already shaking my head.

"We sleep together. Remember?"

Meredith nodded.

I didn't want to set a false precedent. Hell. It was going to be hard enough keeping my hands off her for the rest of the night.

But she hadn't been truthful when she said she wasn't sore.

I could tell by the way she gingerly sat on the mattress, and I frowned.

I should probably kiss it and make it better.

Mmm. Good idea.

I planned to do just that after we rested a bit.

"Good morning, Mr. Aziz. Would you like breakfast?" the steward on the private jet asked as I boarded the plane with my new wife.

"No, thank you. I've already eaten. How about you, Wife?"

I grinned, watching Meredith's cheeks burn a dark pink color at the seemingly innocent question, and my not so innocent answer.

This Big Bad Wolf had breakfast earlier. Remembering the taste of my wife's pussy, and the way her cunt quivered around my tongue when she came, made me want to drop to my knees so I could taste her again.

"Very good, sir. Can I get you anything, Mrs. Aziz?" the steward asked.

"I'm fine, thank you."

Just like on the flight there, I sat beside my wife. I

was going to need to rein this shit in. Hell, I was unable to leave even a seat between us.

Shit. I frowned.

Maybe this was a mistake. But how was I supposed to know one touch would be enough to rekindle the flame of my obsession with this woman?

I grabbed my cell phone and scrolled through my messages.

No, my company would not burn to the ground after one day's absence.

But I sure as fuck was not about to sit there staring at my wife for the entire five-hour flight back to New York like a lovesick teenager, for fuck's sake.

My phone buzzed, and I frowned at an incoming message from Marat, the younger Volkov brother.

MARAT

Heard you got married. So, you pussy whipped yet, brother?

I ignored the asshole. I was not pussy whipped.

My gaze flicked over to my wife. My dick hardened. My heart pounded.

Fuck.

Maybe I was. Maybe that was the issue.

Gritting my teeth, I glanced at his text, mocking me, and I huffed out a sigh.

I couldn't even formulate a response. Growling, I

closed the text box. It was better to simply ignore his annoying ass.

"Everything okay?" Meredith asked, her pretty green gaze focused on me.

"What? Oh, yeah. Just work," I replied, not quite truthfully.

I couldn't exactly explain to my wife the cacophony of emotions roiling through me at the moment. Especially since she was the cause of it all.

Speaking of which, I opened my email searching for the latest information my team had stockpiled on Meredith. Glancing through it, I frowned.

It was more a report of where she lived and what she did there, as opposed to *who* she'd done it with.

What about her exes?

I needed to know. Jealousy fueled the terse email I sent to my team. I wanted them to dig deeper. I wanted to find everyone she went on a date with over the past fifteen years. And I wanted to bury them.

Fine. So, I was a little possessive of my new wife.

Fucking sue me.

CHAPTER FIFTEEN
MEREDITH

Waking up to find my sexy new husband's head between my thighs had been quite thrilling. Sitting in the seat beside him on his private aircraft while he studiously ignored me?

Not so much.

I wasn't being fair.

He had work to do. And if that wasn't a reminder for me to notify my bosses I was leaving, hopefully transferring to one of their locations in the city, I wasn't sure what was.

I went to my email app and sent a quick letter to my boss, explaining my sudden marriage and move to NYC.

Josef had explained he worked out of his Manhattan

apartment, and that was where we would both be living.

He was rich, yeah, but I enjoyed my work. He hadn't mentioned me quitting, so I was not about to bring it up.

My job as an intake counselor was meaningful and brought me solace. It gave me a purpose beyond myself, and I'd met so many wonderful people. People who really cared about people and tried to make a difference.

God knew, I tried.

I'd worked to help women get out of dangerous situations. But I didn't think I'd be able to continue at the Jersey City location. The commute was just too much, and there were three volunteers waiting in the wings for a position to open up, so I wasn't leaving them short-handed or anything.

Fortunately, *or unfortunately*, depending on your perspective, places like St. Elizabeth's Shelter for Women and Children had more than one location. I had no doubts my services could be of use elsewhere. Somewhere closer to my new home.

Chills ran up my spine, and I tried not to imagine what living with Josef was going to be like. I mean, last night was, well, it was amazing.

The ceremony was succinct, and dinner was bizarre,

but our wedding night was everything I'd ever dreamed of.

He'd loved me so exquisitely—*no, not loved, just fucked.*

My heart seized, and tears pricked my eyes. But I had to remember the distinction.

We weren't in love. We were married. But love was not part of our deal.

And it never will be.

Sadness came on so suddenly, I almost didn't catch myself in time.

I bit back my sob, concentrating on my email.

It was difficult, trying to separate teenage me from adult me. My hopes, dreams, and heartache all centered on him.

On Josef Aziz.

He was back in my life in a role I once upon a time could only dream about. But it had a different meaning now. I'd saved Gray Corps, but I might have damned myself in the process.

No, I couldn't allow myself to think he cared for me. I mean, sure, he was careful with me, with my body. And last night he'd shown me more than we'd managed to discover the first time we'd been together.

Intimacy was not an easy thing for me.

Not liking the turn my thoughts had taken, I grabbed my ancient, beat up earbuds from my bag and stuck them in my ears. I found my book app and opened it, looking for my most recent acquisition.

Thank you, Z. Wolff!

Listening to an audiobook from my favorite author sounded like a plan. The narrator was just so good, and I'd been waiting for this installation of this series for weeks.

I found the conversational style storytelling of the author combined with the narrator's voice just so easy to slide into.

No matter where I stopped, I could always get right back into it.

Laying my chair back, I closed my eyes and listened.

I must have nodded off at some point because the next thing I knew, Josef was gently, taking my earbuds from my ears. His handsome face was so close, I couldn't help it, I rubbed my hand along his beard, noting the surprise in his gaze as he looked at me.

"Are we there yet?" I asked, stifling a yawn.

"Almost. You need a new phone. Any color?"

"What? I don't need—" I stopped arguing, knowing it would get me nowhere.

Josef straightened in his seat and turned his own top of the line smart phone, showing me what was available.

It was a long time ago when I used to have the best

of everything. I bit my lip, guilt warring with excitement.

"I am getting you a new phone, Little Red. So pick it out or don't and I'll just order you black everything."

"No! I don't want black," I said, biting my lip. "Okay, the phone can be white, but can I choose a case?"

"Yeah, here," he replied, handing me his phone, which already had a selection of case options on the screen.

I chose a dark pink one with gold trim and grinned. Pink really was my favorite color. It was hard to find the right shade for my complexion, but when I did, I was all over that.

There was an old cliché about pink not looking good on redheads. But society could fuck itself, far as I was concerned.

Besides, according to one of the nannies I had in my preteen days, I was fairly certain Molly Ringwald changed the entire world's mind about that in the cult classic 80s film *Pretty In Pink*.

I was born after that movie's heyday, but it was still one of my favorites.

Anyway, the point was I loved pink. So when Josef showed me the available cases, I didn't hesitate.

"Finished?" he asked.

"Yes. Thank you," I replied.

"It will be waiting for you when we get home. Oh,

and I need to know what you want to do with your father's house."

"Stepfather. And I don't know yet. Is that okay?"

"I could have movers pack it up if you want?"

"Well, maybe the kitchen and neutral areas, and his bedroom. But I should probably do some of it myself. See if he kept any of my mother's things," I mumbled, not really wanting to think about it.

"Okay. I will keep the staff on for now, give them instructions to pack the kitchen and common rooms, and Franklin's bedroom. You can just let me know when you're ready and we will discuss when to go together," he said.

"You'd go with me?"

"Of course," he said, like I was being dumb.

"Oh," I said and hummed my approval.

Grateful for his efforts, I watched my husband as he sent off a couple more texts.

He was just so different from what I remembered. This part of him, at any rate. The business owner billionaire part.

"What is it?" he asked, eyebrows raised.

I blinked and smiled tightly. I hadn't meant to get caught staring, but I couldn't help it.

"Is it strange? Having all that money now?" I asked, curious.

"At first, it was," he agreed, perfectly in tune with my

question. "I grew up with nothing. No family. The military was not my choice. It was either enlist or die in the street. I refused to be another victim or worse, a perpetrator in some pointless war between rival gangs."

"I never thought about that. I never thought about much, I suppose. Like how you ended up in the military. I only know why you got discharged because you told me," I whispered.

"I remember. It was one of the first times we really talked, wasn't it?"

Josef's eyes darkened, and I thought maybe both of us were trapped back in the past.

F*ifteen years ago.*
School was done for the day. The library was closed. But I hated studying at home, so I made Josef drive me to the park.

It was chilly, and stupid me, I had nothing but my uniform sweater and my short plaid skirt, paired with knee high cable knit socks and penny loafers.

Luckily, he had a clean towel in the trunk and a jacket he let me borrow.

"How did you get into bodyguarding?"

"It was an easy transition after I left the military," he explained.

"Why did you leave?"

"I was encouraged," he said, a sneer marring his handsome face.

God, I loved looking at him. He was so handsome. The darkness I saw sometimes behind his eyes was so vast, so big, but it called to me.

It scared me, but I trusted Josef. I knew he wouldn't let me get lost.

"Encouraged? By whom?" I asked.

"By my superiors. I was dishonorably discharged for beating my sergeant."

"Why did you do that?" I whispered, staring at him with nothing less than hero worship shining in my eyes.

"It's too dark a story for you, Little Red," he murmured, but I wasn't letting him get away with that.

"Tell me. Please," I begged.

"Sergeant Diggs started off innocently enough, teasing one of my fellow soldiers. But he went too far. He forced himself on her and she, well, she just couldn't live with it," he paused, but by then I was standing and gripping his forearm.

"After her death was ruled a suicide, the higher ups refused to take action. All charges were dismissed. So, I did a bad thing, Little Red."

"Was she your girlfriend?" I asked, needing to know.

"No. She was just a friend."

"Was he a friend too?" I asked, biting my lower lip.

"I thought so. But it turned out I didn't really like Diggs. I sure as fuck didn't cater to his misogynistic attitude."

"What did you do?"

"I followed him. And I killed him," he said, letting that sit between us.

"I'm not a good man. I see the way you look at me, and you have to stop, Meredith. You're too young. Too innocent. And you should know what kind of man I am. I'm a killer. I'm not for you," he said.

But he was wrong. He was the only one for me. I felt the truth down to my marrow.

I belonged to Josef Aziz, and he belonged to me.

"I know what kind of man you are, Josef. And believe me, you're good."

"I tell you I murdered someone, and you call me good?" he scoffed.

"No. You told me a story of a woman who'd been killed. And you avenged her."

"She killed herself."

"No, that's just what other people say. My mother committed suicide, but it was my father's callous treatment that drove her to it. I don't know why he acted that way, but he was cruel and terrible to her," I told him.

"That sergeant killed your friend when he raped her.

And I know it doesn't have to end that way for everyone, but it was the end for that soldier. Just like it was for my mother. You avenged her. You're a hero. So don't tell me you aren't a good man."

"I'm sorry about your mother," he whispered.

"Me too," I said, and then I stepped over the invisible line he'd drawn between us.

I hugged him.

Right there, in the middle of the Morristown Green, I wrapped my arms around him, and I held on tight.

F*rom that moment on, my heart belonged to Josef Aziz.*

CHAPTER SIXTEEN
JOSEF

A week after our Las Vegas wedding.

Volkov Towers stood tall and ominous against the graying skies.

We were expecting another fucking thunderstorm.

Nothing unusual for New York City in the Spring. But it was so damn tedious.

Summer was just around the corner, and any day now, there would be nothing but blue skies and sweltering heat.

I usually hated the summer. But I was looking forward to it now.

Maybe I hated it because it used to remind me of her. Of what I lost. But she was here now. With me.

My wife.

The same woman I'd been avoiding for the last seven days.

That little trip down memory lane I'd gone on during the flight home from Vegas was like tearing a scab off a raw wound.

I thought I left all the hurt and pain her betrayal had caused behind me years ago. All that angry indignation and insufferable despair from her rejecting me. The way I felt torn up and lost.

But I guess I wasn't as over it as I'd pretended to be. But I couldn't afford to allow all that emotion to divest me of my plan.

I was completely and totally dedicated to seducing my wife. To making her fall for me—*for what? I wasn't going to leave her.*

Fuck. Okay, fine.

I'd lost sight of what the hell I'd even started doing this for the second I saw her, never mind touched her.

And not touching her since our ceremony had been pure hell. Just ask my team. I'd been one ornery motherfucker the last seven days.

But working myself to death wasn't helping. I wanted her now more than ever. Hell, I wanted her so badly, I could taste it.

I'd had her stuff moved into the penthouse condominium located beneath Marat's, even though he was currently staying more and more at the house he'd bought next door to his brother's in Long Island.

Meredith hadn't commented on the penthouse, or on the fact her things were already there waiting for her when we arrived.

The day after we returned from our wedding, we held the private funeral for Franklin Gray. Meredith and I went alone.

Well, it was us along with a team of my men whose sole job was to ensure we were undisturbed.

I watched my wife as she sat silently throughout the mass.

She'd been raised Catholic, and while I wasn't particularly religious, I'd been to my fair share of funerals. The priest was perfunctory. The ceremony was brief.

None of that surprised me.

What did surprise me was that Meredith did not shed one single, solitary tear for the man.

Also, she'd refused to place a rose on her stepfather's casket before he was sealed inside the mausoleum.

I wasn't judging.

I just didn't understand.

Meredith was the most compassionate person I knew. Well, once upon a time she was. The girl I'd known was a bleeding heart.

I supposed this just solidified the fact we were sort of strangers now.

Married. But strangers.

Fuck.

The night of the funeral, she went to bed early.

I slept in the guest room. Working the hours I'd started to keep, I continued to sleep there every night since. It was easier that way.

Until it wasn't.

Not touching her. Or smelling her. Or talking to her was driving me mad.

It was torture. Hell. I was in actual Hell.

Without her, it felt like I'd been thrust back into the cold, dark void after only the briefest, sweetest glimpse of the sun.

I'd barely spent two minutes in her presence since Vegas. I left before she woke up. I returned when she was in bed.

According to Mario, she never left the condo.

Except for this morning.

I began my morning commute before the sun was up and was on my first travel mug full of coffee when my phone buzzed, signaling an incoming text.

I almost dropped the fucking thing on the floor of the SUV when I saw it was from her. I'd added her contact information under the nickname I loved to call her. It was how I thought of her all the time, might as well make it easy on me.

LITTLE RED

Hi, I'm not sure how all this works and we haven't had the chance to talk, but would it be okay if I took a car? I need to go to my new job site. My boss needs me to fill out some forms before I start my new position at our Manhattan location tomorrow.

JOSEF

Mario will drive you wherever you need to go. You're not a prisoner, Meredith. But I need to know the address of the Manhattan location.

LITTLE RED

Thank you. Of course. Sending it now.

Of course, I'd send the car. I wasn't a complete asshole. And she wasn't my prisoner. She was my wife.

Maybe you should treat her like it then, shithead.

Rolling my eyes at my inner asshole voice, I rubbed a hand over my face. It had been a long fucking week, and I hated that the only way she felt she could talk to me was via text.

Your fault, shit for brains.

All. Your. Fault.

I'd already assigned Mario as her permanent bodyguard. He'd reported to me in regular half hour intervals. Just as I demanded.

That's it.

Meredith was making me lose my mind. She'd turned me into a goddamn stalker.

I gritted my teeth just thinking about her working in that place. Exposed to violence and to so much damn heartache.

She didn't cry for Franklin, but I knew she must bring some of this home with her. I only wished she'd confide in me.

When would she have the chance, ass face? You're never there.

I was going to strangle my inner voice if he didn't shut the fuck up.

"Everything alright, Boss?" Edgar asked, pulling up outside the towers.

"Fine. I'll call when I'm ready to leave," I told my driver.

I knew what it meant to the women and children who went to St. Elizabeth's Shelter for safe harbor. I wasn't that much of a monster to pretend it wasn't a good thing my wife was doing with her time.

But it left me uneasy.

I didn't like her working some place I hadn't thoroughly vetted. So yes, I set my people to work.

My team had only just finished going through the

files of all the staff and residents at the Jersey City location. Today, they started doing the same for the Manhattan shelter.

I needed them to be fast and thorough. Not just current employees and residents. They needed to go back three years, minimum, before I'd be satisfied.

As I rode the elevator for my morning meeting with Adrik and Marat, I sent half a dozen texts to my top team with new tasks and specific instructions.

I wanted the rest of the background check I'd asked for on my wife now.

One week was more than sufficient for them to find every skeleton in Meredith's closet. And I needed to know every fucking thing there was about her.

"Whoa! You look like shit, brother!"

Marat raked me over from head to toe with his black gaze and chuckled obnoxiously as I stepped out of the elevator.

I rolled my eyes, checking him with my shoulder as I passed, and headed straight for Adrik's office. I was in no mood.

"Seriously, is married life not agreeing with you?" Marat asked, his grin even wider.

"Shut up," I grumbled.

My phone buzzed, and I looked down, exhaling a slow, steady breath. It was more of the report on Meredith. Actually, it seemed like it was everything.

Everything she's done. Everywhere she lived. Every person she came into contact with over the past fifteen years.

This was everything I'd been waiting for.

So why did I feel like a fucking monster for even considering opening it?

"Josef, do you need to answer that? Or can we get on with our meeting?" Adrik asked from behind his enormous desk.

"Sorry. I'll do it later," I said, putting my phone away.

"Good. Andres, proceed with the predictions for the next quarter. Afterwards, we can go over what went wrong and right this quarter," Adrik directed the newest member of our circle.

Andres Ramirez started as a low level clerk for Volkov Industries, but after years of busting his ass, he'd made it past his already coveted position of administrative assistant to one of the inner circle entrusted with running the Volkov Industries.

Andres was given a new office, a penthouse in Manhattan, a substantial raise, and the official title of president of business acquisitions for Volkov Industries.

"With Marat's new greener incentive program hitting all of our major mines by the end of the fiscal year, we are looking at better profit margins all around."

"Explain please. It's my understanding the greener initiative almost doubles costs for us," I said.

"Because, costly as it is, major tech companies are very aware of how they're presented to the world's media. One false move, and entire product lines are canceled. By signing with Volkov Industries, even with our new increased rates, they are securing their images as environmentally conscientious."

"I see. Smart," I said, dipping my chin in acknowledgement.

Andres went on for about thirty more minutes, and I did my best to listen. But the phone in my pocket was burning a goddamn hole in the fabric.

I needed to read that fucking report.

I needed to know more about my wife.

But I couldn't read it. I shouldn't.

Fuck.

But I had questions damn it. Like when she said she hadn't been with another man. Was she just feeding me a line? Or was she telling me the truth?

My blood heated with the possibility I was the only man she'd ever taken to bed.

Barbaric? Maybe.

But what could I say? Hope sprung eternal, it would seem.

So, like a fucking fool, I sat there dreaming that maybe, just maybe, it could be true.

Maybe Meredith remained chaste for fifteen years.

I didn't.

Suddenly, I felt ashamed. I could blame the demands of my job or biological need, but however infrequently I indulged over the years, I always felt empty afterward.

I sated my lust with whoever was willing to indulge me on my terms. I could argue that just made me human. But I still felt guilty. It always felt like betrayal.

In the years we were apart, I fucked, but I didn't date. Never wanted anyone like that. Hell, my stomach turned at the mere idea.

I shouldn't feel like I needed to apologize for being human. But I wanted to.

Christ, I wanted to confess everything to her. How I tried to drown her out of my brain and heart with booze, battle, and women. How sick I felt during and after. Every. Fucking. Time.

God, how I'd punish myself after.

Rigorous training, dangerous assignments. You name it, I did it. Anything to ease the taint of my sins.

Killing men was simple compared to sleeping with a woman who was not her.

Now that we were legally bound, I would never touch another.

Neither of us would.

Just admitting that to myself eased the burden on my soul.

I inhaled, feeling lighter, unaware of the eyes on me.

CHAPTER SEVENTEEN
JOSEF

The atmosphere inside Adrik's enormous office shifted as everyone's attention turned to me. I pretended not to notice at first.

New York City was shrouded in clouds, visible through the window wall behind Adrik's massive desk and chair. I huffed out a sigh.

Fucking busybody motherfuckers.

"Alright, Josef. We've waited a week, but you're still keeping to yourself. No more hiding. Tell us," Adrik said.

"Fuck," I muttered, rubbing my hand across my face.

"I know I was fucking with you before, but you are family, Josef. You can tell us anything," Marat said.

"Fine, You know I married her. I married Meredith—"

"Wait. Meredith? Why do I know that? Holy shit. You married Meredith Gray! The girl you used to bodyguard?" Marat asked, his mouth dropped open.

"She's thirty fucking two years old. Not a girl. Not underage. And she's *my wife*," I growled.

"No! I mean, yeah! But she was in high school—"

"I never fucking touched her until she turned eighteen. And it was only once. One time and she fucking sent her Daddy to me with a check to buy me off," I snapped, pissed off at everyone, me included.

"We know you would never touch an underage girl, Josef. But you only touched her once?" Adrik asked, cocking his head to the side.

"I remember how she destroyed you. You were with this girl one time, but you mourned her for years, Josef. Never got over your obsession with her then, did you?" he said it like there was even a question.

"Obviously not," Marat scoffed.

"Shut up, Marat," he told his younger brother.

I was always amazed by the way Adrik had so completely reinvented himself in the states. Hell, his voice barely held any trace of his Russian roots.

Unless he was angry or pissed. Then I could hear his accent just fine.

Adrik wasn't angry now, only concerned. I, on the other hand, was volatile as fuck.

I grew up bouncing around from one foster home to

another until I was old enough for the group homes. Three years in that hell was all I needed to convince myself to enlist in the armed forces.

I was good at soldiering. Good at the physical stuff, at any rate.

The listening to assholes part?

Not so much.

I was sure others had a different experience of that life, but for me, it was what it was.

I wasn't there to judge anyone else.

We were all our own witnesses in this life. Each of us had a piece of our consciousness dedicated to simply surveying all we went through.

Didn't we?

I mean, I was pretty sure I'd read that somewhere.

After the military, I met Adrik on a job. Working as muscle for some fucking lowlife mobster in New York City was not my idea of a good time.

But I needed the money.

We worked well together. Soon after, he introduced me to his younger brother, Marat. They had their own crew. And they were doing big things. Taking over territory and making legitimate business from shady ones.

I was interested. Very interested. So, from then on, we were a team.

Adrik had his own crew, and he hired me. Eventually, I was his right-hand man. When an interesting prospect showed up that would make a ton of money for all involved, I wanted in.

I needed seed money. So, I took a job as a bodyguard for some Morristown millionaire's teenage daughter.

And that was when my whole world shifted.

Sometimes it was like I witnessed my own life through hooded eyes, my heart clenched tight against my emotions.

The shit I'd seen and experienced would make most people's hair turn white. But that was my story to keep and to sift through when I was all alone in the dark.

Men didn't do shit like that out loud. And definitely not in front of others.

But it seemed my brothers by choice wouldn't let me do this alone. I didn't know whether to be grateful or pissed. I sucked in a sharp breath and went over what Adrik had just said to me.

He was right. I only touched her once, but I never got over her. If they only knew how I went at her like a rutting animal on our wedding night.

It was safe to say my obsession leaped to new heights.

Fucking Meredith wouldn't get her out of my system. If anything, kissing, touching, caressing, and worshipping her soft, supple body was only imbedding her deeper into the very fiber of my being.

"Did it take you more than once to know Sofia was yours?" I asked hotly. "What about you, Marat? The moment you saw Destiny, I could tell you were done with your single life. So yeah, it happened that way for me."

"You're right, of course," Adrik murmured.

"I'm so sorry, Josef. I didn't even think about it like that. But all those years without her? I had no idea you suffered so, brother," Marat said quietly.

I inhaled roughly.

It sounded insane.

How could I still be so torn up over this woman?

Fuck.

What was that feeling inside my chest?

It wasn't good. I knew that much.

Heavy. It felt heavy. Hard to breathe. Angsty. Unsettled. And nervous.

All terrible feelings for an ex-soldier who'd honed his skills by tamping down his emotions.

I just couldn't afford to be reckless about this.

About her.

Not again.

Adrik and Marat were the closest things I had to brothers. I appreciated it when either of them called me that. More than I could ever express.

I supposed confiding in them would suffice.

"When I knew her then, she was spoiled, sheltered,

perfect. She's different now. More beautiful, older, wiser, still perfect."

"So, what is the problem?" Marat asked.

"The problem is she told me something on our wedding night. Something I don't believe. And I can't do this if she is lying. I need the truth," I confessed.

"And you don't trust her?" Andres asked, speaking up for the first time.

"I don't know if I can afford to," I confessed.

"Meanwhile, you've been avoiding her bed, haven't you?" Marat asked.

He was all sage observation, no wise-assery. So, instead of punching him in the face, I just nodded.

"Well, there is a simple solution, brother," Adrik said, a grin toying at the corner of his mouth.

"Oh? What's that?" I asked.

"You need to seduce your wife into falling in love with you."

Yeah. Real simple.

CHAPTER EIGHTEEN
MEREDITH

The penthouse that was my new home was absolutely stunning. I mean, I grew up wealthy, but I never dreamed I'd live on Billionaire's Row.

I wasn't one of those Jersey Girls who ran to the big city every chance she got, so I was sort of a tourist in Manhattan. I liked it, though.

The energy. The history. The architecture. Even the crowds.

But I was lonely. Even working again, I felt so damn alone.

Mario was always around. Not in the penthouse. But downstairs if I needed something. Today, he escorted me to and from the Manhattan location for St.

E's. Afterwards, he informed me that would be the way of things.

So, I didn't need any of those bus routes I'd printed.

That was twenty minutes of my life I wasn't getting back. Oh well.

Chewing my lip, I thought about the glass of white wine I was going to pour when I got home and sighed.

Almost there. Just as soon as traffic clears.

Right now, we were sitting at an intersection, and it would be a few minutes before we could move again. Well, at least it gave me time to think about the real problem. The thing that had me worrying day and night.

I was sleeping alone, and it bothered me.

Also, it bothered me that it bothered me.

I should be relieved. Right? I shouldn't want that from him.

But now that we'd been intimate again, I was feeling sort of, well, needy.

Goddamnit, why should I feel ashamed about that? I was human, too.

I wasn't the one who sought Josef out or asked him to marry me. He was the one who said I wouldn't be sleeping alone.

Putting ideas in my head.

Smelling so damn good.

Dragging me off to Vegas to get married. Fucking me like the god he is until I came screaming his name.

Then we come back, and poof, nothing? Oh, fuck him!

Did I do something wrong? Was I not any good? I had no idea. Because he wasn't even talking to me. I never even saw him. Like at all.

The only proof I had that he was here were his dirty clothes he left neatly in the hamper inside the guest room.

Douche canoe.

Couldn't he at least be an inconsiderate prick? If he was rude to the housekeeper, or made a mess, I could maybe hate him a little.

But no. He paid well. He was polite. He worked hard.

He just didn't like me.

Fucking fantastic.

Nope, I didn't know why Josef stopped coming to bed after our wedding. And right now, I didn't care.

If I wasn't good enough for the experienced Josef Aziz, well then, he could just take a long walk off a very short pier. The jerk!

My cheeks burned as I rode in the back of the SUV. I needed to sort through everything that had happened over the past week. I needed to try to process what I was going through.

This was as good a time as any.

The day after we returned from Vegas, we buried my stepfather.

That was pretty damn traumatic.

And I'd appreciated Josef taking point and then standing quietly by my side for the duration. But maybe it would have been better if he'd asked questions.

Or maybe it would have been better if I simply told him the truth.

But how did you start a conversation like that?

Hello Husband,

So the guy you thought was my bio Dad was actually my stepfather, a fact I hadn't learned until the same night you took my virginity.

But hey that was only after he'd slapped me and tore my shirt when trying to grab me inappropriately.

You see, he was mad that he couldn't give his virgin redheaded daughter to some oil tycoon he was trying to make a deal with.

Crazy, right? So yeah, in case you were wondering why I didn't want to put a rose on his coffin and why I didn't cry, that's the reason.

Any questions?

Yeah, I didn't think that would go over so well, either.

"How long till we get there?" I asked Mario, my permanent chauffeur/bodyguard, recently appointed to that position by my husband.

"About fifteen minutes, Mrs. Aziz."

"You can call me Meredith."

"I don't think so, ma'am."

"Whatever. Thank you," I replied.

Being driven to my job at a woman's shelter by Mario, the six foot tall, half as wide man with a shaved head and a face that looked like he never smiled a day in his whole life, had been difficult to explain to Sr. Elise, my boss.

The shelter was for victims of domestic violence, and Mario, while I knew he was a good guy because Josef wouldn't have hired him if he wasn't, was likely a bit much for the residents to deal with.

"Um, Mario, I wanted to thank you for understanding about not coming inside with me today. That was cool of you."

"Oh, I, uh, I was there."

"What? I didn't see you," I said, stunned by the revelation.

"Sorry, Boss said I had to. But no worries. I cleared it with Sr. Elise first."

"You called Sr. Elise?"

"Yes."

He didn't offer any more information, and I was too damn stunned to ask.

Did Josef do a background check on me or the staff?

It was the only explanation for Mario knowing where I worked and who my boss was.

Hurt and anger warred within me.

Why didn't he just ask me himself?

I sniffed, forcing myself not to cry while Mario parked the SUV in the underground lot.

If my husband couldn't be bothered talking to me directly about my life, then I supposed I didn't have to worry about sharing any of my past with him. It wasn't like he was offering me any information about him.

Fine. He could just keep his business and his stupid-talented hands to himself!

My stomach clenched.

It all made sense now.

He was using sex as a form of punishment! Making me experience what I'd missed these past fifteen years only to withhold his attentions after.

That giant asshole!

I was such a fool. I knew he'd married me for revenge, but I didn't think he hated me so much. I just wished I could hate him back.

I closed my eyes, feeling the car lurch forward as Mario released the break.

Fuck Josef. Fuck him so much.

CHAPTER NINETEEN
MEREDITH

The next day, I didn't bother texting my husband. He texted me first.

JOSEF

Good morning, Little Red. Have a good day.

I stared at the message for the fiftieth time since getting in the SUV. The rain had finally let up and there was a patch of blue sky peeking between the rolling clouds and skyscrapers.

"Mrs. Aziz, are you ready?" Mario asked, and I realized we were already at the shelter.

"It's Meredith," I tried again.

"I don't think so," Mario replied and exited the vehicle.

Trying to get inside was chaotic, which was usual. There was a front guard, and another on the floor of the shelter.

Weird. He wasn't there yesterday.

When we finally made it to the interior office, Sr. Elise was openly sobbing. She ran over and hugged Mario enthusiastically, thanking him.

"No worries, Sr., Sigma International is happy to do this," he said, allowing her to pinch his cheeks.

A crazed sounding laugh escaped my mouth as my gaze flashed from Sr. Elise to Mario and back. It took me a second to get over my initial shock.

"Oh, Meredith, my dear, your husband is such a gem!" she said and hugged me next.

A gem? That wasn't how I'd describe him, but okay. I was curious.

The petite nun was a hundred pound soaking wet, and seventy if she was a day. But she was a right spitfire, that nun.

A true hero to the women and children who'd come through the shelter's doors since they opened in 1974.

"I know Jersey City misses you, but Manhattan is so lucky to have you, my dear," Sr. Elise said hours later as she walked us to the door. "And you, young man, are a godsend!"

"That's a first. Thank you, Sister," Mario said, and nodded his head.

"Thank you and have a great night," I said.

All my paperwork was done. I'd even spent a couple of hours on a conference call with my old boss in Jersey City, where I managed to help her resolve staffing issues my leaving would have otherwise caused in the hours since we'd arrived.

I admit, I was shocked at the donations Josef had sent in my name.

In. My. Name.

He'd sent over two hundred thousand dollars in cash, ear-marked specifically to help those who needed immediate re-housing accommodations.

I didn't understand. Not one bit. He'd ignored me all week, but then made this grand gesture.

What did it mean?

He'd also sent Mario and a team to install Sigma Security approved locks, doors, and windows on every entryway and exit of St. Elizabeth's.

And not just the Jersey City location. Sr. Elise let it slip that Josef had done the same for all eight of their shelters.

"Did you need anything while we are out, Mrs. Aziz? Or would you like to go straight to the home?" Mario asked.

"Just home. Please," I replied, not even questioning why I'd called it that.

I was exhausted. Every revelation I learned about

my husband seemed to be from others.

He shared nothing of himself with me. I knew it was early days, but given his attitude, I feared the worst.

This is a mistake. I shouldn't have married him.

Whatever dreams I'd had about this second chance we'd seemed to be given were crushed. Josef was a good man.

But he wasn't in love with me.

No matter how sweetly his body had joined with mine. One night was obviously enough.

Sex was just physical for him. Even so, I'd obviously come up short. Hence the whole spending each night since alone.

Oh well. I was done pining for a man who didn't want me. A week was enough.

There were boxes with my belongings stored for the time being in the hall closet. One of them was marked *bathroom.*

When Mario drove me home, I was going to march myself right to that closet, and I was going to find that box.

Next, I was going to pour a glass of white wine and put all thoughts of Josef and his lack of desire for me right out of my head.

I was going to go inside the master bathroom, fill the luxurious tub, and me and *Walter*, my waterproof clitoral suction and thumping vibrator, were going to have ourselves a night.

I t took an hour of sorting through boxes Josef's team had packed from my old apartment.

But finally, I found what I was looking for inside a small plastic box, labeled Band-Aids. Only there weren't bandages inside. There were adult sex toys.

It was a private joke between me and a woman I'd met in England years ago. Peggy was a fun sort of woman, and she'd joked that vibrators were like *plasters for relationships.*

"They hold together the broken bits by giving the woman a little relief whenever her man runs her down."

God, I missed her. I should probably write.

After years of moving from place to place around Europe, and living with the bare minimum, I thought I'd learned better than to acquire so much useless crap. But apparently not.

I sighed and put the top back on the final box I'd been looking through.

I hated going through stuff.

Much of what was there could be donated or tossed, but I'd likely wait to see what the residents at St. Elizabeth's needed before I did that. That reminded me I still had my stepfather's house to sort through.

Ugh.

That was it. No more. I pushed the thoughts right out of my head.

It was only five thirty, and I knew Josef wouldn't be home for hours. Not that it mattered.

He wouldn't touch me when he got here, anyway.

And I was aching.

Emotionally wrung out and physically exhausted. I needed a release, and *Walter* was my only option.

Yes, I named my vibrators. Why not?

They were my only source of sexual release over the past fifteen years, and they did a damn fine job of it. I'd all but proved I didn't need a man to get off.

Even though being with Josef was so much better. But he didn't want me and that was a reality I needed to face sooner rather than later.

Did it suck?

Yes.

Too bad, so sad.

It was this or nothing.

And I was tired of nothing.

CHAPTER TWENTY
JOSEF

"R eport," I said, stepping onto the private elevator.

I was fucking exhausted.

I'd been sitting on that goddamn background check for two days now, and I still couldn't bring myself to read the whole thing.

Fuck.

Mario joined me inside the elevator, having already notified me that Meredith returned home about an hour ago.

He'd been stationed in the lobby at the elevator entrance, and no one could enter or leave without him knowing it.

Of course, we had state-of-the-art tech, cameras,

locks with biometrics on every door and window of the building, my home, especially.

"I drove Mrs. Aziz back and escorted her to the condo, texting you right after she was safely ensconced inside. She has not ordered dinner, and she has not left the premises."

"Good," I replied.

Anxiety and nerves wrestled for dominance, and I fidgeted with my sleeve before I caught myself.

Fuck.

I didn't fidget.

I was Josef Aziz.

President of Sigma International Security.

I'd killed men with my bare hands. Toppled governments with only a team of men. Made my first billion dollars by simply backing the right horse.

But one fiery redhead was my goddamn kryptonite.

Marat was right. So was Adrik. I had to stop running and face my fears.

I had to talk to my wife.

The second I left Adrik's office after the meeting yesterday, I'd sat at my desk and opened my laptop.

Downloading the report, I decrypted the file and opened it. I had every intention of scouring those pages for details about my wife's life. Her past. Her present.

But what I found out about myself while doing this was shocking. I was a total fucking idiot.

Obsessing over my wife. Thinking the worst. Thinking she'd lied when she said there'd been no one else but me.

Now, I did not read the details.

But I did skim the highlights.

And she was telling the truth.

About all of it. About living abroad and not being in contact with her father. About not having any lovers other than me.

I didn't read the facts. It felt wrong to steal them.

Yes, I wanted to know if there were men in her past. But I wanted the details from her.

The few acquaintances she had, my team tracked down, and they were interviewed. All of them had the same story. Meredith was an ice queen.

A blue ball maker of the finest order, to quote one asshole.

Of course, my men beat the shit out of the guys who'd said such about my wife.

It was obvious she hadn't slept with them.

But fuck them for badmouthing her.

Besides, I fucking knew better. The woman was as far from frigid as a goddamn inferno.

She was passionate. Wanton. Acting with complete abandon in my arms.

And I loved her every action and reaction to my touch.

I cherished that about her.

A savage part of my genetic makeup wanted to beat my chest and roar in the hypocritical victory of being the only man on this planet whose cock had ever felt her sweet cunt convulse around him.

Yeah. I was sick.

Borderline fucking nuts.

Completely unreasonable.

I can't help it.

Not when it comes to my Little Red.

If we had any chance at having a future, it was time for me to tell her how I felt. Time for us to live as man and wife. Time my Little Red knew just how fucking unhinged I was when it came to her.

The elevator doors opened and before I could say anything to Mario, I noticed something off.

The lights were low. Like real low.

A deep bass was pumping through the sound system, and I recognized an older R&B song was playing.

It was the kind of song that made you think about sex and nothing but sex.

I breathed in, and the scent of candles burning reached my senses. Without thinking, I drew my weapon.

What the fuck was going on?

"I thought you said no one came up?" I growled at Mario, who, mimicking me, also drew his weapon.

"No one did, sir. Not from the elevator."

But that left the emergency staircase.

"Check the footage of the stairwell—"

"On it," he growled, seemingly angry with himself.

The sound of moaning reached my ears, and if I heard it, that meant Mario did as well.

Red tainted the edges of my vision as I walked deeper into the condo.

My fucking condo.

Where *my wife* was currently moaning, listening to sexy, *let's fuck* music when she was supposedly by herself.

My nerves were on edge. My hackles rose and my inner beast, the Big Bad Wolf, growled inside of me.

My muscles bunched, and I was ready to attack.

"Stay fucking here," I ordered.

"Yes, Boss," Mario replied.

His eyes were on his screen, and I assumed he was checking footage for the last hour.

There were alarms supposedly in place for those stairs. No one should have been able to access them without my knowledge.

But something was fucking going on, and I needed to know what.

Gun high, I turned towards the master bedroom, where the sounds were louder.

Running water. Heavy bass. Soft, breathy moans.

What. The. Actual. Fuck.

Exhaling slowly and trying for a calm I sure as fuck didn't feel, I opened the door to the guest bedroom stealthily.

My mouth dropped fucking open.

Holy. Shit.

The adjoining bathroom door was wide open, giving me a perfect view of what, or rather, who was inside.

The thing about this condo was it was all window walls and mirrors. I mean, *every* bathroom had mirrored walls.

So many fucking mirrors.

I didn't know where to look first. Every panel showed my wife from a different angle.

My Little Red. My Meredith. Completely naked. Legs wide. Cheeks pink. Eyes drunk with lust.

Her skin was flushed from the warm water surrounding her inside the sunken tub. Her knees were spread wide. Her eyes half-closed. Lips parted.

It was like a collage of X-rated pictures of my sexy as fuck wife were staring at me from every angle.

But these weren't photographs. These were living, breathing, moving images.

Each reflection was a vision that would forever be burned into my brain.

Her small hand pressed against her pretty pink pussy, and was she holding something in it?

My gaze zoomed in on that hand.

Yes. There was something in her grip. It was pink. And it was smallish.

I couldn't make it out.

But I could guess.

Her eyes were still shut, an expression of impending bliss on her face, and the music was loud, so, *no*, she didn't hear me.

"Boss—" Mario said, drawing near.

Fury sped through my blood, and I turned around, shoving the man back through the bedroom door, a snarling growl on my lips.

"Get the fuck out and lock the door. Put guards on the ground floor. Two by the elevator and two by the emergency staircase. I want them there twenty-four hours a day from now on. And no one comes in here. Not one fucking person. Not ever," I said with a finality that brooked no argument.

"Yes, Boss," Mario replied, eyes wide.

He was just fucking lucky I'd been quick enough to push him back before he saw something he shouldn't.

Something that would have been his last vision on earth.

Oh, but what a fucking vision.

When I heard the front door close, I went back inside the bedroom, slamming the door this time so my freaky little wife could hear.

She jumped.

I watched the pulse at the base of her neck throb wildly.

Her mouth gaped open, and she bolted upright, sending rivulets of water cascading between her heavy breasts.

"Josef? W-what are you doing here?"

"What am *I* doing here? No. What are *you* doing here, Dirty Girl?" I grunted, pulling off my jacket and kicking off my shoes.

She cleared her throat. Holding her head high like a fucking princess as she stared at me.

"I was trying to take the edge off since you don't seem interested in the job, *Husband.*"

She was trying to be a brat, but the breathless quality of her voice told a different story.

My Little Red was still turned on.

Whether it was an aftereffect from the still vibrating sex toy in her hand or the fact I was now naked, and her emerald eyes were glued to my rock hard dick, I couldn't be sure.

I hoped it was because of my big dick.

"Oh, I'm interested, Baby. I told you. You just have

to ask," I grunted, gripping my shaft, and giving it one hard pull.

"Josef," she whined, her pretty pink tongue darting out and wetting her lips.

Fuck.

She was so damn hot.

So sexy.

Her tits bounced with every breath, and I couldn't wait to suck the hard peaks into my mouth.

I was starving for her.

"Josef? Nah. Call me *Husband* when we're going to fuck. Say it."

"Alright," she said, not complying with my ridiculous demand.

I stopped walking, one eyebrow raised.

"I mean, are we going to—*Husband*, are we going to fuck?" she asked.

I could tell she was excited by the prospect. Her emerald eyes sparkled, and her cheeks were flushed with desire.

Jesus. Fucking. Christ.

Pleasure rocketed through my blood when she called me *Husband* in that husky little voice of hers.

I wanted to hear it again. I wanted to hear her scream it while buried balls deep inside her hot cunt.

"Yeah, Baby. We're going to fuck. Now, tell me what you want. Tell me you want this dick."

I was so fucking hot just looking at her.

All that smooth, soft, pale flesh. Those juicy, thick thighs. Her big tits, all those soft curves.

One tug on my dick wasn't enough. This woman made me fucking crazy with need.

"I want it, Husband. I want your dick inside me."

Fucking. Fuck. Me.

Meredith's eyelids lowered to half-mast as she watched me cup my balls with one hand and stroke my cock with the other.

She looked intoxicated with desire, and I felt that way, too.

We were explosive together.

I'd known it from the second I saw her all those years ago. She was too young for me then.

Too young and sheltered for the only kind of life I had to offer her at the time.

But things were different now.

We were both different now.

And there was no one else on the entire planet more suited for me than her. She'd seen her share of ugliness in this world.

She'd learned all about life when she'd made it on her own in Europe, and then again, when she returned home.

Everything I learned about what she'd been doing

over the past fifteen years had been on paper. And everything I read only reassured me this was right.

We were right. Together was exactly what we were supposed to be.

I'd made the right choice in marrying her. But I was a greedy bastard. I wanted more.

I wanted her body, her heart, her soul, and her secrets. All of them.

And I wanted her to give them to me. Freely.

Even if I had to seduce her to get them.

There was only one thing that really mattered in any of this. One fact no one could refute.

Meredith was always meant to be mine. Just like I was meant to be hers.

It was time I fucking showed her.

CHAPTER TWENTY-ONE
MEREDITH

When Josef slammed the door, alerting me to his presence just as *Walter* was getting to the goods, I almost died from a heart attack.

"Yeah, Baby. We're going to fuck. Now, tell me what you want. Tell me you want this dick."

I suppose I should tell him. What else did I have to lose?

"I want it, Husband. I want your dick inside me," I said.

After a beat, I stood up in the tub.

"Come here," he growled, and my body obeyed.

My feet moved of their own accord, my entire being complied with his demands. I didn't even realize I still held *Walter*, my bright pink suction vibrator, until Josef took it from me.

He hummed deep in his throat, his gaze traveling down my dripping body.

"On the bed, Wife. Legs open."

I scrambled onto the bed and gasped as the cool blanket touched my warm, damp skin.

My breathing was wild and unsteady as I flipped onto my back and watched Josef approach.

He was so fucking beautiful.

My mouth watered. My heart pounded. My pussy clenched.

He was built and inked like some hero warrior from one of those dystopian romances I couldn't stop reading. Scars dotted his torso. Old wounds from battles I knew nothing about.

But I wanted to. I wanted to know how he got them. I wanted to know what they felt like beneath my fingers, and how they tasted on my tongue.

I wanted everything from Josef.

"You're fucking soaked, aren't you, Little Red?" he grunted, his gaze locked on my pussy.

Goddamn. Why did his dirty words have such an effect on me?

I should have closed my legs. I should have shielded myself from his seductive, burning stare.

But before I could even think of moving, he was there.

Josef, my larger than life, sexy as all get husband, was kneeling on the mattress between my splayed legs.

I swallowed.

Thick, blunt-tipped fingers parted my folds, lazily collecting my arousal and smearing it up and down from my entrance to my asshole, then back to my aching clit.

Oh shit. Oh damn. Fuck.

He was so good at that. Too damn good, and I didn't want to think about how or why that was.

"So fucking pretty," he murmured, leaning forward.

I wound my fingers through Josef's thick mahogany hair as his mouth closed around my clit. I moaned at the friction he caused.

Loudly.

His cool tresses grounded me to reality while his hungry mouth devoured me. I couldn't speak. Could hardly breathe. The only thing I really could do was feel.

There was nothing slow or gentle about his erotic attack. And it was an attack. Meant to disarm me. To defeat me.

I shouldn't let it. I shouldn't let him. But I was as powerless to stop it as Josef was relentless in pursuing it.

"Oh god," I moaned.

Close. I'm so close to coming completely undone.

Seeing Josef on his knees, bent over as he worshipped my pussy with his mouth, was just too overwhelming.

I slid my eyes closed, only to receive a sharp slap against my clit.

Fuck.

It was shocking.

The pain lasted only an instant.

And after, it felt good. His mouth soothed the sting, and I moaned his name. Everything he did felt so good.

"Eyes on me, Baby," he commanded.

I obeyed, helpless to do otherwise. I watched as he slid his entire palm over my wet lips.

That same hand disappeared between his thick, inked up thighs, and I could hear him stroking himself as he went back to lapping at my sex.

Fuck. He is so hot.

And I am so close.

"God, I need to come. Please," I begged.

"Not god. Husband. Say *Husband,* when you're going to come, understand?" he corrected right before he speared my cunt with two thick fingers while his mouth sucked hard on my bundle of nerves.

Walter was completely forgotten.

I clutched at my husband's head. Sharp tendrils of unfettered pleasure began to pulse deep in my core before rocketing up my spine.

"Husband, oh fuck, yes. Husband, I'm coming!" I yelled.

I went completely cross-eyed as Josef hummed with pleasure. His mouth sealed over my rippling sex, the vibrations pushing me even further off the edge into the beautiful oblivion of carnal bliss only he could bring.

And just like that, I gave a little bit more of myself to the only man in the world who had the power to destroy me.

The man who once upon a time sold me and our future for twenty-five thousand dollars.

Tears pricked my eyes as a shameful prayer filled my head.

But I couldn't stop the litany of words from filling me as he reared up, stroking his cock faster and faster until hot ropes of cum splashed across my tits and belly.

"Fuck, Baby," he grunted as he fell on top of me, making a mess of both of us.

Please, Josef, please keep me this time.

CHAPTER TWENTY-TWO
JOSEF

After that day, when I walked in on Meredith with her little sex toy in her hand, I couldn't keep my hands off her.

I started coming home earlier and earlier.

Sometimes meeting her at the elevator door.

I texted her during the day. Kept tabs on her through Mario, and I knew she was doing fine.

No threats.

Good.

That had been my biggest worry.

Women trying to escape abusive or violent situations often found themselves with the unfortunate side effect of having their exes turn into stalkers.

Dangerous stalkers.

I appreciated my wife's dedication to the residents

of St. Elizabeth's, but I wasn't about to allow any harm to come to her.

So yeah, I doubled the fucking security in a permanent endowment to the shelter.

"Husband," she greeted me with a smile, and I saw she had a bag of takeout on the counter.

Dinner would be nice. But I wanted dessert first.

"Wife," I growled, backing her against the wall and dropping to my knees.

It was amazing how a position of supposed submissiveness made me feel so damn powerful.

But hitching my wife's thick thighs over my shoulders as I pressed my face into her sopping wet folds made me feel fucking incredible.

"Husband, yes, oh yes," she cried out.

The taste of Meredith in my mouth was the single best intimacy I'd ever shared with another human being, and it got better all the time.

Every. Single. Time.

The heels of her feet dug into my back, and I moaned against her sweet cunt.

She clutched at my hair, pulling the strands I usually cut by now, but left longer because I knew she liked to pull them.

Christ.

I was obsessed with this woman. I was even changing my haircutting habits for her.

But it was worth it.

To have Meredith ride my face with total abandon?

Yeah. It was definitely fucking worth it.

"That's my Good Girl," I growled against her slick lips.

She was like ambrosia to me.

All cocoa butter warmth and spicy need.

My delicious Little Red.

Big Bad Wolf had a new meaning for me now. If Meredith was my Little Red and I was the Big Bad Wolf, it only made sense I would eat her.

And keep on eating her.

Swallow her whole.

Fuck. Yes. Mine. More.

Her arousal was still dripping down my chin, and I wanted more.

I couldn't get enough. Would never get enough of her. And that was the truth.

I would never be satisfied when it came to Meredith.

I would always want more.

And that was perfectly fine with me. I had a lifetime to work on satisfying my hunger.

I stood up with my hands on her ass, making sure she didn't slide off as I walked us to our bedroom.

"Husband! I'm too heavy!"

I frowned and swatted her on her sweet ass before I fell backwards on the bed.

"Don't you fucking move, Baby," I told her, making sure she stayed right where I wanted her.

Her dress was up around her waist, and her legs were open.

"I'll suffocate you," she said, exasperated and maybe embarrassed.

But I just shook my head.

This was exactly what I wanted. My Little Red, hair loose and tangled, sitting on my face.

"Take your dress off," I commanded, holding her by the thighs so she couldn't wiggle away.

Meredith inhaled shakily, then pulled the stretchy fabric up and over her body. I'd already gotten rid of her panties, so she only wore a nude bra.

Goddamn.

Not that the bra was particularly sexy. It wasn't.

It was plain, perfunctory. What made it sexy was my wife's big tits.

Her creamy, soft skin. The indent of her waist. The smattering of freckles across her shoulders. Her delicious cocoa butter flavor.

It was her. All her. Only her.

My wife was a curvy, soft goddess, and I coveted every inch of her.

"Tug the cups down," I growled.

She did, and my cock ached desperately beneath my fly.

I really needed to convince my wife to let me titty fuck her.

But not now.

I wasn't finished eating yet.

"Husband," she moaned, and I grinned wickedly.

"Needy, aren't you? It's alright. I got you, Baby," I breathed against her dripping slit. "I want you to play with your tits, Wife. Tug those nipples and sit on my face."

I felt her hesitation, but I was having none of it.

I grabbed her ass, pulling her down so her wet folds were lined up with my mouth.

I lifted my head, then I feasted.

With my mouth closed over her clit, I sucked on the tiny nubbin, and Meredith lost her battle to remain above me.

Her thighs shook. I sucked harder. Then she sat down. Giving me more of her delicious weight.

My dick throbbed. I was leaking precum inside my boxers. But I didn't care.

My sexy as fuck wife was sitting on my face.

I groaned and shoved two fingers inside her channel, teasing her asshole with my other hand as she rocked against my mouth.

Then I felt her come apart, and it was the sweetest

victory.

Her pussy rippled.

Her back arched.

And my Little Red moaned long and hard.

Before her orgasm ended, I flipped us over, sliding up her soft body, and I pushed inside her still convulsing pussy without any resistance at all.

My cock catapulted her orgasm into a second one. Her sheath tightened around me, trying to suck the cum right out of me.

"Fuck, Baby, you feel so goddamn good. Say it again, call me Husband."

"Husband, Husband, I need you," she moaned.

Meredith lifted her hips to try to get me to move, but I held still. I was determined to ride this out and build the next one from the ground up.

"Kiss me, Wife," I murmured and pressed my lips to hers.

She opened for me like a flower begging for a bit of rain, and I answered her call. Letting her taste the release that still clung to my lips.

I poured everything I had into that kiss. Everything I felt for her. And for the first time in years, I felt complete.

Then I moved. Her hands clutched at my sides. The sharp bite of her nails was drugging. Adding just the right amount of pain to the immeasurable pleasure soaring through me.

Every stroke grew heavier, harder, more intense until I felt like this was more than fucking.

More than sex.

This was a claiming.

A total fucking branding.

Meredith was mine.

All mine.

No one else's.

"You're mine, Little Red. Tell me," I demanded.

I felt her nod, her lips pressed against my throat as I worked my body over hers, pressing my cock so deep I didn't know where she ended, and I began.

"Words. I need the words. Tell me you're mine. No other man's. Just mine," I growled.

My wife was so fucking good at doing what I asked. So good at taking directions. I just needed her to take one more.

I needed her to accept my claim.

"Yours. I'm yours, Husband. No one else's. And you're mine," she groaned, scratching me, marking me with her nails.

"Fuck."

I was hers. She said it.

And I never realized until that moment how much I needed to hear that.

I spread her legs wider, lifting them over my forearms as I pounded into her. I rutted her up the mattress until we were right against the headboard.

I used one hand to stop her head from banging into it.

I should have done more.

I should have moved or something.

But I couldn't stop fucking her.

My body was on a mission.

To claim and be claimed. To imprint myself on her fucking soul.

I felt my balls tighten. I was so damn close.

Her tits were bouncing, and the tips were pebbled so tight. I dropped my head and sucked on one, earning me another long groan from my wife.

She was so goddamn beautiful. Her expression was so raw, so wanton.

It drove me wild.

She drove me wild.

Pride surged inside of me that I brought her to this level of madness. That I was the only one who'd ever filled her sweet cunt.

"Come on, Baby. Give me more. Give me everything," I demanded.

"It's yours, Husband. Everything is yours," she moaned.

Her emerald eyes were burning with feverish need. I

was fucking lost inside them. A willing victim to her flames.

There was nothing I wouldn't do for her. Nothing at all. Even if I only admitted that to myself.

Fuck.

I needed her to come. Like now.

Growling, I ground my pubis into her, rubbing her sensitive spot just right.

Her pussy clenched and tightened, rippling around me. Sending more jolts of pleasure through my blood.

I hadn't used the name Big Bad Wolf in years, but when I was with her, I felt the animal inside my soul roar to life. Like a ravenous beast. But all my hunger, all my yearning was for her.

My Little Red.

"Tell me again," I demanded.

"I'm yours, Husband. And you're mine. Please," she begged.

She called me hers again.

The words seared into my mind.

Like a burning hot, neon pink ribbon, those words wrapped around me, around my entire body and hers, too. It tensed and squeezed until I felt it sear my fucking bones.

Tight. So tight. And tighter still.

Then it broke, sending me spiraling into oblivion.

I reached between us, pinching her clit between my

forefinger and thumb, and her pussy squeezed me hard as she cried out, joining me in bliss.

"Yesss. Fuuuuckk!" I moaned, my voice turning into an incomprehensible roar at the end.

Shivers ran through me. My eyes were so fucking wide.

I clutched at my wife, pulling her into my embrace.

I needed her, her warmth, the evidence of her thunderous heartbeat against mine, to anchor me.

Something happened right then. Something I didn't fully understand.

"I need a minute," I gasped, my face pressed into her neck.

She nodded, seeming to need a moment of her own. I felt her arms around me, her fingers threading through my hair as she hugged me back.

Finally, the emptiness I'd carried around in my soul started to fill. That void in my heart, the chasm that had only widened when she rejected me, began to close.

"Baby. My Baby. My Little Red. Are you okay?" I finally asked, still not daring to let go.

"I think so," she whispered, and the shakiness in her voice made my heart clench.

"What is it?" I asked, moving only my head back.

"After all this time, is it possible you forgive me?" she whispered after what seemed like minutes, *or was it hours*, later?

"What did you do that I need to forgive you, Little Red?"

"That night, the note—"

"You were so young," I replied, kissing her temple before easing out of her.

"I wasn't. And you know it," she said, and I couldn't bear the hurt in her eyes.

Ignoring the messy realities of sex, I rolled onto my back and pulled her on top of me.

"Josef," she gasped.

"Shhh. You should know, I ran a check on you," I began, feeling guilty, but needing to clear the air.

"I know. I figured it out when I went to the shelter and Sr. Elise showed me everything you did. Thank you, by the way. That place needed it," she said, surprising me again.

"I don't usually apologize, but I think I should for stealing some of your past like that. I'm not sorry I did it. I mean, I need to keep you safe, and to do that I need to know everything. But I didn't read the details, Meredith. Those are your stories, and I want you to share them with me when you are ready. Not before."

"Really, Josef? Do you mean that?" she whispered, and I held her closer.

"Yeah, Baby. I mean that."

"Because," she hedged. "I don't think your reports told you everything."

CHAPTER TWENTY-THREE
JOSEF

I felt her tense, and I rubbed my palm up and down her back.

God, I loved touching her.

She was so soft, so warm.

"Do you want to tell me?" I asked, allowing myself to hope.

"I think I have to tell you," she replied, and I frowned.

Have to wasn't the same as *want to*. I tensed.

A bad feeling crept through me as I held my wife in the dimly lit guest room. We should probably move to our bed, but I was too comfortable to get up just yet.

Besides, I didn't want to break the fragile trust we were building.

"I need you to understand what really happened all those years ago."

"Okay," I whispered.

"That night, at the stroke of midnight, when I turned eighteen, I could hardly breathe when I found you in the garden," she whispered.

I was immediately thrust back in time to that night. Fuck, she was so beautiful. A redheaded angel, skin so soft and pale, she'd glowed in the moonlight.

"It was the sweetest thing, making love to you that first time. Giving myself to you so completely," she whispered. "I know you didn't believe me then, but I was telling the truth when we got married. I never touched another man like that—"

"Shh. Baby, I believe you. I know you told me the truth," I interrupted.

I couldn't stand to let her think I didn't trust her.

"I just couldn't do this with anyone else," she said.

"I'm glad," I told her, knowing I sounded like a dick.

"Wait, how do you know I'm not lying?" she asked.

"Because I had my team hunt down every man you ever dated, and they interrogated them."

"What?"

"I won't apologize for it, Meredith. I needed to know," I said, feeling as though I just closed a door on something.

Fuck.

"You could have just asked," she murmured, and I could feel the hurt rolling off her.

I said nothing.

How could I reply to that?

When Meredith tried to move off me again. I allowed it.

"I know what we have is unconventional, but I'm a person, Josef. I have feelings. I don't lie. And if you want to know something, you should ask. Or I should tell you. Excuse me, I have to use the bathroom," she said, sounding choked.

Fuck.

However close we'd been moments ago, even if it was mostly physical, I couldn't help but feel like an ocean had just sprouted between us.

Good thing I can swim.

CHAPTER TWENTY-FOUR
MEREDITH

"Y ou're just like your whore mother! Giving it away to every guy who blinks at you! Slut! You ruined everything!"

"Dad? What are you saying?"

"Dad? Don't call me that! I'm not your father! I never was. Your whore mother tricked me. But look at you, Meredith. The evidence of another man's DNA is written all over you."

I cried. Shocked and horrified by what the man I thought was my father said to me.

His face was frightening. Sweat dotted his brow. A crazed sort of drunken madness glittered in eyes nothing like mine.

"You're gonna write a note, telling him it was a just a game."

"No!"

"Yes, you will. You'll do it or Josef will die! I know people. You know I do. Now write!"

My hand shook as I held the pen and his fingers dug into the back of my neck as he held me in place. His breath stunk of booze, and it made me want to puke.

"Since you're giving it away. Why not?" he grunted, pulling on the neckline of my shirt.

I screamed and backed up, but his grip never wavered. He tore it. And his clammy hands closed over my breast.

"Stop it! Dad stop!" I screamed.

He backed away, eyes wide, and ran a hand over his face.

"Oh no. Merry, I didn't mean. Shit. Stop crying. Stop it! Just stay here," he told me, locking me in his office before he left.

Sorrow, confusion, and pure, abject misery filled me.

"Please let me out! Let me out!"

"Let me out!" I screamed, sitting up.

"Hey, hey, easy," a familiar voice broke through the foggy haze of my nightmare.

"I got you. You're safe," Josef whispered.

His powerful arms wrapped around me, and I clung to him, my chest still heaving.

I stared behind him at the floor to ceiling windows in our bedroom.

Our bedroom. In New York City. I'm married. To Josef. I'm with Josef.

The nightmare loosened its grip on me as I caught

my breath and stared at all the shimmering lights of Manhattan, glittering beneath us like some magical, everlasting festival.

New York was the *City That Never Sleeps*. A place that held more opportunities than anywhere else. Frank Sinatra's *New York, New York,* played in my head, and I shivered.

My stepfather had been a huge fan of Ol' Blue Eyes. Most folks from his generation, and New Jersey especially, since the famous crooner had been born in the Garden State, were.

I couldn't stand to listen to him anymore. Not without thinking about that horrible night.

I trembled again, and Josef's arms tightened around me.

I was being dumb.

In my line of work, I'd seen true horrors, and I knew what I'd been through was nothing.

But I allowed myself a moment of self-indulgence, and I burrowed into my husband's strong, warm chest.

Tracing the tribal tattoo on his shoulder, I steadied my breathing.

Yes, I'd had nightmares over the years, but they'd gotten a lot better. I'd had some counseling, but not much.

Still, having Josef there to comfort me was more than I could have ever wished for. He kissed my temple, rubbing my back in soothing circles. I breathed in his spicy masculine scent and felt his chest move with each breath he took.

He grounded me. And I was so damn grateful to have him.

"Wanna talk about it, Baby?" he rumbled.

I shook my head. I didn't. Not really. I just wanted him to hold me.

"Okay, Little Red. Whatever you want," he said, kissing me again and leaning back against the pillow with me firmly in his embrace.

I sighed. Happy and content for the first time in what felt like ever.

I'd fallen asleep still feeling hurt by him. I was upset he'd checked on my story. But really, of course he did.

What did I expect? He owned a security firm, for fuck's sake. It was literally his business.

Anyway, I'd never had a nightmare before tonight. But just like with everything else he did, Josef made it better.

He was so big and strong.

A natural born protector.

"You're safe, Baby. I will never let anyone hurt you," he said, reassuring me without me having to tell him to.

"I know you won't," I replied, kissing his chest.

I knew I shouldn't delay any longer. It was about time I let Josef in.

If we had any hopes for a future together, he needed to know the past. He deserved that much. We both deserved the opportunity to make something of this whatever we had.

I felt his arms tighten around me, and I exhaled a slow breath.

The rise and fall of his chest were steadying, grounding me as I started to reveal the truth about my eighteenth birthday.

"I'm going to tell you something," I started,

"Okay, I'm listening."

"That night, after we, you know, in the garden," I began, my voice barely above a whisper. "I tried to sneak back into the house, but Dad, I mean, Franklin, was there. He'd been drinking, and he was angry."

I remembered the all too familiar posture of my drunk stepfather as he sneered at me.

Later, he'd said he was too drunk to remember what he did.

But he wasn't drunk enough to not lie and bribe Josef. So drunk wasn't a good excuse. Drunk was a copout.

"I tried to walk past him. He'd gotten drunk before, and he was never very pleasant to be around, anyway. I knew it was wiser to avoid a conflict when he'd been drinking, so I didn't even reply when he asked where I'd been."

"Did he get drunk a lot back then?" Josef asked, and I shrugged.

"I'm not sure. I was pretty busy senior year, and nursing my infatuation with you," I said honestly.

Josef grunted, his hand still rubbing my back.

"He got mad. Blocked off my exit. Told me he saw us in the garden. Called me a whore. Said I was like my mother. He said a lot of mean things. Then he told me about her, and how she'd tricked him into marrying her, thinking I was his."

I took a big breath. Readying myself for the next part.

"But I wasn't his daughter. He told me my father was just some loser. A low life who never wanted my mother or me. Then he told me I ruined his plans," I whispered, shivering at the memory.

"What plans?" Josef asked, his voice husky and angry.

"H-he was trying to close a business deal, and uh, I was part of the arrangement. Franklin planned to gift me, *his virgin daughter*, to the owner of Petro Star Oil. They went bust a few years ago. Apparently, the man was a fucking pig. Anyway, Franklin knew he lost the deal, and he was mad."

"Motherfucker. Did he—no, I know he did. What did he do?" Josef asked, but I shook my head.

It was clear he was angry, and I didn't want him

angry.

"Please, tell me, Little Red. I need to know."

Josef kissed my temple, holding me tighter, and I knew he was right. I couldn't keep it from him anymore than I could keep it from haunting my dreams.

"He screamed at me. Then, he just pulled my hair and shoved me into his chair at his desk. He forced me to write a note saying I was just playing with you and saying goodbye. He had my hair so tight, and I was so scared. I just did it. I'm so sorry I wrote what he wanted me to, but I didn't know what to do—"

"Oh fuck. Shit. Meredith, you did nothing wrong. I'm sorry. I'm so sorry, I believed him," Josef said, sitting up with me in his arms.

He held me even tighter, cupping my cheek and kissing my head as the memories just poured out of me, like a weeping wound.

"He came to the cabin where I bunked with the other guards a few hours after I left you in the garden. Tears in his eyes, that motherfucker. He gave me the note and a check for twenty-five thousand with his apologies," Josef told me.

I already figured that out, but I was glad Josef confirmed it for me.

It felt cathartic in a way. Like we were mending fences. Building bridges over the past.

"I know. He showed me a copy of the check. Said you cashed it immediately."

"I did. Fuck, Meredith. I left and took it right away. I just couldn't believe someone as special as you would ever really want me," he confessed, and I was stunned.

"I'm so sorry, Baby. A friend needed money for his business, and I was his first investor. I gave him the check an hour after I got it. I was so fucking hurt. But when did you leave?" Josef asked after a few moments.

"After writing the note, right before he went to see you. He, um, well, he'd been drinking. He stunk of booze. He pulled my hair, slapped my face, and then he, he," I stuttered on that part.

"He what?"

"He tore my shirt, and he g-grabbed my breast and twisted it. He was shocked when I started screaming. He called me names. Said it was my fault and called me more terrible names. Then he locked me in his office," I said with remembered shame.

I shuddered against Josef. A strangled sound came from his throat, and he squeezed me tighter, but I needed to finish telling him. So I did.

"I was so confused and hurt and tired, but I couldn't fall asleep in there. The sun wasn't up yet. But I knew he would be back. When he returned, I rushed the door, knocking him out of the way."

"Thank God. Thank God you got away," he whispered huskily.

"I ran. I just took that opening, and I ran. I tried to find you, but you were gone. So I went to the guesthouse where I hid until I finally bribed a maid, her name was Gretchen, to grab some stuff from my room. Then I ran as far away as I could with the money in my pocket and my passport," I finished.

I took a deep breath, gasping when Josef squeezed me. I felt relieved, like I'd just lost about fifty pounds of shame and guilt.

"Fuck. Fuck. Baby, I am so fucking sorry. Sorry you had to go through that, Sorry I left. And I'm fucking sorry he's dead. I want to kill him myself," Josef growled, surprising a laugh from me.

I couldn't help it. I knew it was wrong. I knew it made me sicko or a freak. But I really just could not help myself.

Relief flooded my veins, and it was euphoric.

Just knowing that Josef knew.

That he knew and still wanted to defend me. That he didn't blame me. That he believed me.

Knowing all of that helped so much.

I hadn't realized how much guilt I'd been carrying around. As if I was somehow responsible for Franklin Gray's revolting behavior.

"It wasn't your fault, Baby," Josef said, squeezing me tighter.

"I know," I replied.

And for once, I really did know.

"That was all him. It wasn't you. He was supposed to protect you from the monsters, not be one."

"I didn't know he wasn't my father," I confessed. "I didn't know. I mean, I didn't look like either of them. Not my mom or him. But I didn't know."

"It doesn't matter if he was your biological father or not. He was responsible for you, Meredith. He should have done better. I should have done better, too. I'm so fucking sorry for all of it."

I felt anger and more roiling through him, and I hugged Josef tighter. It wasn't his fault, either.

He had to know I didn't blame him.

"I wouldn't be surprised if you did."

"But I don't," I said, realizing I must've spoken aloud a moment before.

And I meant it. I didn't blame Josef.

But I still loved him.

Oh fuck.

I did. I loved him.

There was no way I could deny it any longer. To hell with the consequences, my reckless heart didn't seem to care.

I loved Josef, and I really wanted our marriage to work. And not just that. I wanted him to love me back.

In fact, I just might demand it.

CHAPTER TWENTY-FIVE
JOSEF

After listening to Meredith's truth, I held her until her breathing evened out.

I did not let go of her. I just kept my arms around her, replaying her words in my head over and over again for the rest of the night.

The next day, I left early and waited for Mario to text me when she arrived at the Manhattan location for the shelter.

I'd already had the place refurbished with new doors, windows, locks, cameras, and everything else they needed to ensure my wife's safety.

She didn't know it yet, but I had Andres in talks with the non-profit who ran St. Elizabeth's.

Sigma International Security was interested in

taking over the whole thing, making Meredith Aziz its head.

"Josef, you're coming tonight, right?" Marat asked from the doorway to my office.

I looked at him blankly. Marat's perfectly symmetrical face stared back at me, a game we'd been playing for years.

Who could stare the longest?

Me.

Obviously.

Satisfaction filled me when he gave up and rolled his eyes.

"Not kidding about tonight," he said again.

What the fuck was tonight?

"Bro, we're celebrating Sofia and Destiny's new audiobook release. The new house on Long Island. Eight o'clock."

"Right. Yes," I said, nodding.

Fuck.

"If you don't show up, they'll both kill you," he added, and I waved him away.

He was telling the truth. I wasn't dumb enough to think he was lying or exaggerating.

I knew Sofia and Destiny, and those two women were scary as hell. Especially when it came to family gatherings.

And for whatever reason, the Volkov women had decided I was to be included in every single function.

Yay me.

All I knew was if they said I needed to be there, I needed to be there.

Whoever named the men of Volkov Industries wolves never met their wives. Those women were scary as fuck when they were worked up.

I opened a new text box. Little Red was going to need some warning.

JOSEF

Wife, Forgot to mention we have plans tonight. A party for the wife of one of my business associates. Well, he's more than that. Like a brother. Anyway. We need to leave at seven. I'll have a dress sent to the condo, so you have time to get ready. -Your thoughtful husband.

LITTLE RED

Husband, Short notice much? Is it her birthday? Should we bring a gift? Why are you always dressing me? -Your anxious wife.

JOSEF

Wife, No gift needed. And I enjoy undressing you so much, I figured I should get to choose the wrapping. -Your lustful husband.

> LITTLE RED
>
> If you're going to send me texts like that at work, I'll have to start bringing extra panties. -Your uncomfortable wife.

> JOSEF
>
> You take your panties off at work, and I'll tan your ass, so you won't be able to sit for a week. -Your very serious husband.

> LITTLE RED
>
> You're just proving my point, Husband.

Fuck.

I grinned and adjusted my now hard cock. Picturing my sexy wife in her wet panties at her desk while texting me had me about ready to come.

Goddamnit. Little Red had me thumping inside my pants.

I really didn't want to share Meredith with anyone yet. But I supposed I had to. Anyway, Sofia and Destiny were truly wonderful women.

The two had become coworkers when Destiny discovered a talent for narrating the sexy little romances Sofia wrote under the pseudonym Z. Wolff.

It was a combination of her and Adrik's names. A sort of nod to her Dark Wolf husband and the Z was short for Zaika, which was Adrik's pet name for her.

Destiny, Marat's wife, and the mother of their little girl, Lucy, had a gift for narration.

She and Sofia were celebrating their sixth audiobook release.

Which got me thinking. Meredith liked audiobooks and reading in general. When we flew home from Vegas, she'd been listening to one.

I wasn't sure of the genre, but I could check her reading app.

What?

Her new phone was on my account. I had access to all her apps, messages, everything, really.

I should probably tell her that.

But I wasn't stupid, and I wasn't looking for a fight.

Plus, I didn't look through her stuff religiously. Definitely not since we decided to make this marriage real.

I still wanted my wife to give me her secrets knowingly, willingly.

Seduction aside.

But it was time I introduced her to the others. And if they had some common interests, like reading or listening to smut books, then it might be easier on her.

When she wasn't at work, Meredith spent her time with me. But I knew better than to think that was enough.

My wife could use some friends, and Destiny and Sofia were two of the best people I knew.

Hell, they were family.

But family and friendships aside, maybe we could leave the party early.

As all those thoughts were dancing in my head, I figured I could surprise Meredith with some new additions to her wardrobe.

I pulled up the catalog for an exclusive boutique on Billionaire's Row and dialed the owner's private number. My company had installed security there, and Adrik and Marat were frequent customers for their wives.

I could just have someone else do this. But if anyone was dressing my wife, it was going to be me.

I adjusted my cock again and paused my scrolling on a sexy little number. The call connected and I spoke first.

"This is Josef Aziz."

"Mr. Aziz! Yes, sir, what can I do for you?" Van Wong, the owner of the boutique, asked.

"I need some things for my wife. I'm texting you her measurements and sizes. It's for a dinner party. Tell me, do you have item 5e023d in pink?"

"Pink?"

"Yes. That's what I said."

"I can have that for you, no problem. When?"

"Have it delivered by five," I replied.

"Yes, sir. Will you be needing accessories?"

"Indeed. Purses. Wallets. Send a dozen of each. Also, shoes. Not too high. She prefers flats or wedge heels. As a matter of fact, send whatever else you have in her size as long as there's pink in it."

"Pink? Yes. Very good, sir."

"Thank you, Van," I said.

"My pleasure to assist you, Mr. Aziz."

Cost was no issue, as Van knew. My account would be paid in full before he could hit enter.

Whatever the price. It was worth it. I was practically salivating, just thinking of how delicious my wife looked in pink.

Yes, leaving the party early seemed like a very good idea.

CHAPTER TWENTY-SIX
MEREDITH

W*hy am I so nervous?*

It was ridiculous.

There was a time when I could afford all the top fashions.

I'd been spoiled and petted and praised most of my early life. But that was mostly because people were sucking up to me or my father, *er*, stepfather.

Anyway, it had been years since I had anywhere fancy to go. I felt nauseated, and the butterflies in my stomach were more like fighter jets.

I barely ate all afternoon.

I knew it was silly. Josef had seen, caressed, touched, and kissed every inch of my soft, curvy body.

He knew where all my freckles were. Saw and loved on all my pink bits.

It was completely ludicrous for me to feel self-conscious. Especially in clothes.

And yet, here I am, chewing my lipstick off.

I ran my hands over my soft belly and bit my lip as I waited for my husband to come pick me up.

But will he like it?

He bought it, so he should. I mean, he told me he was buying me something to wear.

But he went a little overboard.

The dress I had on was completely gorgeous. But it clung to me like a second skin.

And old-fashioned as it was, I wanted to please him with my appearance.

We were going to a dinner party to celebrate the wife of his friend. This was important.

Like an interview.

Truth was, I didn't really know who he was close to, but I wanted to. I wanted to meet the people in his life.

Curiosity had plagued me all day. It was all I could do to focus on work.

Work.

That reminded me. Right before I left, we'd gotten a new admission to the shelter. I hated having to leave early, but the other employees would take care of her. I knew that.

The sweet young mother was sporting a full arm

cast and a black eye. My heart damn near broke when she told me her story.

Well, the bits and pieces she'd shared.

It was a wonder someone who'd been hurt that badly was willing to confide in anyone at all, let alone a stranger.

It was a humbling experience when someone trusted you without you really earning it.

Ellie was her name. She seemed shy and timid. But she'd been hurt so many times, I couldn't be sure if that was her real nature.

All I knew was she needed help.

Leading her to one of the small efficiency rooms in the back, newly secured courtesy of my husband, I gave her my number and one of the mobiles we had on hand for residents.

It was important they did not use any of their own electronics.

Phones, tablets, and computers could all be traced.

I'd confiscated what she'd brought, offering her son an older but safer tablet to use. Then, I locked her things away in a *go dark* bag and stored them in the safe.

I recognized the name brand clothes she wore, and the designer backpack her small son had carried in with him. They came from money. Or her abusive piece of shit husband did.

Ellie was safer than she had been before she arrived.

That was just a fact. Too often did these cases turn fatal, and so many women did not get the help they needed.

That was why I worked at St. Elizabeth's and why I hoped my husband wouldn't mind that I used the money my stepfather had paid into my old bank account for years, to set up temporary housing for those women who didn't want to sleep inside the shelter. Women who just didn't feel safe there.

I understood.

I mean, the shelter was easy enough to track. Plenty of exes had tracked their spouses or significant others to our doors, and the resulting confrontations were difficult and sometimes violent.

Ellie was one of those women who felt she needed to go elsewhere. But where? That was the question.

She was fine at the shelter for a little while. But her husband had money and he would find her. She knew it and I knew it. Which was why I also knew she wouldn't stay there long.

She needed something more permanent. And I was going to find it for her.

With a little over seven figures in my account, that's what I had of Franklin Gray's blood money, I called the shelter's lawyers and asked them to find a place I could buy as a sort of off-site accommodation for women in the tri-state area.

They were looking into it, and I felt a deep sense of

satisfaction knowing I could use the money for something good. Sure, the law tried to help, but I never met a restraining order that could physically stop someone hellbent on hurting another.

Ellie's was just one story, but something about her drew me to the woman. Maybe it was her sweet little boy. Either way, I left work feeling a sense of hope for the first time in a long while.

The night security guard waved goodbye to me when I went into the hall to meet Mario who'd arrived at four to bring me home.

I had no idea the surprises that were waiting for me inside the condo. And when I saw them, I cried happy tears.

Such beautiful surprises.

If my husband was trying to sweep me off my feet, he'd succeeded.

Dresses, gowns, pants, blouses, purses, and shoes. Dozens of the most exquisite items I'd ever seen had been delivered to the penthouse.

Even better, all of them had pink somewhere in the design.

And there, placed right on top of the bed, was a small envelope with my name scrawled across the back. I opened it, and there was a note tucked inside.

Pick something delicious, Little Red. I'm feeling ravenous. Your Big Bad Wolf.

Excitement filled me and I'd giggled for five full minutes as I flitted from bag to bag and hanger to hanger.

Everything was so beautiful. So colorful. And all the right sizes.

Someone had obviously been inside the condo, because all the dresses and clothes were in the closet on velvet-covered hangers. I couldn't wrap my head around it.

I felt like a teenager getting ready for prom. Something I'd missed in my youth.

We were going to a party. Tonight. And he wanted me to meet his friends. Squeal!

I was nervous, but also eager to be introduced to the people close to him.

I took a quick shower, careful to keep my long hair dry. I dressed with care, rubbing the new jar of imported body butter my husband had bought me all over my skin first to make it soft.

Josef had truly outdone himself. I only hoped he was happy with the result.

The dress I'd chosen to wear was a deep, dusky shade of rose. The material was soft and stretchy, so it fit perfectly over my wide hips and large bosoms.

It even did a fine job of camouflaging my soft tummy with its ruched bodice and sweetheart neckline. Tight sleeves came down to my elbows, and the fitted skirt ended a few inches below my knees, giving me a very 1950s glam look that I adored.

I wore black accessories, low heels, and a matching clutch, and I pulled my hair up and away from my face in a simple twist. My make up was all done, and I already used the restroom one last time.

I just had to wait for him to show up.

Sighing and shaking out my hands. I was in the middle of my *get yourself calm girl* stretches when the elevator pinged, and the door opened.

"Wife—holy fuck!"

Next thing I knew, Josef had blurred across the room and had me by the hips. His gaze was frozen on my body in a stare I felt down to my toes.

Gulp.

"Um, do you like it?"

CHAPTER TWENTY-SEVEN
JOSEF

I was going to have to kill everyone who stared at her, I realized when I saw Meredith in that dress.

My heart had been beating double-time ever since I'd sent that note home with Mario for the housekeeper to put inside our bedroom.

We had a cleaning service that came daily, and I requested someone to stick around to arrange the clothes I ordered for Meredith in our closet as a surprise.

Not like I would allow Mario or any of my men to put one fucking foot inside the room where my wife slept, ate, showered, dressed, and fucked.

I was the only man who was allowed in that space.

Me. Only me.

And yeah, I did not give two shits if that made me a fucking barbarian.

All damn afternoon I'd been picturing my sexy Little Red in one of those dresses I'd picked out.

Jesus. Christ.

The reality was so much better than my imagination. And I could daydream like a motherfucker.

"We're not going," I said, shaking my head.

"What?" she asked, shocked.

"Nope. We're staying right here," I said, pressing her back towards the bedroom.

"Josef!"

Meredith raised her hands and her eyebrows at the same time. Like either would stop me from slamming my lips to hers.

Cocoa butter sweetness burst across my tastebuds as I licked into her mouth.

"Fuck, you always taste so good," I grunted, cupping her face, and angling her head where I wanted her.

"Mmm, Husband," she moaned softly.

I pressed my forehead gently against hers, trying to calm my thundering heart by just breathing her in.

"Sorry. I'm acting like a beast," I murmured, suddenly ashamed of myself for coming at her like a beast.

"I'm not sorry. I guess that means you like the dress," she said.

Meredith's emerald eyes glittered mischievously as she blinked her long lashes at me.

"Like it? You look delicious, Wife," I growled.

She looked like a goddess.

She looked like mine.

"Really?" she asked.

I picked up a tiny note of doubt in her voice, and I frowned. I wasn't having any of that, I cupped her cheeks in my hands.

"Meredith, you look beautiful."

"Thank you," she replied, her voice soft and breathy. "It would be a shame to waste it. I mean, you did buy it so I could wear it out tonight to meet your friends, didn't you?"

"I did," I relented.

"Good. Shall we go then?"

"Yes. We'll go. Give me a moment," I said, and went to change my suit.

It took seven minutes, but it was worth it when I exited the bedroom and found Meredith unable to look away.

"I thought I would wear something new, too," I said, smirking at the way her gaze traveled up and down my form.

I was a fit man. The perfectly tailored suit only enhanced my physique, and the black color matched her accessories perfectly.

"You're always in black," she commented.

The breathy quality of her voice told me it wasn't a criticism. It was true. I did favor dark colors.

Black, mostly. But that was a force of habit.

You couldn't really get blood and other bodily fluids out of many others. So black was as much a necessity as it was a fashion statement.

"You're my color," I said, pausing to take her hand.

My breath caught at the verity of that statement.

Meredith, with her milky white skin and her flaming red hair, with her emerald fire eyes, and penchant for wearing pink.

She was the color in my world.

Without her, I'd been living in the shadows. A half-life. A broken one. A near dead thing.

But I had her back now. And with her, she brought the sunshine.

She brought life.

I kissed her knuckles, catching the surprised grin on her face, and fuck, but it warmed me.

Silently, I held her hand the whole way down to the garage and the waiting SUV, contemplating the very real possibility that I was head over heels for my wife.

I'm in love with her.

I love my wife. So damn much.

My chest tightened as I opened the SUV door,

HIS WILD SEDUCTION   241

glaring at Mario when he moved to do it until he stepped back.

No one got to touch my wife's door when I was present. She was mine in every sense of the word, and I was fiercely protective of what I considered mine.

My man understood that and backed away towards the front, where he would ride with my regular driver.

"How far is the trip?" Meredith asked, seemingly unaware of the tension brewing within me.

"Not far. I would have driven myself, but I thought maybe you'd like to talk with me?" I asked, feeling a little stupid about it, really.

The truth was, I wanted her to talk to me.

I looked forward to that time of day after we both came home from work, between eating dinner and making love, when Meredith would share little stories and tidbits about her day.

Yes, Mario sent me updates. Every hour on the hour.

Possessive prick that I was, I demanded it.

But that was not the same as hearing it from her sweet lips.

"Today was rough," she said, and I watched her frown as she chose her words.

I already knew about the woman with the broken arm and small scared son who came to the shelter seeking safe harbor earlier in the day.

Mario had informed me immediately, as he'd been instructed.

Within an hour, I had all the information I needed on Ellie Maxwell-Peters.

She was the Maxwell heiress. Due to inherit billions that stemmed from an old mining fortune.

Her people were from Pennsylvania, originally, but she'd moved to Manhattan with her husband.

Gary Peters was a fucking prick.

The guy worked for his wife's father, came on strong, got her pregnant, forced a marriage, then lost his shit when he realized the company wouldn't go to her.

Oh, she inherited money after her father's demise. But it was spread out.

The big deposit wouldn't hit until she turned thirty, and that wasn't for another year.

Maxwell Mining had taken a deep nosedive when Ellie's father passed on. The whole thing was going on the auction block.

I already sent Andres what I had on the company and asked him to investigate. If he thought it was a good investment, Andres would bring it to Adrik and Marat.

It was kind of what Volkov Industries did. I'd take my piece, of course.

But the real benefit to everyone was that I had plans to sink that fucking asshole for putting his hands on his young wife.

I hated abusers. And Gary Peters was the worst fucking kind.

Hitting a woman because he wasn't smart enough or good enough to build himself up on his own? Oh, I didn't fucking think so.

I turned my attention to my wife. My sweet, caring, beautiful wife who worked so hard to make a difference.

"I'm just worried she won't want to stay in the shelter. So, um, I wanted to tell you, I took that money I had, that Gray Corps had been paying me all those years, and I asked Fr. Augustus, he's the head counselor for St. Elizabeth's, to find some properties that might be worth buying as a secondary location for some of our tri-state residents."

She bit her lip, as if she thought I would object. I narrowed my eyes and dipped my chin.

"God, you're incredible. Do you know that?"

"What?" she said, shaking her head.

"You are so good, Meredith. St. E's is lucky to have you. Your idea sounds really good. Will you let me help?" I asked.

"You want to help?" she asked, eyes wide.

"Yeah. Can I have Fr. Augustus' contact information? My lawyer and personal realtor can definitely help."

"Really? You would do that. And you're not mad," she whispered, and the most authentic smile I'd ever seen broke out across her pretty face.

"Of course not. I'm serious. I'm proud of you, Baby. You know, I can pay for whatever you need—"

"I know. But I want to use this. I hate the idea of Franklin's money sitting there. It feels wrong. And I, well, I used it before to help people get away," she confessed.

I squeezed her hand. I knew she did something with that money, I just had no idea how selfless she was.

But I understood what she meant. She didn't need her stepfather's dirty money, anyway.

I would work myself to the bone to make sure Meredith had everything she wanted, everything she needed.

My wife would want for nothing. If she wanted to buy other properties for the shelter to use as lodging for its residents, that was more than okay with me.

I leaned forward and captured her lips in a hard, fast kiss. Smiling against her mouth, I breathed deeply. Just sucking in all the flavors of her.

I really loved this woman.

More than anything.

She owned parts of me I didn't know existed.

Deep, dark, secret parts.

Meredith elicited emotions I didn't think I was capable of feeling.

Protective instincts. Possessive ones, too.

Hell, I knew I would do terrible things to keep her safe and warm and happy. And most importantly, with me. Because that was where she belonged.

With me.

"We're here, Boss."

My gaze darted to the front of the SUV. I almost smirked.

Marco was waiting for me to tell him what to do. I nodded once, dipping my head to the front of the SUV.

He got out of the vehicle and stood there, on guard. But he made not one move towards my wife's door.

Nice job.

"Wait for me, Little Red."

"Yes, Josef."

"That's right, Good Girl, always wait for me," I whispered, touching her chin with my forefinger and thumb.

I knew she would.

Meredith was mine. I felt the truth of that down to my marrow as I circled around to her door and held it open.

"You ready?" I asked, and she nodded, assuming I meant to go inside.

But what I was really asking was she ready for this?

Ready for me to take this whole thing to another level?

Because I was so fucking ready.

CHAPTER TWENTY-EIGHT
MEREDITH

The elegant beachfront mansion was located on the Long Island Sound. It took almost an hour and a half to get there, and Josef's driver had been moving way past the speed limit.

I was still in a warm daze after chatting most of the trip with my husband. I talked about work mostly, and I wasn't sure what to expect at first.

But he surprised me. Wonderful man. He was just so understanding.

It was like he knew I needed to do this, and he let me. He didn't take over. He just offered help. He respected me. And I loved him a little bit more for it.

Once upon a time, the Big Bad Wolf broke my heart, but every day since we met again, he worked hard to put it back together. And I wasn't really sure how to deal with that.

Watching him move as he walked around the vehicle to open my door had me licking my lips. I was married to a handsome man.

He turned his head, and the sunlight caught his mahogany hair and the twinkle in his whiskey eyes, and damn, my mouth went completely dry.

I mean, I knew Josef was fine as fuck. The way he filled out his suit and everything, but it was that rare glimpse of happiness on his face that made him sublime.

Pride filled me as I thought maybe I was responsible, even if in the smallest way, for bringing him that look of contentment.

Of joy.

Appreciation filled his gaze as he watched me slide out of the high SUV, careful to keep my skirt down.

His possessiveness was something I loved, and honestly, I wasn't much of an exhibitionist, and I didn't want anyone to steal a glimpse of the little bitty panties I was wearing. Those were a surprise for Josef's eyes only.

He had one hand on my hip, the other holding my hand, as he pulled me against him and kissed my temple before stepping back.

"You look fucking perfect in pink," he said, and I felt the compliment to my toes.

He placed a possessive hand around the back of my neck as we walked up the stone path to the entryway.

It felt so good to be with him like this. In public. Technically, it was still early days for us, but our history made it so I felt like I'd known him forever.

Josef was a part of me. A part of my past, my present, and hopefully, my future.

I didn't get the impression he was growing tired of me, but I admit I had small doubts sometimes. But that was for me to work on.

Josef had done nothing but make me feel wanted and desired.

If only I knew what was in his heart.

But I was going to take it one day at a time. That was the best advice I'd ever heard in all my travels, and it applied to just about every situation.

One day at a time.

And today was a good day.

I watched as Josef's face changed before my eyes as we approached the two men standing by the door. He looked hard, unreadable. The man on the left nodded his head.

"Mr. Aziz," he said.

Josef's chin dipped down slightly. A small confirmation he'd heard the man as he guided me inside.

They must be part of his security firm, I thought.

The men did not bother stopping us, and for the

first time I understood just how powerful my husband was. There were a few more imposing men and two women, dressed all in black with cleverly concealed weapons on their persons.

They stood at three foot intervals, stopping guests from trying to make their way around back as they checked their lists.

Everyone entering the party was expected to announce who they were and show their invitations. Everyone except for us, it seemed.

I'd been nervous as we bypassed the small queue that had formed outside, but Josef didn't even slow down. He moved with an air of arrogance and complete ease that on anyone else would have been obnoxious.

But on him, it just enhanced the muted strength he carried so well. The hand on my neck lowered to the small of my back and I shivered at the heat coming from his fingertips.

"Are you cold?"

This man.

"No. I'm good," I said, leaning into his powerful body.

He hummed appreciatively, and his hand flexed against my back. I knew this was a party for one of Josef's friends' wives, and I wanted to be there. But I also wanted to be alone with my husband.

Later.

Turning my head away from my husband's heated stare, so I didn't melt into a puddle of *take me I'm yours* goo at his feet, I took a moment to look around. The house was stunning.

I hadn't expected all this. The ceilings had to be at least sixteen feet high, and everything was done in shades of blue and gray. It was the perfect mix of old and new.

Framed paintings and stained glass lined the walls. Large vases with fresh flowers decorated tables. The floors were highly polished wood, stained a slate gray, but somehow the wood itself added a warmth to the décor I wouldn't have expected.

The party was taking place in what looked like a large, comfortable sitting parlor whose back wall was made entirely of glass that opened up onto an outdoor terrace.

I saw small glittering lights outside and grinned. It was like a magical fairyland out there between the beautiful wrought iron fence, the lights, and the dozens of potted lemon trees and blooming shrubs.

It was brilliant. Cozy somehow, despite the obvious opulence. Deep blue leather couches and velvet chairs were strategically posed to make the most of the space and offer guests a respite.

I was thoroughly impressed. The home was positively beautiful.

"Josef!" a female someone called out to my husband with a familiarity that, at first, sent jealousy spiking through me.

I frowned as I watched a pretty woman with beautiful dark curls wearing a stunning sapphire jumpsuit approached us.

"Thank God you're here," she said, clapping her hands together. "Will you please find my husband and tell him there is nothing wrong with allowing guests to wander around the ground floor?"

Josef chuckled beside me as he looked at the woman with an indulgent expression on his face. He obviously knew her and cared about her. But who the fuck was she?

"I would love to do that, Destiny, but Marat's not wrong," Josef said apologetically.

"Ugh, you're just like them! I'm sorry to interrupt. Hi, I'm Destiny," she said, offering me her hand.

Destiny. Marat. Oh shit.

It all came together, and my cheeks burned with embarrassment.

"I'm Meredith," I replied with as best a smile as I could manage, considering I'd just been plotting ways to get her away from my man.

Oopsies.

I was a little more possessive about my husband

than I thought. But Destiny didn't seem to notice. She was open and friendly, and welcoming.

"Destiny, allow me to formally introduce you to my wife. Meredith," Josef told her, and the way he said *my wife* sent shivers racing through me.

"Little Red, this is Destiny, Marat's wife," Josef explained.

"It is so nice to meet you. Thank you for inviting us to your beautiful home," I exclaimed.

"Of course and thank you. We only moved in full time a month ago, and it's been crazy trying to get everything ready, especially with Lucy teething. Plus, my overbearing husband is giving me fits. Josef, please go talk to him," she begged.

"Will you be alright?" my husband asked me, and I smiled and nodded.

"Oh my God, I'm not going to bite her. Get outta here. We have womanly things to discuss, and we don't need any more Alpha male overprotective nonsense right now. So shoo!"

Destiny made a moving motion with her hands.

I couldn't help it.

I laughed out loud.

Like really loud.

Then I snorted.

Oops.

Josef raised one perfect eyebrow at me as I covered my mouth. But the giggling wouldn't stop.

The woman was a riot.

"Alright, I'll be right back. Behave yourself, Little Red," he murmured, brushing his lips against the corner of my mouth.

"Shoo, go away already," Destiny mumbled, grabbing me by the arm.

"I thought he was never going to let go of you. Come on, Sofia's in the breastfeeding suite, but she is dying to meet you."

"A breastfeeding suite?" I asked.

What a marvelous idea!

"Oh, yeah, it was Marat's idea, actually. He's ridiculously protective and always trying to make my life easier, which is probably why I am so dang in love with him," she said, shaking her head.

"That jerk," I joked.

"Right? I mean, bad enough my husband looks like Lucifer, but he has to be good to me, too. Total loser," she teased.

"Anyway, the suite was his idea to make feedings easier on me when we have guests. In fact, Lucy, my daughter, is probably throwing a fit right now. Sof is entertaining her for me. I was going to run interference with security and a couple of guests who tried to go into one of the other smaller parlors for a bit of quiet, but I decided to just argue with my husband instead. I swear, Josef's security teams can deadeye you like no one's business. I mean, you'd think we invited total strangers to this thing the way he's behaving."

She wasn't wrong. From what I knew of Josef, I had no doubt Sigma International employees were the best of the best at what they did. Even when he was my bodyguard all those years ago, Josef's professionalism stood out.

Pride filled me. I looked around at what had to be over a hundred guests. There were a lot of people. I didn't know how she knew so many, but people did.

There was a fairly even mix of men and women. Everyone was dressed for the occasion. So I didn't feel out of place at all. The clothes Josef had picked for me were all beautiful, and this dress, well, I'd been super excited for him to see me in it.

I followed behind her. People were smiling and milling about, drinking wine, and eating cleverly plated tapas passed around by servers dressed in white.

"Are all of these people close friends?" I asked, increasing my pace to keep up with the surprisingly spry woman.

She was wearing the cutest little ballet flats that matched her blue jumpsuit. It was sparkly and clung to her lovely frame. The sapphire blue pant legs were wide and swirled about her legs as she walked.

The front was low, and I noticed the discreet clips on each shoulder, realizing that must be for easy access to nurse her baby. How clever! The bodice cinched beneath her breasts, and the overall effect was really something.

She looked like some sort of marine goddess. The fact she was curvy, like me, had me making a mental note to ask where she got it.

"Well, not exactly," Destiny answered my question a few seconds later, after smiling and nodding her head at a few of her guests.

"There are people from the publishing house I don't really know here. And some of the scary-looking men in suits are business acquaintances of Marat's. And some are new neighbors."

"Ah. Well, then maybe your husband has a point," I hedged, not wanting to start anything.

But I could see why her husband would not want people wandering unsupervised through their new homes. Especially not when they had their baby there.

"Oh, that is so cute! You and Josef have the same attitude about safety!"

"Well, I don't know if it's cute. But, um, I was raised to respect proper security. Someone broke into my childhood home when I was in high school and they broke my things, took some jewelry that had been my mother's, and they wrote nasty slurs on the wall," I explained.

"Oh no! That must have been horrible," she said, her big blue eyes filling with tears.

"I was fine. Please, don't cry—"

She opened the door to a private room, and I was stunned at how beautiful it was. I'd never seen a breast-feeding suite, but this was amazing. There was every convenience a mother could want.

A couple of cushiony rocking chairs lined one wall with matching ottomans. A pair of changing stations. A mini fridge. A play area with toddler appropriate toys. A flat screen television. An en suite bathroom. Bassinets decorated in soft blues and whites. And even a sofa.

A stunning woman in cropped silver pants topped with a black silk blouse turned around. Her smile was warm and friendly, and she was holding a precious bundle in her arms.

I never met her, but she looked vaguely familiar.

"Hi! I'm Sofia, you must be Meredith! I am so excited to meet you. I'm Adrik's wife," she said while handing the little girl to Destiny.

"Oh my God," I exclaimed as recognition hit. "You're Z. Wolff. I read all your books!"

Excitement short-circuited my brain, and I was two seconds from full on fangirling.

"You do? Thank you," she said, laughing.

"And you're her narrator! D. Wolff?! Holy shit! I love you guys!"

"Hear that Lucy, Mama's got a fan," Destiny cooed while she snuggled her baby to her breast and began feeding her.

"I really am a fan," I said, clapping my hands awkwardly. "Sorry, I am making this weird."

"Not at all. And thank you so much. Josef didn't tell Adrik you were a reader," Sofia said, gesturing to one of the seats beside Destiny.

I thought it might be awkward for her to have us sitting there while she nursed her baby, but she didn't seem bothered. She had a soft-looking blanket draped over her chest, and a serene smile on her face as she rocked the chair back and forth.

"Oh, well, um, Josef didn't tell me you were an author, and you a narrator," I said, and shrugged.

I couldn't help the momentary panic that filled me.

Why hadn't Josef mentioned me? Was he ashamed? Embarrassed? Was our past too fraught for explanations?

"Hey, don't look like that," Sofia said, her tone gentle. "I've been married to Adrik for three years now. I know he considers Josef a brother, but that man is probably the most close-guarded human being I've ever met."

"Josef? But we talk all the time," I replied, frowning.

Slowly, I started to see her point. The more I thought about it, the more I realized *I* was the one who talked all the time.

"Um, how did you two meet? I'm dying to know," Destiny asked, her tone hushed so as not to disturb little Lucy.

"Oh, well, we met years ago. My stepfather hired him as a bodyguard when I was a senior in high school."

"Wow! I know you don't know us yet, but I promise you can trust me and Destiny to keep your secrets, Mer."

"Mare? Like a horse?" I asked, confused.

"No, she means, Mer, like your name. M-E-R. Don't mind her. Sof is all about the nicknames," Destiny replied with a teasing eye roll.

"What are you talking about? This is kismet! I'm Sof. You're Des. And she is Mer! It works," Sofia replied with a pout.

"It's fine, I mean, at least it's my name. Josef just calls me Little Red for obvious reasons," I confessed, and waved my hand towards my hair.

"Oooh, I sense a forbidden romance," Sofia said, her eyes bright with humor.

"It's funny cause a few weeks ago thinking about Josef and our past would have made me sad and angry, but you're right. I guess it was a forbidden romance."

"You don't have to, but if you want to share, we are all ears," Des said quietly.

"And I promise not to use anything you say as book fodder," Sof added.

I laughed. For some reason, I felt comfortable with these women. It had been such a long time since I had a real friend, if I ever did.

So, I told them everything.

All of it.

My tumultuous past with Josef. Everything that had happened with my stepfather. Running away to Europe. Coming back to the states. Working for the shelter.

And the more I told them, the better I felt.

Less alone. Supported. Comforted.

I should've probably realized from my experience and all the time I spent counseling women and children who'd left abusive situations that I could benefit from a little therapy myself. I mean, I tried counseling years ago, and I thought it worked.

But I never considered maybe it was something I should have continued.

"I know it might seem like what he did was cruel, like the way he backed you into a corner. But I think maybe Josef needed you and didn't know how to deal with that. His ultimatum solved that problem," Destiny whispered.

HIS WILD SEDUCTION   261

Lucy was asleep, so I understood why she was being quiet.

But it felt like maybe this conversation was too precarious for loud words.

I thought about what she said for a moment and felt hope rising inside me like an unstoppable tide.

Could it be true? Did Josef maybe care about me like I cared about him?

The sound of voices outside the nursing suite brought our attention to the door. A soft knocking sounded, and Sofia stood to answer it.

"Yes? Oh! Sure, she's here. I'll tell her," Sofia whispered, coming back with a wide grin on her face.

"What is it?" I asked, curious.

"Your husband is outside waiting for you, and he looks fit to be tied," Sofia remarked, highly amused if her expression was anything to go by.

I frowned and stood up, turning back towards both women.

"Oh, um. Thank you for letting me talk and for welcoming me."

I was a little embarrassed that I was moved to tears by something as simple as the ready friendship these women offered. But I was.

Things like that didn't happen every day. The women I worked with were healing and guarded. As was their right. But now and then, I wondered if their situations couldn't have been avoided. If maybe they couldn't have gotten help sooner. If only they had a friend.

But that was what abusers did. They separated you from your people so they could dominate you. So they could exact control.

Josef did the complete opposite. He brought me here, introduced me to these women, creating a place for me to thrive and feel good about myself. He was giving me a support system that didn't just revolve around him.

He thought he was a bad man. But he was the best man I knew.

God, I love him.

"Hey, we're bound by womanhood and our husbands. The *wives of wolves* need to stick together!" Destiny said, and I wondered at her turn of phrase.

Wives of wolves?

Sof grabbed me in a short, tight hug, then eased back with a genuine smile on her face. Her eyes twinkled with mischief.

"I'll call you this week for lunch, okay? I want to talk more about your job and what we can do to help."

"That sounds great," I told her, and I meant it.

A feeling of rightness settled over me as I bade both women goodbye. I never had close friends, but maybe I did now. It felt good.

Curious about what Josef could be so upset about, I walked into the hall and was shocked when the big man grabbed my hand and tugged me to him.

"Damn it, Little Red. I didn't know where you were," he growled, wrapping me in his arms.

Startled by his reaction to my absence, I hugged him back, kissing his neck and cheek, whispering soothing words.

"Where's your phone?"

"Um, I don't know, I must have left it in my bag when I checked it at the door," I said, shrugging.

"Were you worried?" I asked, biting my lip.

"Yes, I was worried. I walked away for a minute and then you were gone!"

He looked angry. Pissed even. But the worry lines around his eyes told another story.

He'd been scared. Scared I'd left him.

"Hey, I'm yours and you're mine, remember? I'm never leaving you," I said, looking into those whiskey colored eyes I loved so much.

My heart was pounding so hard. His hands tightened on my shoulders as he pulled back and just stared at me. That was okay. I was doing some staring of my own.

I studied my handsome husband, noting the slight flare of his nostrils before he moved.

He was so damn fast.

Josef blurred to me, closing the space between us. Spicy cologne and male musk filled my nostrils.

His big, muscular body crushed my softer one in his frenzied embrace, but it felt so fucking good.

Were it not for his arm around me, I would have tipped over. But Josef wouldn't allow that. He would always keep me safe.

Trust and delight bloomed inside me.

And desire—always desire when it came to this man.

At first, I thought maybe I'd said the wrong thing.

But I didn't have to worry. It was the absolute right thing to say because my sexy as fuck husband was crushing my mouth with his.

His hand cupped the back of my head, so it didn't connect with the unforgiving wall as he ravaged my mouth.

"Um, are you coming back to the party?" an amused voice said from behind us.

Josef slowed us down, breaking our connection only to come back for several more plucking kisses. He pressed his forehead to mine, not turning around or releasing me.

"We'll be right there."

"Alright, I look forward to meeting you formally, Mrs. Aziz," the masculine voice replied.

I couldn't reply.

I was still trying to catch my breath.

CHAPTER TWENTY-NINE
JOSEF

When I came back from checking the security teams and the biometric alarm system I'd installed personally in Marat and Destiny's new home, I couldn't find her.

My Little Red was missing.

At first, I thought maybe she'd gone to the restroom. So, like a fucking stalker, I waited outside the one designated for ladies for ten full minutes.

But no Meredith.

Then, I texted her. I waited another couple of minutes.

No reply.

I tried to track the thing, but of course the security system I installed also messed with any tracking software inside the home, so that was moot.

Curiosity turned to annoyance.

Annoyance to anger.

Anger to rage.

Then rage to worry.

And that was the fucking worst of it.

I was worried my wife of less than two months had walked out on me. Like some lovesick fucking boy, I panicked.

I was so scared that Meredith, my Little Red, had finally wised up to the fact that I was so fucking beneath her she decided to leave me.

No. I can't let that happen.

I was about to race outside when Marat caught up with me. His amused expression told me he knew exactly what I'd been thinking.

"I believe I know where she is," he'd said quietly, turning as if I'd just follow him.

Fucker.

He was right.

I followed him blindly.

"We converted one of the sitting rooms into a nursing suite for Destiny, and anyone else who might be breastfeeding. I just wanted her to be comfortable, but my Dumplin' loved the idea, especially after she'd joined a few mommy groups out here," he explained.

"Meredith's not nursing," I growled.

The sudden vision of my wife swollen with my seed,

then breastfeeding the yet to be born baby, had my cock so goddamn hard, I groaned.

My hands were shaking.

No, it was worse.

My entire body was vibrating. And I didn't know if it was from worry, fear, or lust.

Fuck.

I had better control than that.

Or at least, I should have better control than that.

It took a few seconds for me to get myself calm enough to form words. I nodded my thanks and Marat pointed out the door to the nursing suite before he discreetly left.

Knocking on the door, I waited. But it wasn't Meredith who answered. It was Sofia.

Adrik's wife looked positively delighted by the fact I was there, searching for Little Red.

But I had no time to worry about her or how ridiculous I looked.

The scent of cocoa butter reached me, and I closed my eyes, breathing in deep.

She was there. She hadn't left.

Relief filled me, but that happy sensation darkened, turning into something else as my wife, deliciously wrapped in pink, approached me, her head canted warily.

All those carefully worded things I wanted to say

that I'd had readied in my head prior to knocking got blown away in the hurricane of my feelings for her.

My wife. My Little Red.

I managed a few sentences. But it wasn't enough. Hardly articulate at the best of times, I felt choked with emotion and I couldn't get past that initial fear I'd felt that she'd run away.

From me. Again.

Then she spoke, and the words she said rocked me to my fucking core.

"Hey, I'm yours and you're mine, remember?" she whispered, cupping my bearded face with her small hands.

So much damn emotion surged through me, I couldn't help myself. I pinned her to the wall, claiming her with my mouth.

I was so fucking worried she would push me away. But I didn't give her the chance to talk or to refuse me.

Not knowing exactly how Meredith felt about public displays of affection, I took a chance.

But this was hardly a hug or peck on the cheek in front of friends.

This was a full on claiming.

A consummation without it actually turning into sex.

I wouldn't do that. I wouldn't fuck her in public.

The idea of anyone else seeing or hearing my sexy as

fuck wife in the throes of passion made me positively homicidal.

No one got to hear her moans or see her body, ever. No one but me.

She's mine.

But I needed her to know that. I needed her to understand how much *mine* she really was.

I pushed my tongue into her mouth, kissing her so damn fully, branding her with my lips, so all she could see, hear, feel, breathe, and taste was me.

I wanted to consume her. To carry her around inside of me forever.

She was in my blood.

My Little Red.

She was the beating of my heart. My rhyme, my reason, my whole fucking life. I'd do anything, give anything just to keep her.

This woman owned me.

Me.

Josef Aziz.

The Big Bad Wolf.

Killer of men.

Black-hearted monster living in the shadows.

But maybe I wasn't only that. Not anymore.

Maybe, with Meredith, I could be something else. I could be more than I was. More than the shadowy boogeyman.

With her, my life wasn't so cold and dark. With her, I wasn't alone.

Meredith was the sun in my sky. She brought color back into my life. And warmth.

So much fucking warmth.

I needed her like I needed air. Like the earth needed the rain and the sun.

She was necessary to me. To my existence.

All those years apart, I'd been missing her. But no more.

I'll never let her go again.

"Um, are you coming back to the party?"

I could hear Marat's smirk, and my chest rumbled with aggravation.

Not wanting to move away from her soft body or her cocoa scented kisses just yet, I leaned my forehead against hers, pleased she looked as flushed as I felt.

"We'll be right there," I told him.

"Alright, I look forward to meeting you formally, Mrs. Aziz."

Marat walked away, but I could hear him stop by the nursing suite to get Destiny, assuming their nanny took over watching baby Lucy after she was fed.

"Come on," I said, standing up straight and adjusting myself so my hard on wasn't too noticeable.

"Are you sure you're alright? Maybe I can help with

that," Meredith said, her green eyes glittering with mischief.

"Minx," I growled, lunging for her.

She giggled and ducked my outstretched arm, but I caught up to her easily and swatted her on her heart-shaped ass.

Fuck. I really loved her ass.

"How long until we can leave?" she whispered as we rejoined the majority of people.

"An hour at least. Want something to eat?"

She nodded, and I lifted my hand, calling over one of the servers circling the room with tapas and drinks.

I handed Meredith a glass of wine and fed her some prosciutto wrapped melon from my hand, finishing what she didn't.

We ate like that for a little while. Me feeding her bites of this and that from whatever small plates were being served.

Feeding her was quickly becoming one of my favorite damn activities. She moaned appreciatively around a cracker slathered with olive tapenade and a sprinkle of fresh thyme.

The mini lamb skewer with a mint sauce reduction was delicious. But the chicken croquettes were my favorite.

Meredith tried it all. She was game for everything.

Even the fried squid and raw oysters served on a spoon with a mignonette sauce.

She almost went cross-eyed when we shared the goat cheese stuffed strawberries.

Feeding her was a goddamn aphrodisiac. I couldn't wait to get her home to try it again.

Only next time, I was thinking of feeding her my dick.

An image of my Little Red, her pink lips stretched around my girthy cock filled my head and I wanted to groan.

Fuck. Me.

"Oh my God, no more, please. It's so good, but I can't eat another bite," she said.

I frowned, thinking we hadn't even had dessert yet.

"Glad you enjoyed everything," Marat interrupted, approaching with his brother and their wives in tow.

"Hello, I'm Adrik Volkov. This is my brother, Marat," he said.

"It's good to finally meet you! Anyone who can put up with Josef must be a saint, for sure. Oof," Marat grunted the last, and I grinned at Destiny who'd just elbowed her husband.

Jerk.

"Sorry, Mer. Our guys can be a bit much," Destiny said, nodding at Meredith and rolling her eyes at her husband who was now pouting like the overgrown toddler he was.

"You didn't mind my muchness this morning, Dumplin'," Marat whispered to his wife, but I still heard him.

And when she elbowed him again, I chuckled.

"It's a pleasure to meet you all," Meredith, ever the diplomat, said, fighting against her smirk.

It might have looked odd to outsiders, but the fact neither man offered his hand to my wife, and that Meredith made no move to touch them, just proved my earlier point.

Meredith was mine.

And fuck, I really liked that.

CHAPTER THIRTY
MEREDITH

After chatting for a little while with the Volkov brothers, who were intimidating as fuck, Josef found us a small corner to sit down in one of the rooms off the main parlor.

Destiny got her way, I mused.

There was plenty of open space for the majority of the party dwellers to mingle, and though Marat did not want people just walking around willy-nilly, Josef had managed to convince him the two smaller parlors off the main room were perfectly secure.

It made Destiny happy, so Marat relented. And I, for one, was glad, too. Growing up with money, I'd attended plenty of parties, but that was so long ago.

I didn't really fit in with that crowd, despite appearances. And I relished the privacy of the small parlor, and sitting with Josef as he handed me a small demi-tasse cup with a shot of perfectly brewed espresso inside.

"Thank you," I said, smiling appreciatively.

"It's decaf," he warned, and I hummed my approval.

I didn't want to have the jitters all night. It was only ten o'clock, but still. I was tired after my long work week, and Josef looked about ready to leave, too.

Our earlier encounter not forgotten, I hoped we'd make it home before sleep won out.

There were things I needed to say, *and do*, to my husband.

"Adrik is signaling me over. Do you mind if I go talk to him for a moment?"

"Of course not," I said easily.

"Promise not to move?" he asked, and I grinned.

"Promise. I will be right here," I told him and meant it.

Josef nodded, taking my hand, and pressing his lips to my knuckles before turning on his heel.

I hated to see him go, but I sure didn't mind watching him leave.

I was so distracted by the view of my husband's firm backside, it hardly registered when someone took the seat across from me.

"I never expected you would cavort with the enemy so publicly, Meredith," a sharp voice said.

I turned my head towards the sound, startling when I saw Richard Hamilton sitting there. His expression spoke volumes.

I was stunned. I'd only met the man via Skype call with the attorneys after Franklin's death.

There was no reason on earth he should address me so informally. We weren't friends.

What was he doing there? I didn't think Volkov Industries had any connections to Gray Corps.

Other than them owning it, I reminded myself.

A bad feeling settled in my stomach. He crossed his legs, relaxing back into the chair as if he had the right, and the overall wrongness of it was like a slap to the face.

Richard swirled whatever he was drinking in the crystal tumbler—*scotch, maybe*—and flicked his gaze back to mine.

"Looking for your thug husband?" he spat.

Leaning forward, Richard grabbed my wrist with his clammy hand.

"Excuse me?" I said, shocked and more than a little uncomfortable.

I tugged my arm back, but he tightened his hold. Not wanting to make a scene, I froze and steeled my spine.

"You know, your father never got over your betrayal and your running away. I thought when you returned, maybe we could perhaps make a merger ourselves. What a waste, Meredith," he seethed.

"Let go of me," I hissed, but he ignored my request and leaned closer.

"To think you're now in bed with the man who destroyed him, who killed him, I suppose you could say, is the best portrayal of your corrupt character as any."

"What are you talking about?" I asked, shocked and sick to my stomach.

"I'm talking about you and your loose morals. You think I wouldn't find out how you had an affair with your bodyguard when you were just a teenager? Just like your mother. Franklin told me all about her. I guess the apple didn't fall very far from the tree."

My heart thudded inside my chest and my palms grew sweaty.

Where was Josef? I needed him.

Panic threatened to send me to my knees. But I held on. Barely.

Wait? Did he say my mother? Franklin spoke about my mother to this cretin?

"Your poor father tried to save you, and you were so ungrateful. Now you've gone and delivered his company right into the hands of the man who defiled you, and he is nothing more than a gangster!"

I glanced around, noticing we'd gathered a bit of an audience. Emotions slapped at me, but I tried to keep still, not wanting to embarrass Josef or his friends.

Anger. Shame. Humiliation.

As if he knew exactly how I felt, Franklin laughed. It was a vile sound, and finally, he released his hold on my wrist.

I rubbed at my skin, wanting to erase his touch. I tried to swallow down my embarrassment, my rage, and disgust, but they swirled around deep in my gut.

Each emotion threatened to topple the other, and none were good. But if I had to feel anything, anger was probably the best bet.

If Richard Hamilton expected me to run off tearful and sobbing, he was grossly mistaken.

"That's right, just sit there speechless, like the little whore you are. It was worth the five thousand dollars I paid my neighbor to give me his invitation just to be able to say this to your face," he spat.

I flinched at the insult. Then I narrowed my eyes.

"Listen to me because I will say this once and one time only. Franklin Gray was my stepfather. Not my father. I left his house when I was eighteen and made a life for myself away from his ill-gotten wealth. I had absolutely nothing to do with his financial affairs or his poor business decisions," I said anger heating my words.

"As for my husband, your libelous insults and filthy

insinuations of his character couldn't be more wrong. My husband is a hundred times the man you are. He would never corner a woman in the middle of a party and try to embarrass her by spewing misinformation and lies. I don't know who this neighbor of yours is, but he's going to have a lot to answer for since this is a private event. Now, I suggest you leave on your own two feet before I have you tossed out on your pompous ass."

"Too late for that, Little Red."

My gaze flashed above Richard's frowning moue, and I had one second to appreciate the menacing beauty of my husband's suppressed rage before he grabbed Richard Hamilton by the back of the neck and hauled him to his feet.

"Take him outside," he said, handing the sputtering man to Mario, who looked almost as furious as he did.

"Apologies everyone," Marat said, smoothing things over with a joke or two, but I couldn't hear what he said.

Josef was crouched in front of me, one hand cupping my cheek, the other holding the wrist Richard had grabbed. Whiskey fire eyes stared into mine.

"Are you alright? Did he hurt you?"

"No. He didn't hurt me. He was trying to get a rise out of me. Maybe out of displaced loyalty to Franklin," I whispered, exhaling the breath I didn't know I'd been holding.

"But he did touch you. Don't lie to me."

"Never, Josef. I would never lie to you, Husband. He grabbed my wrist. But that was it."

"Alright. Destiny is going to sit with you while I take care of this. I'll be right back, then we're going home."

"Yes, Husband," I replied, swaying closer to him.

There was something so hot about my man wanting to defend me. Maybe it was a base human reaction to that kind of display. Whatever it was, I found myself completely turned on.

Josef stood, taking me with him, and I leaned into his embrace, my hands on his wide shoulders. He kissed my temple, and I closed my eyes, seduced by the power I felt simmering beneath my fingertips.

Maybe it was foolish of me, but I didn't want to pretend I wasn't affected by him.

By his possessive display.

The way he handled that creep, Richard.

All of it.

All of him.

Everything he did was just so damn seductive.

I couldn't deny my feelings for my husband. And I wouldn't.

Not anymore.

"Meredith, are you alright?" Destiny asked, coming to my side with Sofia right behind her.

"Yah, I'm fine," I reassured my new friends.

Josef gave my hand one more squeeze before walking in the same direction his men had just gone.

I knew he was going to confront Richard.

More than that.

I knew he was going to do bad things to that horrible man. And it should bother me. I mean, that probably wasn't okay. I shouldn't just dismiss his proclivity for violence.

I sure as shit shouldn't get wet thinking about him coming to my defense so readily.

But I was. I was so fucking wet.

Who knew the fact he would champion me, using physical force to bring down any threat to my honor, would be such a total turn on?

Hot, so hot.

"Will he be long?" I wondered aloud, already planning the ways I wanted to thank him.

Marat surprised me by turning towards us, the three women who belonged to the most powerful men in the house. Hell, maybe even the state. His bright smile was wide as he tucked his wife into his side.

"I shouldn't think he will be long at all. In fact, I believe Josef will have his business handled before I finish this sentence."

He wasn't wrong.

My ears had just caught up to his words when I felt a domineering presence behind me. I turned towards my husband, his stony face betraying nothing at all.

But I knew better.

Josef was great at hiding his emotions, but I could feel the fury simmering beneath the facade.

"Husband," I whispered, and his whiskey gaze flashed to mine. "Ready?"

He nodded. I turned back to our hosts.

"Thank you for a wonderful evening."

"Our pleasure, I'm sure," Marat replied.

"I'll call next week for lunch," Sof added.

I wanted to tell her I was looking forward to it, but Josef was already dragging me out the door.

I smile as I jogged to keep up with his long strides.

It seemed I wasn't the only one in a rush to get home.

CHAPTER THIRTY-TWO
JOSEF

When I heard what that weak fucking excuse for a man said to my wife. When I saw his slimy fucking hands on her delicate wrist.

Fuck.

It was all I could do not to snap his fucking neck right there.

Witnesses be damned.

Shock was the only thing that stayed my hand the second it happened. Sheer surprise that even though I'd fucked up in so many ways with this woman, she'd stood up for me against that prick.

Goddamn. What a woman. I was a lucky man.

And Richard Hamilton was a dead motherfucker.

When I heard he'd bribed his way into Marat's

party, a sleight of hand I should have foreseen and wanted to kick my own ass for allowing, I fumed. And when he started to disparage her in front of those people, it was more than I could bear.

I would make my apologies to Marat about the infiltration to his wife's and Sofia's party tomorrow. That wouldn't be allowed to happen again.

My team already received quite the fucking talking to about that.

Someone had gotten lazy, and that was not allowed.

Not on my watch.

All the invitations were supposed to be double checked against properly issued photo identifications like driver's licenses or passports.

It seemed old *Dick Hamilton* had slipped a few hundreds to one of my newer guys, and the moron allowed him entry.

He wouldn't be working for me, or anyone, in security ever again.

It was difficult to do our line of work when you were missing certain body parts.

As for Dick.

Accidents happened.

People had swimming mishaps all the time. The Long Island Sound had unpredictable tides.

And really, you should never go for a dip, especially

not a moonlight one, without the proper backup or the safety of a lifeguard on duty.

Strong currents had been known to take swimmers out and into the ocean. Especially when the tide was just right.

Even if he could tread water while unconscious, I suspected the blood trickling from the head wound he got when I punched him in the face, and he fell onto the pavement would attract plenty of our local sea life.

The Sound was full of predators from sand sharks to bull sharks, and even the occasional Great White.

Hmm.

I wondered briefly if Meredith would enjoy a trip to the local aquarium.

She used to like things like that. She'd make me drive her to museums, botanical gardens, the zoo back when I knew her before.

I'd have to ask her.

Later.

Right now, I just needed to get her home.

"Josef," she said, and her voice sounded light, teasing.

"What?"

"Thank you, Husband," she whispered and flexed her hand.

I looked down, realizing I was squeezing her too tight.

Oops.

"You don't have to thank me for taking care of you, Little Red."

I released my hand, loving how she leaned her body into mine.

"But I will," she replied.

Goddamn. This woman. My wife. My love.

I felt like a piano wire pulled too tightly.

Any moment now, I was going to snap.

"It's okay," she said softly, placing her head on my shoulder.

I closed my eyes and just concentrated on the moment. Meredith was okay. She was right there.

By my side. Leaning on me. Trusting me.

I had so much to atone for with this woman. So much to make right. By some quirk of the universe, I'd been given a second chance.

I wouldn't squander this opportunity to be with her. To show her I could be a good husband.

That prick had come too close to my Little Red tonight, and I wouldn't let anyone get that close to hurting her again.

I was going to do right by my wife.

I was going to honor her and cherish her for the fucking angel she was.

Meredith was mine now and once more I was consumed with the need to show her what that meant.

And I'm going to start right now.

CHAPTER THIRTY-THREE
JOSEF

"**G**ood morning," my sweet wife murmured as I kissed her temple gently.

Poor thing needed extra sleep.

I knew why. I caused her exhaustion. And the knowledge made my blood sing.

Last night, I'd been wild for her. My sexy Little Red had been just as hot for me.

I'd been nervous about her reaction to the way I'd handled the man from the party, but she didn't seem concerned.

Not in the least.

The way she reciprocated my feelings with sensual overtures of her own was just a fucking bonus.

I leaned back and watched her pretty green irises, glassy with sleep, as she slowly blinked herself awake.

So beautiful.

I smiled and turned back to the tray I'd filled with pastries from the café down the block. I'd had one of my guys fetch my order and bring it up while I made her some coffee.

I made a mean pour over, using freshly ground and ethically harvested coffee grounds imported from South America.

My men were fast, eager to please me after last night's blunder. They were none too happy that one of their own had caused such a mess last night.

I'd already sent word of my displeasure to each of the team leaders working for me at Sigma International.

I demanded a company-wide background check on every single employee that worked for me, Volkov Industries, Gray Corps, and St. Elizabeth's going back ten years. And I wanted the reports as soon as possible.

Every single person who had even the slightest chance of coming into contact with my wife needed to be thoroughly vetted.

Darius, my top guy, had questioned the need for such drastic measures. But one glimpse of my face through the video call had shut him up.

That was good. I did not like being questioned.

Darius had good instincts. He was loyal. And he took commands well.

That was why he was my number one. He was the one I trusted to manage things while I was otherwise occupied.

As for Mario. The man who spent the most time around my Little Red.

He was the man I trusted with the personal safety of my wife.

I could not emphasize the importance of his role. So I made sure he understood.

I described in great detail what would happen should one hair on her precious head come to harm.

Mario believed me.

Then he thanked me for trusting him with the job.

Good man.

I gave him a fucking raise for having the balls to stand there while I spelled out the torture that would await anyone who tried to hurt her.

He'd only nodded. He did not break down, cry, or puke on the floor like one of his team had.

Fucking weak link.

I had no use for weakness in my firm and definitely not on my wife's personal security team.

Mario fired him before I could. He'd been furious at the security breach last night, and I knew he was riding his team hard for the fuck up.

He'd already sent men to pick up the neighbor Destiny had invited to her party.

The one who'd sold his invitation.

That guy had one lousy night, I guaranteed it.

As for me, well, I had my wife back in our penthouse. Safe and sound. Exhausted from me keeping her up all night.

Perfect.

Everything was as it should be.

My life didn't feel so dark anymore.

I wasn't alone in the shadows, just a Big Bad Wolf hunting for something to fill the emptiness inside of me. Not now.

Now, I had what I'd been searching for the whole time. I had what I once lost.

I had her.

Meredith brought the sun with her.

She brought the color back. And she sated my hunger like no one else ever had.

"Good morning, Little Red," I replied.

"Is that for me?" she asked, nodding at the tray.

"It's for *us*, yeah. I thought we could share some breakfast in bed to start our day."

"I'd like that. Um, bathroom first. Close your eyes," she said, giggling as she hustled her naked ass out of bed.

"Not a chance, Wife. That's mine to look at and enjoy," I said, openly staring at every soft pale curve on her.

She giggled. And the sound sent joy singing through my soul.

Christ.

She was perfect. Meredith was like joy personified when she was happy.

Her brightness touched every part of my soul. Sometimes it felt so bright I had to squint, but I would never look away.

Fuck.

That she gave me even one second of her inner joy made me ache. I knew I didn't deserve it.

I wasn't like her.

I wasn't sunshine.

I wasn't good.

But the thing about sunshine was it cast shadow. So maybe that was why we belonged together.

You couldn't have light without dark.

She was light, and I was dark.

But we belonged to each other.

Together, we were better.

She gave me so much. She gave a lot to everyone. The women and children she helped at the shelter. The easy smiles she gave Mario and his men.

She made the day brighter for so many people. I had to share her with the world. I knew that.

But I was greedy. I wanted all of her.

When I thought about what really happened all those years ago, all the time wasted, fuck, I got so mad.

I wanted to go back in time and kill Franklin myself. That piece of shit.

She was so strong, my wife. So brave.

To have gone through all that fucking shit. Having to deal with the trespasses of the only father she'd ever known alone.

Then, to take that painful experience and use it to help others?

That took a strength, a power, a self-discipline, and a heart I could only imagine.

Meredith amazed me.

I spent the whole night just holding her, going over everything she ever told me, wondering how she must have felt. Trying to put myself in her shoes, to see it from her perspective, was one of the hardest things I'd ever done.

Meredith had been eighteen, alone, and lost. Abandoned by me. Abused by Franklin. Made to feel alone, shameful, and unworthy.

I fucking hated myself for what I did to her. For not trusting her. And I hated that motherfucker.

What I hated most was that he'd died before I could deliver the end he truly deserved.

But I had to push my anger aside.

Today was not about that. Today was about starting our lives together. Our real lives.

As husband and wife.

As man and woman.

As Big Bad and Little Red, a darker part of me whispered.

When I saw Adrik and Marat with their wives clinging to them so openly, I'd been filled with envy. I wanted that for me.

But I had no idea how to seduce my wife into caring for me like that again. I really wanted her to love me.

Today, I was doubling down on my efforts. I didn't just want Meredith to care for me.

I wanted her to fall for me. Like head over heels.

Because if there was one thing, one single thing I was finally man enough to admit now that I'd stopped and listened to her truth and faced how I'd feel if she left me, it was this.

I was completely in love with my wife.

Irrevocably. Interminably. Totally batshit fucking crazy in love.

I had never stopped loving her.

I would never stop loving her.

Meredith was my reason. She was my purpose.

Whether it was bullheadedness or sheer stupidity that took me so long to realize it, now that I had, I was going to do everything in my power to ensure she knew it.

"Oooh, that smells so good."

Her breathy whisper reached me as she walked across the room, wearing one of the button-downs I must have left in the bathroom.

Fuck. Me.

She looked good dressed in my clothes. Even better without them.

I cleared my throat, waiting for her to sit in bed so I could settle the tray across her lap, opening the legs before I did that.

"Oh my god, is that a chocolate hazelnut croissant?" she asked, her green irises sparkling.

"Yeah," I replied, wanting to high-five myself for knowing her weakness for chocolate hazelnut anything.

The fact this bakery got their cocoa from the same town in Switzerland where she got her body cream was just a bonus for me.

"Gimme gimme," she said, giving a little wiggle that almost upended our coffees.

"Stay still or we'll end up wearing this," I chided, lifting the delectable pastry to her lips.

She tried to take it from me, but I pulled back. Meredith rolled her eyes playfully, but she opened her mouth.

This was a new obsession of mine.

I needed to feed her. In fact, I was all but consumed by the desire to do just that.

Just another one of those pesky biological imperatives that seemed to sprout like weeds where she was concerned.

"Open wide, little Red," I said, and like at the party, my mind filled with images of me saying those exact words with her on her knees.

She must have had the same idea cause her gaze heated, and her breathing changed.

Mmm. We are definitely doing that later.

"You know, you don't have to feed me," she said shyly.

But I could tell from her pink cheeks and bright eyes that she liked it as much as I did.

"I know I don't have to, but I want to."

"Okay," she said agreeably.

"So, I was thinking, Baby. There's some stuff we need to cover," I said, and she frowned as she chewed.

"Like what?" she said, covering her full mouth with her hand.

I grinned and tugged her hand down. She giggled more, and we made a little mess.

That was okay. Messes could be cleaned.

"Mm, delicious."

I leaned forward, licking a dollop of chocolate from

the corner of her lips and moaning as she turned at the last minute and kissed me.

For several minutes we ate cocoa dusted pastries filled with chocolate hazelnut ganache with sliced strawberries on top and freshly whipped cream.

In between bites, we took sips of delicious mocha lattes.

Chocolate.

Always chocolate.

I loved the stuff. It was because my girl always smelled of cocoa butter. And I loved her.

So fucking much.

"So, what do we need to talk about?" she asked after I fed her the last strawberry.

I was so goddamn hard, I thought my cock would bust through my boxers. Meredith sighed and patted her belly contentedly.

Fuck.

She was so sexy. All curves and pale skin. Her flaming hair tumbled around her shoulders like solid wildfire.

Jesus. Christ.

She was a vision. A goddess.

So full of life and color. So bright, she was blinding. Was this what they meant when they said love was blind?

I wondered.

In that moment, Meredith was all I could see. My heart squeezed painfully, and I knew I could never live without her again.

Luckily, I didn't plan to.

"First, I need to apologize for everything—"

"For what?"

"The way I did this. Making you marry me," I murmured.

"You regret marrying me?" she asked, her voice shaky.

"No! Not at all, Baby. I regret I let you think I was marrying you for reasons that weren't true. But when I saw you that day in the boardroom, I wanted revenge."

"I know, and I don't blame you. But it's not something I enjoy thinking about," she mumbled.

Sadness tainted her shining eyes, dimming the glow. I wanted to kick myself for doing that to her. But I was going to make it up to her.

Right fucking now.

"Wait. Hear me out. I was stupid. I was lying to myself."

"Josef, you don't have to explain," she interrupted, but I shook my head.

"That's where you're wrong, Little Red. I do have to explain," I said, and I ran my hand over my face.

Don't fuck this up, I told myself.

"All I ever wanted was you. You that's it. My whole

fucking life, I had no one. Then I took that job and there you were," I said, shaking my head when she looked like she was going to interrupt.

"You were too young for me. Too good for me. Way too fucking pretty for me," I said, and she shook her head, tears clinging to her copper lashes.

The sun winked at us from the sky outside the tall windows in our bedroom.

The special tint was designed so the light was never too bright, but it still made my wife look like a goddess.

All shimmery and soft, the pure sunshine filtered through the room, landing on her.

Like the sun itself couldn't stay away from her, either.

"What are you saying?" she whispered.

"I'm saying, let's start again. Me and you. Let's forget the past. Forget the world. Let's start fresh. Let's build something together."

"But there's so much history between us, Josef. Some of it, I don't want to forget," she argued, and yeah, she was right.

"Maybe we don't forget, then. Maybe we just forgive. Maybe we just build from here. Is that better?" I asked, needing her to say yes.

A sob escaped her lips, and my heart clenched. She gasped, cupping a hand over her mouth.

"Please, Baby," I begged.

"We're already married, right? But what are you really saying, Josef?"

"Fuck, you're not going to make this easy, are you?" I asked, grinning when she smiled at me through the tears trekking down her face.

"Nope."

"Good Girl. You shouldn't. You should always demand more of me, and I will always give it to you," I said, loving her more with each passing minute.

"I'm saying what I should've said 15 years ago. I am saying *I love you* and I want you and I will do anything to make this work. I want our marriage to be real. Not one of convenience, for the sake of Gray Corps, or some shady fucking prick's perversion of our past."

"You love me?" she whispered.

Why was she so surprised?

Of course, I loved her.

What sane man wouldn't? She was perfect.

"Yeah. Yes. Of course, I love you," I said, cupping her cheeks and kissing away her tears.

"Well, are you just gonna leave me hanging?"

"Oh, Josef, I love you, too. I never loved anyone but you," she confessed, and her words were like a balm to my wounded heart, healing it almost immediately.

Fuck. Thank fuck. She loves me.

"Okay. Good. Now our real life begins."

Crashing into my wife, I sealed my mouth to hers in a desperate kiss I couldn't contain.

She welcomed me with open arms, and I reveled in it.

This was the first time we'd both admitted how we felt.

The first time we loved with abandon, and it was glorious.

It was everything.

Life altering.

Heart healing.

I tore my borrowed shirt from her sweet flesh and flipped her over onto her hands and knees.

I needed to taste her everywhere. To take ownership of my woman.

"Fuck, you're dripping for me. Such a Good Girl, Wife. So pink and wet, soaked that little cunt just kissing your husband," I told her, pushing her head down into the mattress as I settled behind her.

I grabbed her pale cheeks in my hands, spreading them wide. Meredith gasped, her hips flexing instinctively.

"Stay still, Little Red. Stay still so I can see what's mine," I growled, then I bent my head and slid the flat of my tongue over her tight little rosebud.

"Mmm, Baby. You taste so fucking good," I told her, licking her from asshole to clit and back again.

"Josef! Husband!" she cried out with every swipe.

Now that I knew she'd never been touched by another man, I couldn't wait to touch her everywhere. I wouldn't fuck her ass yet. But I was going to finger it. And she was going to fucking love it.

"You ready for me, Wife? Is that cunt ready to be filled?"

"Yes, Husband. Please," she begged.

"Good Girl," I praised her, pressing through her slick folds.

And she was.

My very Good Girl.

CHAPTER THIRTY-FOUR
MEREDITH

Even if I wanted to stay still, I couldn't.

The second Josef filled me with his gloriously thick cock, I was no longer in control of my actions.

My back arched, and I pushed back, taking him deeper inside my needy hole. A keening wail escaped my lips, and the rest was all begging and moaning.

It would have been embarrassing, but this was Josef. How could I be ashamed of what he made me feel?

My husband was a total sex god. His skilled body seemed made for mine.

No wonder I never let anyone else touch me. How could I?

He was the only man I'd ever allowed inside my

pussy. The only man who would ever see me pant and beg.

Something about knowing that, about acknowledging that he was the only one who made me wild with need, amped my pleasure up another notch.

Another.

And another.

"Goddam, Baby. Look at you. You're dripping all over me, Good Girl. That's it. Show your husband how much you like it when I stuff you with my cock," he grunted, his pace punishing as he fucked me from behind.

"Look at you," he said some more, his hands gripping my cheeks and spreading them apart.

I tensed.

I moaned.

And when he said more dirty words, I almost came. *Almost.*

"I need some of this virgin ass," he growled.

I felt something wet and warm against my crack. I wasn't sure what it was. But then I felt pressure *there*.

"That's it, let me in, Baby."

Josef's finger teased the outer circle before he started pushing, pressing it inside my asshole.

I whimpered as he shoved his slick digit deeper inside, past the tight ring of muscles.

"Fuck. Damn, Josef!" I moaned.

It was almost overwhelming. I never thought I would like that sort of thing. And maybe I wouldn't if it were anyone else.

But this was Josef. My husband. And this man owned me.

Body, heart, mind, and soul.

There was something freeing in admitting that. In just surrendering myself to him.

"That's it, Little Red. Take it. Your cunt is squeezing me so tight when I push my finger inside your ass. You like that, Baby? Want me to fingerfuck your ass while I pound your pussy with my cock?"

Josef pulled back, almost withdrawing both his finger and his dick from me, and I whimpered at the loss.

"Yes! I want that. Please, Husband," I begged, needing him to come back, to fill me again.

"Anything you want, Baby. I told you, just ask me and it's yours."

His words whispered against my skin as he filled me completely. The sounds of our combined breathing and the slapping of our bodies reverberated in the room.

Maybe it was the entire wall of windows or the impossibly high ceilings that made it sound so loud. I couldn't be sure.

All I knew was it filled my head. The feel of his body, so hard and hot thrusting into me, the naughty words he murmured, and the praise I didn't know I needed, it was all too much.

Josef was everywhere, filling my senses, making me believe. And I wanted to. God, how I wanted to.

"Take it. Take it all. Take everything I give you," he grunted into my ear, and wrapped his one free hand around my throat.

That was all I needed to explode around him.

"Fuck. That's it, Little Red. Suck the cum right out of me. Show me how good I make you feel," he groaned.

Josef's body arched, his dick spasmed inside of me, filling me with hot cum, and he yelled with his completion.

Still in the throes of my own orgasm, I hardly recognized him falling forward until he was crushing me into the mattress.

Neither of us could catch our breath just yet, and to be honest, it felt good.

His weight trapping me beneath him. His heat warming me from the outside in. Our combined cum sticking to my thighs.

It feels good. Really good.

"Fuck, Baby. That was," he started, rolling off my well-used body.

He took my left hand and lifted it to his lips. His brows furrowed as he looked at it closely.

"What is this?" he asked, holding my hand up and sliding my ruby ring up to my knuckle.

I froze.

I knew what he was looking at, and suddenly, I felt a little silly.

Around my finger was a single pink line with a small bow on the inside of my digit. *Pink curly ribbon.* I'd had it tattooed years ago.

It was exactly the same as the pink curly ribbon Josef had once tied around my finger as a promise to me. Just a silly thing people did when they were young and in love.

He must have remembered because his whiskey colored eyes flashed to mine, and I saw it there in his gaze.

"Why, Baby? Why did you do this?"

"So I would never forget," I whispered, and two fat drops rolled down my cheeks.

"I'm gonna make it up to you, Meredith. I promise."

"You already have," I said, and my heart never felt so full.

"I love you," Josef said and pressed his lips together like he was trying to contain his emotions.

He slid the band back into place and grabbed me by the neck, pulling me into his arms.

We kissed for what felt like hours then. Unrushed and unbound by lies or secrets.

He knew everything now.

And I knew how he really felt.

I felt close to him, and my wounds while raw, were finally starting to heal. I felt safe and loved, and in loving him, I felt like I had a real chance at happiness.

Finally.

"We can make it up to each other. We have a lifetime, Husband. We can heal together now," I said, cupping his face in my hands and kissing him softly.

"I love you, Wife. You brought color back into the world for me, and warmth into my heart," he whispered.

God, he felt big. So big. I held him tight, telling him how I felt without fear.

"I love you so much, Josef. My first. My last. My forever."

His chest rumbled with his hum, and I grinned, holding on as tight as I could.

CHAPTER THIRTY-FIVE
JOSEF

I sat on the private jet, staring at my phone and the last text Meredith had sent me. It was a picture.

Of her.

My sexy, sweet, gorgeous wife.

She'd been laying down on our bed, her red hair billowing out behind her like a crimson pirate sail on a sea of dusky rose-colored silk when I took the photo.

After our Vegas wedding, I had the cleaning service replace all the sheets with different shades of pink.

Little Red loved them. And I loved her, so making her happy was a priority.

I'd sleep on sheets with fucking unicorns on them if she wanted me to.

She'd send me the picture when I texted her, I'd

arrived at the private airport to meet Adrik and Marat for an unexpected business trip.

Since I was a major shareholder in Volkov Industries, any disruptions in the mining business affected me too.

This one should be easy enough. A new political party was in power in the small east African country where one of the rare earth metal mines was located.

Palms needed greasing, and an understanding needed to be reached.

I knew without checking there would be piles of money in metal suitcases in the luggage area and I'd brought two dozen men from my elite ops teams with us.

The trip would go as dozens of others had gone before. There would be the usual exchange of money, a bit of posturing, and a real possibility of violence.

That was what had me anxiously gritting my teeth. Not the violence. I was used to that. Hell, I'd trained and fought my entire life.

But there was a difference now. One very real, notable difference.

This time, I had something to lose.

This time I had Meredith.

My chest constricted, and I closed my eyes, willing this horrible suffocating to pass. What the fuck was wrong with me?

I should have been checking the most recent reports and land surveys. Making sure the house we'd rented was being seen to by the first wave of men I'd sent over when it became clear we were heading out last night.

But no.

I was sitting there like some pussy whipped shit-head, mooning over my wife.

My beautiful, sweet Meredith. The woman who brought the color and warmth back into my life.

My Little Red.

I was so fucked. But for some reason, that didn't scare me or upset me. Not in the least. Instead, it filled me with something I never thought I'd feel.

Happiness.

That feeling was pure fucking happiness.

"It doesn't get any easier, bro, trust me," Marat said, taking the seat beside me.

"What are you talking about?" I asked, turning my phone down on my lap.

Only her face was visible in the picture. But she'd been naked when I'd left her, and her skin was still flushed and pink from our feverish lovemaking.

No one else got to see her looking all soft and warm in my bed. No one but me.

"I'm talking about leaving your wife. Even for necessary trips like this. This shit is just as difficult for me now as it was the first time I left our bed to travel for the business."

"So, you feel like this too?" I asked.

"Anxious? Worried? Sick to my stomach at the very thought of being separated for any real length of time never mind all the fucking miles between us? Yeah, I feel like that, too. And if you think this is bad, wait till you have kids. Am I right, Adrik?" Marat said, and fuck, his words were not a goddamn comfort to me like at all.

My heart stuttered inside my chest as Adrik joined us.

Children? Did Meredith even want children?

We hadn't discussed it yet, and I'd pictured it before.

Her pregnant. Her nursing our baby.

The second Marat mentioned it, I had that vision again. My Little Red softly swollen with our baby in her belly.

Fuck. I wanted that.

It would be up to her, of course, but I was down to be a father to our children. However many she wanted. And if she decided she didn't want any. That was okay, too.

The real truth was I just needed her in my life. We could play aunt and uncle to Marat and Adrik's brood, if that was all she wanted.

Shit, I wished I could go back home to talk about it with her. I wanted to know her thoughts on parenthood and whether she thought we should or could bring a baby into the world.

I don't think I would have ever considered it before. But now, I couldn't stop thinking about it.

Fucking Marat and his big, stupid mouth.

I glared at him as Adrik pulled his seatbelt securely in place. The big bastard sat across from me and he laughed.

Fucking laughed.

But it was a mirthless sound, but he was already nodding his head, agreeing with Marat.

"Oh, Josef. You understand now, yes? Why I was so crazy when I met my wife? You know, every time I leave Zaika moya I feel like I can't breathe until I am with her again. And I swear my sweet Michaela grows five inches overnight every damn time I go. But I must do what I must do to keep them safe and secure."

"It's the same for me and Destiny. She knows I'd do anything for her and Lucy, and I know she'll be waiting for me when I get back. Knowing that helps," Marat said.

I couldn't believe these two badass motherfuckers were just admitting this shit to me.

I frowned.

"So, what do you do? I mean, how do you stop feeling like this?" I asked.

"Stop? Why would you stop?" Adrik looked down-right confused.

"Because I feel like I can't fucking function without her!" I roared.

"Ha ha! Man, you are just as screwed as we are, but relax," Marat said, slapping me on the back. "Being in love like that is the best thing you could hope for."

"How?" I asked, truly perplexed.

"Because love is the only thing that makes any of this shit worth it," Adrik replied.

I exhaled, feeling that familiar neon pink ribbon tightening around me, only this time it was wrapped around my heart.

I closed my eyes, counting the minutes until I'd be with her again.

It was going to be a long fucking week.

CHAPTER THIRTY-SIX
MEREDITH

D ay one since Josef left.

SOF

Okay ladies, I am starting this texting chain because I have an idea.

DES

God help us. (SNORT)

MER

How did you guys get my phone number and why are your contacts already in here? And OMG is my name shortened?

SOF

Sweetie, just breathe. Your husband is not called Big Bad for nothing. He handles all Volkov Industries securities, so if you think exchanging all our info so we can text chat is wild, just wait!

DES

Sof, be nice. Meredith probably thinks we're creepy!

MER

I don't think you're creepy. LOL. I was just surprised. Okay, Sof, so what's the idea?

DES

Please don't say yoga.

SOF

Yoga? Yuck. No, thank you! Saturday Night Live killed that for me with the whole hot yoga skit. My idea is this: sourdough.

MER

Your idea is sourdough?

DES

Pretty sure someone beat you to that Sof.

SOF

Har har. Yes, sourdough! While our
hubbies are away, we are all going to
try to create a viable sourdough starter,
and if we succeed there, it will be home
baked bread goodness once a week!
We'll have sourdough eating parties!

DES

I'm sorry, what?

MER

Guys, I hate to tell you this, but I am a
shitty cook.

SOF

That's the beauty of sourdough!
Anyone can do it!

DES

Where did you get that bullshit? Bakers
are professionals, Sof. And Mer has a
job at an office. And we have kids, and
books to write, and record.

SOF

I know, but this takes like no time.
Look, anyone can do it! The internet
said so, so it must be true. Anyway, I
already sent you guys everything you
need to start. Come on! Let's do this
together. It only takes a few minutes
each day to get started and it will give
us something to concentrate on other
than the guys.

DES

You're not going to give up on this,
are you?

SOF

Nope.

MER

Okay. I'm in. I'll do it!

CHAPTER THIRTY-SEVEN
MEREDITH

D ay three since Josef left.

SOF

Does anyone know if your starter is supposed to smell like bananas?

DES

Yeah, I read that's normal. Mine smells like feet.

SOF

That is so gross.

MER

Mine doesn't smell like anything. But
let's keep trying, ladies!

The promise of homemade carbs was a poor substitute for my man. I was making a mess out of our kitchen. Wasting flour by the pound. And I was pretty sure the housekeeper was a second away from quitting.

God, I missed my husband.

CHAPTER THIRTY-EIGHT
MEREDITH

Day six since Josef left.

My phone buzzed as I rode the elevator up to the condo with Mario, and I cringed.

Every day since Josef left, my bodyguard escorted me to and from work, insisting on door-to-door delivery.

I felt a little bit like a parcel, but I understood.

Josef was a powerful man. He had powerful connections. And powerful enemies.

It had been a while, but I wasn't a stranger to that kind of life.

After all, the only reason I met Josef was because my stepfather had similar enemies.

Ugh.

I hated thinking about him. Franklin Gray. That fucking monster.

I could not recall a single time in my life when that man treated me as anything other than an obligation or a burden. And that was only during one of the rare and far between visits I'd had with him after my mother died.

Nannies took the burden of my upbringing, and as lonely as that had been, I was grateful for it now. Anything would have been better than that man.

I remembered so very little about my mother. She'd killed herself when I was barely in kindergarten.

I remember her having dark eyes and hair. She was beautiful.

Too beautiful.

She used to laugh a lot, and it sounded like bells tinkling.

What I remembered most vividly was her dancing with me. She used to make me stand on her feet as she moved to no music at all.

Franklin had always hated that.

He would always barge in and say something sharp. I couldn't remember the words, but the tone was always cruel or snide. Even a child knows when someone is being ridiculed.

I hated him for treating her that way. For making her feel so small, so useless, unloved, and uncared for.

I couldn't pretend I understood all the reasons she left me. And I was angry at her for that, too.

People had always assumed I was a spoiled rich princess, but not everyone had a storybook upbringing. I knew that firsthand.

Josef had been my first taste of the real world.

How could I have known he would be the best of it?

My heart warmed whenever I pictured my handsome husband. He'd been gone six days, and I missed him like crazy.

My phone pinged again as Mario opened the condo door, but I waited until I was inside to get it from my purse.

Josef had left strict instructions that no one was to be inside with me, except for this.

Every time I returned, Mario did a check of every room while I waited inside the closed, locked front door.

Then he would leave, and I'd secure the double bolt and re-engage the alarm system.

"Everything is good, Mrs. Aziz," Mario said before exiting.

"Thanks, Mario. Goodnight."

I took off my shoes and dropped them on the little rack by the door. Today had been a tough one.

Josef's lawyers and realtors worked with Fr. Augustus on securing a property with the money I had from those payments I'd received from Gray Corps over the years.

The historic Victorian was in the same town where I grew up. Morristown, New Jersey, was one of the oldest towns in the entire country.

It was the site of the winter headquarters for George Washington himself, during the American Revolution. There were tons of museums and parks dedicated to our country's beginning, places with historical significance.

The house itself was on a nice little cul de sac. Quiet, secluded, close to the local school.

It wasn't a mansion or anything, but it was clean and there were plenty of bedrooms. Eight to be exact.

Ellie and her son were moving in first. Josef had arranged for a construction team and building inspector to fix the place up first, and they'd moved like lightning.

I'd offered to take them to the new house before I'd known Josef wouldn't be there to help.

Tomorrow was the day, and I was not about to back out.

Mario and his team were going to accompany us, but I already asked him to ensure everyone else rode in a separate vehicle.

Ellie was skittish around men. As I would be, too.

Her ex had come by the shelter asking for information once or twice, and I wasn't there either time. I understood he was a nasty piece of work.

The other staff had sent him packing, which was easier now that Josef had sent men and women from Sigma International to see to the safety of the shelter and its inhabitants.

I didn't ask for any of that, but still, Josef did it. And it wasn't like he just made empty gestures or offers. He didn't try to take over or muscle me into doing things his way.

Josef simply saw a need and filled it. He was just that good.

Warm feelings filled me, followed by an ache inside my chest because I missed him so. I walked to the kitchen, checking on my latest batch of sourdough starter with high hopes that quickly sank when I saw the neon mold floating on top of the jar.

Fuck.

"Back to the drawing board," I muttered, and my phone pinged yet again.

Oops.

I'd forgotten about that. Maybe it was the girls. I hoped they had better luck with their starters.

The sourdough kits Sofia had sent were awesome. They came with everything. Plus, she sent five pounds of organic bread flour and a canister to hold it in.

I was never much of a cook. Growing up the way I

did, it was no wonder. Even after I left home, I was more an instant noodle kinda gal than a Cordon Bleu chef.

But I have to admit, it's been a fun distraction.

Ping. Ping.

Sighing, I grabbed my cell phone, expecting Sofia, but was very pleasantly surprised when it was Josef. Or Big Bad, as he named himself in my contacts.

BIG BAD WOLF

What's this I hear about your turning the kitchen into a science lab?

LITTLE RED

When did you hack my phone and change everyone's name? And when did you decide to give Des and Sof my number without telling me?

BIG BAD WOLF

Figured you'd need friends while I'm gone. Having fun making your sourdough starter? I suppose you're an expert by now.

LITTLE RED

You suppose wrong. (sends pic of neon mold being flushed down the drain.)

BIG BAD WOLF

Poor baby. Sorry that happened.

LITTLE RED

No worries. So, are you coming back?

BIG BAD WOLF

You saying you miss me?

LITTLE RED

Nope. Just need to know so I can
cancel my next clandestine meeting
with my secret admirer.

BIG BAD WOLF

Anyone trying to meet with you
clandestinely or not won't live to see
another day, Little Red. And teasing me
when I'm missing you this bad is not a
good idea, Baby.

LITTLE RED

So…you really miss me?

BIG BAD WOLF

Is that all you got from that?

It really was.
Swoon!

LITTLE RED

Yep.

BIG BAD WOLF

Yes, I miss you, Baby. And I am man
enough to admit it.

LITTLE RED

Me too. Not the part where I'm a man
though. I mean, you know that.
Obviously, you know that. Never
mind…

BIG BAD WOLF

Yeah, Baby, I do know that. Now, send
me a pic of you so I can dream about
something good tonight.

LITTLE RED

(sends pic)

BIG BAD WOLF

I like your face.

LITTLE RED

I like yours back.

BIG BAD WOLF

Good. Cause when I get home, you're
going to sit that sweet ass right on my
face and ride it till you come screaming
my name.

Oh my fucking fuck.

My core clenched, and I whimpered just thinking of
how much I missed him in that way. Seemed being
married had jumpstarted my starving libido in ways I
hadn't anticipated.

BIG BAD WOLF

I gotta go, Baby. Don't make me wait.

LITTLE RED

I miss you. I love you, Husband.

BIG BAD WOLF

Just a few more days, Wife.

I closed my eyes and kissed the screen, feeling anything but stupid.

No, he didn't say he loved me back every time we texted or talked. But I felt it.

The weight and warmth of his love was like a living thing, and it wrapped around me in his absence.

I couldn't wait for Josef to come home.

Meanwhile, I had work and sourdough starter to feed.

CHAPTER THIRTY-NINE
JOSEF

The clean up crew I'd brought with us were almost finished destroying all evidence of our being anywhere near the resident of the former army general who thought he could shake more money out of Volkov Industries than he was worth.

Sometimes it was simpler and better to just take out the trash.

Adrik and Marat were eager to return home, and so was I. We just had to wait for the new party in charge to reopen the mines before we left.

Should be any minute now.

The flight home would take eleven hours, and I felt tired and irritable.

"You ready to leave?" Adrik asked, walking towards me with his Ruger still in his hand.

I nodded. Fuck yes, I was ready to leave. Ready to get back to my Little Red.

Marat followed behind his brother, his cell phone pressed against his ear. The smile on his face let me know he was talking to Destiny.

Good idea.

I dialed the number for my wife eager to hear her voice.

"Hello, this is Meredith."

"Hey," I said when she answered.

"Josef!"

"I just wanted to let you know we're leaving in a little while. Should be back by dinner."

"Oh, that's great! Oh, um, what time?"

"About six. Why? You got a date, Wife?" I asked only half-kidding.

"Don't be silly. I'll be home by then. We're driving Ellie and her son to the offsite house in Morristown."

"You personally?"

"Yeah, I told you about it."

She had. I just forgot.

"It's all been arranged. Mario will drive the three of us and his team will follow in another vehicle."

"Not sure I like that, Wife."

"Please, Josef, she has been through so much," she began, but it wasn't necessary.

I already planned on giving in.

"Okay. Then you come straight back to the condo, alright? Wait for me there, I'll take you out to dinner," I told her.

"Sure, we can go out, But um, we can also order in," she *whispered and there was no mistaking the tone of her voice.*

My wife really had missed me, and I missed her.

"Yeah, Baby, we can stay in," I replied.

"Okay, Josef. Ill see you later. I love you," she said, and *fuck, but I never tired of hearing it.*

"See you soon," I replied, wondering why it was so fucking hard for me to tell her how I felt.

It wasn't like I hadn't said it before. Maybe I just wasn't used to throwing those three words together all the time.

It was something I had to work on, and I would. Meredith deserved to hear how much I loved her every fucking day.

I'd start by telling her in person the second we landed.

"We fucking going or what?" I yelled out loud and headed for the door.

I was done with this country. I needed to get back to New York.

Back to her.

The neon pink ribbon tied around my heart gave a

squeeze and I rubbed my fist over the ache in my chest that started the second I left her and the country.

It would get better once I had her in my arms again. I knew that. But I hated waiting.

Just a few more hours.

We loaded the plane, the deal with the new government in place. Adrik and Marat were busy with whatever, and I was too amped up for small talk.

In the meantime, I had a whole stack of reports and emails to catch up on. A lot of it involved the transition of ownership of Gray Corps.

My wife had just agreed to sell the whole business to Volkov Industries, wanting nothing to do with the company. And I didn't blame her.

But I'd make sure she got top dollar for it, and I would protect as many of the employees as I could, saving the jobs of those who deserved it.

As I scrolled through the latest reports, which had been fudged by a few of the more dubious managers, including the recently deceased Richard Hamilton, I uncovered some rather nefarious activities.

Someone had been siphoning funds from several accounts in tiny increments so as not to be noticed. My team traced that money to a dozen offshore accounts.

One of which was emptied the same day Franklin Gray supposedly died.

The hairs on the back of my neck stood up.

"Everything alright?" Marat asked.

"I'm not sure," I said, and told him and Adrik what I found.

CHAPTER FORTY
JOSEF

The condo was empty by the time I arrived from the private airport.

At first, I hadn't called Meredith because I wanted to surprise her.

But when I dialed Mario's number from the car, it had gone straight to voicemail.

That was when my hackles started to rise.

You didn't get to where I had in my business without learning to trust your instincts.

After what I'd discovered before takeoff, my instincts were setting off full fucking alarms.

I took a deep breath and pulled up the tracking app I had installed in every vehicle and every cell phone belonging to all Sigma International and Volkov Industries employees.

And yeah, I had the software on my wife's phone, too.

I'd apologize later for the invasion of privacy. It was hardly the first time, and it would not be my last.

Fucking sue me.

I'd never be negligent about my wife's security again.

"Fuck," I cursed aloud when both Mario and Meredith's phones pinged at the same location.

A location neither of them should have been at.

I dialed Mario's second in command, a man named Tom Fields. Tom's location was not showing up. Neither were the three men purported to be with him, nor their vehicle.

"What the fuck?" I growled, already moving for the elevator.

I called Darius first.

"I need everyone available to meet me at the address I just texted you—"

"Yes, Boss. What's going on?"

"Just tell Adrik and Marat what is going on. And I want you to meet me there."

"How many should I send?"

"As many as we have," I growled.

Thunder roared in my ears as I blurred out of the elevator through the garage to my SUV. My driver,

Edgar, hadn't even had the chance to start washing the thing.

"Boss?"

"Key! No time!"

I grabbed it and jumped into the front seat of the SUV, and I took off without him.

The mass text I'd sent had probably been delayed because the garage was underground. Even with my juice, Wi-Fi sucked in the garage. But he'd learn what was up soon enough, and he'd find his own way there.

I had no time to spare. Meredith was in trouble.

Hold on, Little Red. I'm coming for you.

CHAPTER FORTY-ONE
MEREDITH

few hours earlier...

A"There! That's the last box," I said to little Sammy, Ellie's son.

It wasn't unusual for residents of a shelter to be reticent about sharing their names, but Sammy was too young for that kind of subterfuge. After the first few days seeing me St. Elizabeth's, he'd lost his shyness.

"Sammy, what do you say?" Ellie chided, kneeling down to help her son look through the small box of toys I'd just set down in his new room.

The fantastic thing about this house was that each of the four floors, plus the attic where Ellie and Sammy were going to stay, were their own suites. My idea was to have single families, or two women without children, on each floor and each floor had its own entryway complete with a door and a lock that could only be accessed with a special code via the keypad.

I didn't know how the construction crew Josef hired managed it, but it was almost like they turned the home into an apartment building, keeping the hallway stairs separate from each floor.

That way, there would be privacy. No overcrowding. And most important, no fear.

The house was way off the grid. Josef's lawyers and the shelter's decided the best way to do this was if the company who owned the house did not bear the shelter's name.

I agreed.

I mean, even if an abusive ex had any idea his wife or girlfriend ran away to St. Elizabeth's, he would be hard pressed to find this place since it had no paper trail or obvious connection to the shelter.

I only hoped it would work out the way I'd planned.

In my experience, having a place to call home without the guards and the fear of being found was the best way for victims of abuse to return to any kind of normalcy.

Ellie and Sammy needed a place to heal, to grow, to learn to trust again. I hoped this was the place.

"Thank you, Mewedith," Sammy said, his little mispronunciation of my name positively adorable.

"My pleasure, Sammy. Oh, look what I found! I

think this little guy wants to play with some of your other cars," I whispered, pulling a shiny red toy car from my bag.

"A new car! Mommy, look!"

"Mrs. Aziz, you didn't have to do that," Ellie said, biting her lower lip.

"Please, I keep telling you to call me Meredith and it really is no big deal," I replied, watching the towheaded boy play on the carpeted floor.

"Meredith. Okay, I can do that," Ellie whispered. "Um, I just want to thank you so much. For everything. This means the world to me."

"Don't worry about thanking me. Let's just concentrate on getting you two well and fed. I am so sorry there must have been a mix up with the deliveries, but the guys will be back soon. And Mrs. Stevens, the caretaker we hired, will arrive tomorrow. Her room is on the first floor. She'll be living here full time," I said.

"Yep, I remember. I met her last week when she came to the shelter. And no problem about the groceries, I'm just so thankful we don't have to be in the city. It was confusing for Sammy," she said, clearing her throat. "Anyway, um, thank you so much."

Ellie nodded, blinking back tears, and I found myself doing the same.

"It's no problem, Ellie. You two are going to be alright. Now, I'm going to go see—"

My phone pinged, interrupting me, and I grabbed it, expecting an update from Josef. It was only four o'clock, and he wasn't due back for a few more hours, but I was hoping maybe they caught a good jet stream or something.

But it wasn't my husband.

"Is something wrong?" Ellie asked.

"Oh, um, I just got a strange text from one of the staff at my stepfather's estate. She says there is some kind of emergency, something about a possible gas leak, and she needs me right away," I muttered, trying to make out the confusing text.

"Maybe you should call?" Ellie suggested.

"Good idea," I replied, and tried the number.

"Hello? Hello? This is Meredith."

"Miss Merry, thank God! It's Gretchen Meriwether. Do you remember me? Um, I need you to come right away. You must come! There's been a—"

My heart stopped when she said her name. I had no idea Gretchen still worked there, if it was in fact the same maid who'd helped me run away.

Our connection was terrible, and I could barely understand a word she was saying. Before I could ask her to repeat it, the call ended.

"What happened?" Ellie asked.

"I don't know. It was one of the maids working at

my stepfather's house. The call dropped, but she sounded super upset."

"You mentioned you grew up near here, right? So the house is in Morristown? Why don't you go check it out?" Ellie asked, concern marring her features.

"I would, but no, I mean, I'm not leaving you until the guys bring back the delivery," I murmured, trying to redial the number, but it wouldn't connect.

I mean, they were just going for a grocery run, but I wouldn't expect Ellie to be okay with stranger men in the house. No way.

"Don't be silly, Meredith. You can leave. It's okay. We've met all the security guards before. Right, Sammy?" Ellie said, and I think she even rolled her eyes.

That was a good sign.

"Yep, Mommy! Mewedith, look!" Sammy said, racing his car back and forth.

"Wow, you are so good at that," I told the little boy, and for one moment I imagined what it would be like when or if Josef and I had children.

My heart squeezed and my mouth went dry. I never thought I would ever have children of my own, but I realized suddenly, I wanted them. With him.

That was probably a conversation I needed to have with my husband. I shook my head and glanced down at another message apparently from Gretchen. I didn't think it was politically correct to call her a maid, but my mind was blank.

She worked for the service that took care of Franklin Gray's estate and had since I was a child. I knew Josef had kept them on until I got around to clearing out the house and putting it on the market.

We were supposed to do it together. But then he got called away.

Whatever this gas leak emergency was, Gretchen sounded frantic, and not being able to get another call through was making me anxious.

Maybe Ellie was right. Maybe I should stop by.

It was only a few minutes away by car.

Sammy squealed and raced his cars across the carpeted floor. I lifted my gaze watching the way Ellie looked after him with a mixture of intense love and sadness in her eyes, it just made me want to cry.

It also made me want to beat the crap out of her ex.

Especially when I focused on her arm, still in its cast.

Thank goodness her eye was better.

Only the faintest yellow remained of the shiner she'd had when she first came to St. Elizabeth's.

"Meredith, we are fine. You have done so much for us, now I insist. Go see what is going on at your stepfather's estate, then go home! You work too hard, and your husband is coming back, right?"

"He is," I said, a smile teasing at the corner of my lips.

Ellie nodded. I liked seeing this side of her. The woman had grit. Sure, her husband did his best to beat it out of her, but there it was all the same. And I couldn't have been prouder.

"Alright, tell you what. You and Sammy stay up here. I gave you the codes to lock the door to this floor, and you can engage the lock until after the guys leave. I'll have Mario have one of them text you, so you know when they delivered the groceries, deal?"

"Deal," she said and grinned.

CHAPTER FORTY-TWO
MEREDITH

I took some convincing, but I finally got Mario to agree to drive me to my stepfather's place, just the two of us.

I really didn't want to wait for the other guys to return from the grocery store. Even though I used the fast pickup app, they were going to be at least another half an hour. And I wanted to get home before Josef got there.

Excitement pumped through my veins, and I bit my lower lip. One week was long enough without my husband.

It was funny, or not, depending on how you thought of it, but we'd been apart for fifteen years. I hadn't realized I'd been living a half-life in all that time without him.

Josef was like my own personal missing link. I needed him like I needed air and water and food.

He was the breath in my body.

My reason. My hope. My dream. My beautiful reality.

Christ, I loved that man.

"Everything okay, ma'am?" Mario asked.

"Do not call me ma'am. You make me feel like I'm a hundred," I said, trying my best to glare at my bodyguard.

"Yes, ma'am," he replied, a slight smirk on the corner of his face.

The fucker.

Mario was a good man, and I felt safe with him, but not like I did when I was with my man, of course.

Still, Josef had handpicked him to be my bodyguard when I left the condo, and I trusted my husband to do what he thought was best.

"The men just alerted me they are en route with the groceries," Mario informed me, and I nodded.

Good.

Ellie and Sammy would get a text when they left, locking the downstairs section of the house, and arming the security system. I voted against having an armed guard at the place.

Mrs. Stevens was a fifty-seven year old widow, an ex-marine who'd also worked for Sigma International.

She was more than capable of handling any security needs, and even better, she was a woman.

I knew from experience it would make it easier on the residents, well, *once I filled the other floors with more residents*, to have a female on site. Especially one with a background in security.

Mrs. Stevens would also manage the house insofar as toiletries, groceries, and what not. I'd set up a fund for such things. None of the women would have to worry about food or towels or the basics until they were ready to move on.

Even then, I had a system in place to help them continue their education, get a job, or move anywhere they wanted. As long as they felt safe to do so. But they were welcome to stay as long as they needed.

"Here we go—oh, I'm getting a message," Mario said, frowning at his phone.

"No worries, just find me when you're done," I told him and exited the vehicle.

He pursed his lips, and I knew he wanted to argue, but I was already on the move.

The quicker I found out what was going on, why Gretchen had called and messaged me so frantically, the quicker I could leave.

The house loomed ahead, and I shivered. It always felt so cold, so big when I was a child.

Everything looked the same.

The landscaping was immaculate. The structure itself, pristine. But that sense of bigness, of heaviness I used to feel as a kid whenever I came home to this place was replaced by something else.

It wasn't hatred. It felt more like regret.

My years working with abused women and children had taught me that I was not responsible for the failures of others. My mother's death was not my fault, and while I tried not to blame her for leaving me alone, I had every right to be angry about it back then.

But I wasn't so angry anymore. I was more sad.

For both of us. My mother was beautiful and wild, far too fragile for this cruel world and her sadistic husband.

I was just a kid. Not responsible for her transgressions in any way. I could forgive her for that, though. I could forgive a lot.

As for Franklin Gray. He was another story.

I did not want to replay the nightmare of when I left his house on the night of my eighteenth birthday.

I already did that when he'd begged me to see him a few weeks ago. The night he died.

I swallowed, fortifying myself as I walked up the stairs and punched in the key code.

"Hello? Gretchen?" I called out, walking inside the house.

Odd.

I knew Josef had told the staff to pack the common rooms. The parlor, the kitchen, stuff like that, leaving the personal items of my childhood bedroom and my mother's belongings for me to sort.

But as I walked further inside, it didn't appear like anything had been boxed.

In fact, there'd been no preparation at all to ready the estate for resale. I'd already planned to donate all the funds to my offsite project for St. Elizabeth's Shelter for Women and Children, of course.

There was no way I'd keep a red cent from anything that once belonged to my stepfather.

"Gretchen?" I called out again, turning when I heard a noise coming from the office.

I opened the door, steeling myself against any lingering feelings I might have against the place.

I hated Franklin's office. I always had.

But even readying myself to go inside, I could never have prepared for what I saw.

"It's Meredith. Are you in here, Gretch—oh my God!"

"Hello Merry, sit down."

"But you're dead," I whispered, shocked.

"That was an excellent trick, wasn't it? Sit. Down."

My stepfather had a gun in his hand, and he had it aimed right at Gretchen's temple.

Horror was replaced by fear, potent and real, as I attempted to back out of the room.

"Not another step or I will shoot her. Now, come inside, Meredith, and close the door," he commanded, cocking the pistol so I knew his threat was real.

I obeyed. I had no choice.

"I'm sorry, Miss. So sorry," the older woman blubbered, and Franklin hit her hard with the butt of his gun.

"Stop it!" I screamed.

Franklin sneered, and Gretchen faltered beneath the punishing blows. Blood gushed from her head wound, making me feel nauseated.

"Stay right there, or she dies. Then you'll be next, little Merry," he hissed.

I couldn't believe it.

He was supposed to be dead. But there he was. The man who haunted my nightmares. The one I once called Dad, who turned out to be not my dad. And he didn't look so dead to me.

Shit.

This was bad. Very bad. I wanted to get away. I wished I was anywhere but there.

I wanted Josef.

I wanted my husband.

Why did I come here without him?

"What do you want from me?"

"What do I want? I want my fucking life back, you little bitch! You gave that lowlife animal you married my company? He is nothing! I am your father—"

"You're not my father, remember? You are the one who is nothing. I love Josef. I always have," I said, lifting my face defiantly.

"Love him? You don't love him. You were a fucking child! You barely put down your dolls. I had plans for you, and you fucked it all up."

"You planned to give me to someone like I was just something you bought and could trade for favors!"

"I did own you! What was I supposed to do? Let this man come in and take you from me? I'm your father! You were supposed to do what I said!"

"The only thing you said that is even remotely true is you *were* my father. At least, I thought you were. You were supposed to take care of me. Not scare me. Not lie. Not slap me or call me names. I've spent my entire adult life in fucking misery because I thought Josef left me for money, but it was all you! You hurt me."

"I never—"

"Yes, you did," I shouted back. "Josef is the only man who has taken care of me. Not you. Never you! I was just a possession to you."

"You're just like your mother. You have no sense of

loyalty," he raged, and while he did, I got a really good look at him.

How had I ever been afraid of this weak, selfish, greedy little man?

Franklin Gray was a caricature of what a real man was. An exaggerated failure of a man.

But he was holding a gun, and guns were dangerous even when handled by selfish weaklings.

As if he realized it too, he waved the gun in the air, then aimed it right at me.

My time was running out.

I'm so sorry, Josef.

"Look, I don't know what you want me to do. You're the one who faked your death, what did you think would happen?"

"You were supposed to come home and save the company. When I found out who owned the note on Gray Corps, you could imagine my surprise. I thought maybe you would throw a piece of ass to your old flame, and he would relent. I didn't think you'd marry him! I was going to show up a few weeks later and we would have reconciled, Meredith. I'm not your father, but I raised you—"

"Nannies raised me. What you did was fucking deplorable!"

"Oh please, don't blow it up into something it wasn't. I didn't rape you, Meredith. I was drunk. I didn't know what I was doing. I barely touched you," he scoffed, shaking off the trauma his actions had caused, as if what he did was nothing.

"You don't get to tell me how to feel about something you did, understand?" I snapped, feeling angry and reckless.

This sonovabitch was threatening me, diminishing my feelings, telling me how I should think?

I didn't think so.

"Shut up! Just shut up! I have to think," he said, grabbing his head, pointing the gun up at my stomach then my chest.

I raised my hands and inched back towards the door, but he was back to aiming at my face.

"I can get you the company if that's what you want. Just let me go, and I'll send the paperwork," I said, trying to placate him.

Empty promises, all of them, but I really didn't want to die at the hands of a madman.

Not when I finally found my happiness.

"You were such a stupid little girl, and you're a stupid woman, too. You think I believe you? You think I don't know, you're going to run back to him, you fat slut," he screamed.

"He's not even here. He's away on business. I just need to contact the lawyers, they will do what I say."

"Bullshit. I read about your *husband*. Aziz is nothing

but a thug working for that fucking Volkov gangster. You think I'm a monster, you married the real monster!"

Fuck you, I wanted to say, but I bit my tongue.

You couldn't argue with crazy. I never realized it before, but Franklin sounded completely insane.

"Just let me go and you'll have the company back in your power in a few hours," I repeated.

"You're lying. This is all your fault. You're going to tell your husband and he's going to come after me," he spat.

Franklin did not look good. He might have faked his prior heart attack, but he was gray and sweating. Whether it was fear or whatever drugs he was on, he looked about three seconds from keeling over.

"You sure he's out of the country?" Franklin asked, and I nodded.

"Yes, he's—"

But the sound of the front door cut off anything I was about to say. Feet pounded down the hallway and someone yelled.

"Meredith!" a familiar voice shouted from outside the house, and I turned my head, relief filling me.

"Josef," I whispered.

"I knew it! You fucking lying bitch! Well, you won't get away with it this time," Franklin growled.

The door to the office flew open just as Franklin squeezed the trigger.

I had one second to react.

One second to say goodbye before I tried to move in front of the speeding bullet aimed at my husband's heart.

"Josef!"

CHAPTER FORTY-THREE
JOSEF

"**N**OOOOOOOO!"

The roar left my body the second I saw what she was about to do.

I had no time.

I raised my own gun, unloading it into that mother-fucker's body while shoving my beautiful wife down onto the ground and twisting us both so that I was covering her with my bulk.

Pain ripped through my side.

I didn't know if it was a clean hit. But I prayed I'd caught his retaliating rounds, and that my sweet Meredith was safe.

As long as she was whole, I didn't care what he did to me.

My team entered behind me. They had Franklin

covered, but I didn't ease off my wife, I didn't drop the still smoking pistol onto the floor, until they gave the all clear.

Then I was all over her. Turning her over and checking her for harm.

"Meredith! Baby!"

I frantically ran my hands over her body, searching for blood, wounds, anything.

Her eyes slowly opened, the green irises so damn beautiful I couldn't breathe for looking at them.

"Josef? Josef, are you hurt?" she asked, struggling to sit up, but I was in the way.

I clutched her to me, unashamed of the tears staining my face, as I held her tight.

"You're okay. You're okay, Baby. I got you," I said over and over again, kissing her head and her cheeks, then her lips.

"Boss?" Darius' voice interrupted our reunion, but I wasn't about to stop holding her for anything.

Hell, I was never letting her go again.

Never again.

"What?" I asked.

"He's gone. The woman is secure. What do you want us to do?"

"Baby, is there anything you want in this house?" I asked, pulling back long enough to see her shake her head.

"Burn it to the fucking ground," I growled, lifting Meredith in my arms as I stood.

She clung to me, tears streaming down her face. I turned my body, holding her tightly in my embrace, so she didn't have to see the gory mess that was all that I left of Meredith's stepfather.

That motherfucker.

I wanted to kill him all over again. Somehow, Franklin fucking Gray had faked his own death. I didn't put it together until the plane ride.

But I had no idea he was this close. I shouldn't have fucking bothered going home. I should have just hunted this prick down from the beginning. Should have demanded to see his body at the hospital—*the hospital?*

"Darius, find the doctor who worked on Meredith and that dead piece of shit. Bring him in," I ordered before stomping out to my car with my precious bundle in my arms.

I could have fucking lost her. Fuck. My arms started to shake.

"Husband, I can walk," she said, thinking I couldn't hold her.

But that wasn't why I was shaking. Fear had me trembling like a goddamn leaf.

"Like hell," I growled. "I'm never putting you down again."

She clung to me tighter, her lips brushing against my neck.

Mario walked behind us, on guard to make sure Franklin had no minions lurking about. It seemed the man was a psycho without an army. More fool him.

My wife's bodyguard was upset, rightfully so. But he had no idea the world of hurt that I was going to rain down on his careless ass for letting her walk inside that fucking house by herself.

Although, really, it was sort of my fault. When I sent the alert out to all my teams, it was encrypted and the moment he spent deciphering it had almost cost me everything.

But whatever.

I was still going to punch him in the fucking face. It was the least he deserved.

"Seatbelt," I said when I put her in the passenger seat.

She nodded, clearing her throat as she grabbed the buckle. That was when she noticed the red stain on her clothes.

"Josef! You're bleeding," she cried.

"It's nothing. A flesh wound," I grumbled, but she was already getting unbuckled.

"Baby, I'm fine. Get your seatbelt on. We're going home."

I punctuated the statement with a kiss. Sure, the

wound in my side was burning like hell, but I didn't give two shits. I needed to get my wife home.

I needed to reaffirm she was alright.

Uninjured. Whole. And mine. All mine.

And I needed to do that now.

Right fucking now.

CHAPTER FORTY-FOUR
MEREDITH

The drive back to Manhattan from Morristown was agonizingly slow.

Josef focused on the road, but I was a bundle of nerves. The stain on his shirt got bigger. I found a handkerchief and pressed it against the wound, and other than a flick of his gaze to where I touched him, he didn't even flinch.

He shifted the vehicle into park the second we reached the garage. Then he jumped out of the seat, opening my door before I even had the chance to get unbuckled.

One of his men was waiting there to take the keys, and more stood guard as Josef lifted me out of the SUV, refusing to put me down.

"The doc is waiting outside the front door, Boss," Mario said, and I wondered how he beat us home.

Then I saw the big SUV parked behind the one Josef had driven and I realized my bodyguard had followed us all the way back.

"Thank you, Mario," I said, and my husband growled.

I pressed closer to him, the move must have been the right thing to do, because he stopped his grumbling.

We got into the elevator. Mario and one more guard got in after us. But Josef still didn't talk.

"I want you to examine my wife," Josef told the doctor as soon as the elevator doors opened.

"No! You're the one bleeding!" I said, exasperated with this man.

I was hardly aware of who opened the door when Josef stepped through and placed me gently on the couch.

"Now," Josef said, and the doctor jumped.

I mumbled through the whole exam, aware the doctor was not touching me any more than necessary. I held my husband's gaze.

"Really, I am fine. Please see to my stubborn ass husband's wound," I said, angry and so over this man's highhandedness.

"Sir?" the doctor asked.

"Fine," Josef huffed, pulling off his shirt.

My mouth went dry.

Of course, I'd seen my husband's body before. I knew every curve of muscle, every line of ink that covered his frame. But every time I saw him, he still took my breath away.

Goddamn.

He was right. It was only a flesh wound, a scratch really, but it still needed cleaning.

The doctor moved with precision and speed, both of which I appreciated because Josef looked like a coiled snake ready to strike.

He wrapped the wound, placed a waterproof seal over it, and gave him a shot of antibiotics.

"Here is some extra dressing, but it should heal shortly."

"Thank you," I told the doctor, since Josef didn't look like he was going to.

He took an envelope full of cash out of a drawer I'd never noticed from the coffee table and handed it to the man.

Once he was gone, Josef turned to me. He took my hand, dragging me over to him, and the enormity of everything we'd just been through came crashing down on my shoulders.

A sob tore from my throat as I clutched at him, careful not to hurt him when I pressed myself to his naked chest.

But Josef was having none of that. He wrapped himself around me like an anaconda, and I reveled in the feeling.

"I'm sorry, Josef. I'm sorry I went there alone. I know you said wait—"

"No. It's on me. I failed. I failed, Baby. I am so sorry. It will never happen again."

"Stop it. You didn't fail. You saved me. You took a bullet for me," I murmured, my heart stuttering in my chest when I realized I could have lost him.

I clung tighter. Kissing him everywhere I could reach. Josef moaned, kissing me back.

"Need you," he whispered, brushing his lips over my cheeks, my nose, my chin, then my lips.

"Yes, yes, Josef," I said, needing him just as much.

"Bedroom," he growled.

He picked me up, and I wrapped my legs around his waist. I leaned back, watching him watch me with his soft whiskey colored eyes full of hunger and secret longings that I shared.

Christ. Jesus Christ. I love him so much.

I loved this man with every inch of my being. I never wanted to be apart from him.

I wanted to grow old in the shelter of his embrace. To live our lives in the fullest way.

I wanted his babies. I wanted his burdens. I wanted his happiness and his pain.

I wanted all of him.

"Meredith," he whispered my name, dropping me gently onto the mattress.

Josef undressed me slowly and with care, kissing every piece of me revealed as he slid my clothes off one piece at a time.

When I was naked and trembling, he stood and unbuckled his pants.

I licked my lips, needing him so damn badly. I slid to the floor, and his shocked gaze met mine as I took over, sliding his briefs down his tattooed thighs.

"Baby, you don't have to—"

"I want to," I said, knowing he wouldn't deny me.

Then I opened my mouth and wrapped my lips around the tip of his thick dick.

Moaning as I got my first taste of him in days. I opened wider, grabbing onto his hips as I bobbed my head, taking him as deep as I could.

"Fuck, Little Red, I've been dreaming of this," he groaned, cupping my head, and pumping his hips.

He was a big man, and it was hard, but I tried my best and was proud of my efforts when he rewarded me with his praise.

"Goddamn, Baby. That's it. That is fucking it. Suck my cock, Little Red. Make me feel good," he grunted.

Tears rolled down my face as I gagged on his dick, but I wanted more. I needed more.

When he tried to pull back, I covered the hand he had on my head with mine, forcing him to push down harder.

"Fuck, Baby, I'm gonna come. Are you ready?"

I wanted to answer, but I couldn't. I could only prepare for the first rope of cum to fill my mouth.

Satisfaction and desire warred within me as my husband's pleasure ran down my throat.

Yes, I was on my knees before him, but I felt like a queen while I swallowed.

"You're so fucking good, Baby. Fuck," he groaned, and flexed one more time before pulling himself out of my mouth.

His eyes looked feral as he stared down at me for a heartbeat before pulling me up and crushing my mouth under his. He didn't seem to mind, I still tasted like him as he pushed his tongue between my lips, kissing me so deep I felt it in my core.

My pussy was dripping with need. My little clit throbbing for attention. And he knew it, too. He grabbed my ass, squeezing with both hands before slapping one cheek. Hard.

"Get on the bed, Little Red. It's my turn to eat."

CHAPTER FORTY-FIVE
JOSEF

I fell face first into my wife's pretty pink pussy and it was the best fucking thing I'd ever experienced.

Well, maybe having her suck the life out of me on her knees was tied with it. But whatever.

I had a lifetime to compare the two.

Yes. Fuck.

I could spend forever just worshipping at her altar. She was such a beauty. Back arched, tits bouncing with each breath she took, eyes closed tight, mouth opened in a silent scream, and her long, red hair billowing behind her like a sail.

So fucking hot. So sexy.

I couldn't help it. I had to own her. Every fucking inch needed to be possessed by me.

Mindless with need, with love, I thrust my tongue inside her pussy. I moaned as her hot little channel squeezed me tight.

Using my thumb to strum her little clit, I fucked her on my face, swallowing every drop of her sweetness.

A long, drawn out moan spilled from her lips, and I wanted to pound my chest like a fucking warrior. But I needed more. I needed her to come on my cock.

Sliding up her body, I notched my dick at her entrance, my hand wrapped around her neck.

Every time I looked at Meredith, desire stirred deep in my gut, my heart quickened, and my breathing became choppy.

"Husband, please," she said, her small hands gripping my sides.

I pushed inside, feeling every shudder and tremble of her body. Fuck, she was perfect.

That cocoa butter scent of hers wrapped tight around my heart, and it was impossible for me to stay still.

Her tits bounced with every thrust, and neanderthal or not, I had to admit just to myself, that missionary was my favorite way to fuck my wife.

She was so wet for me. So hot. And I felt like a god. That this woman wanted me so much was a gift. That she loved me was a fucking miracle.

I didn't deserve her. But I was keeping her. I was

never letting go. And if I had to fuck her into submission every day to remind her who she belonged to, well, I looked forward to the challenge.

My balls tightened. I was gonna come. But I needed her with me.

Fighting against the need to bust inside of her, I pushed a hand between us, rubbing her needy clit. She whimpered, scratching me with her nails. I hissed, liking the bite of pain.

It was all so good. Everything about her was so good. Her scent. Her moans. Her headlong responses to me. So good. Almost too much.

"That's my, Good Girl. Feel me pushing inside you. We're one now. Open those sexy fucking legs and take it. Take me. Take all of me," I grunted, moving to my knees.

I pulled on her hips, lifting her ass so she was almost sitting on me as I fucked her deeper, harder, increasing my speed.

Her sweet, soft body jiggled with every move, and it was so fucking hot.

Perfect. Gorgeous.

"Come for me, Little Red. Squeeze those tits, touch that clit, and come for me," I growled. "Right fucking now."

Her hands scrambled to do my bidding. Juices from

her wet cunt seep down, drenching my cock, and fuck, it makes me want to come.

I watched my wife. One hand pinched her nipple, twisting it, and the other was rubbing her tight little nubbin.

My gaze was riveted to the scene, blazing with hunger as I fucked her and watched my sweet Meredith fall apart in my arms.

"Husband! Fuck, I'm gonna," she yelled a split second before her pussy contracted, sucking the cum right out of my balls.

I came so hard I was almost catatonic, crushing her into the mattress. But I was too damn stunned to move. Every time with her just got better.

I turned my head, needing to taste her again. Kissing her was like coming home. She was everything I ever needed in my life and still, she was so much more.

"I love you," she whispered against my neck.

I tried to say it back, but all that came out was a sort of grumble. Meredith giggled. Her warm breath tickled my skin where it touched me, and I smirked.

She was so fucking cute.

"Think that's funny? You reduce me to ogre-like grunts, and then you laugh?"

"I mean, it's a little funny, Babe," she said, and I smiled.

Did she just give me a nickname?

I mean I had the Big Bad thing, but that felt more like work. Sure, she called me Husband, and I liked it. But her calling me Babe was something else. And it warmed me.

"So pretty in pink, my Little Red," I whispered, brushing her hair across the rose pink sheets with my fingers as I moved to the side of her.

She hummed a sweet sounding noise and cuddled into my side.

For the first time in days, I felt complete. My heart constricted inside my chest, and I dropped another kiss on her forehead.

"What are you thinking about?" she asked softly.

"You. I'm always thinking about you," I confessed.

It was true. This woman took up all the available space in my brain. I tightened my hold.

"Good," she replied. "I'm always thinking about you, too."

"You are?"

I felt her nod against my chest and pride filled me. That she even thought about me at all was more than I could have ever hoped for. I mean, I knew she loved me. But this was more than love.

What I felt was an all-consuming need. Marat and I sometimes teased Adrik about his obsession with his wife, but from what I saw the younger Volkov was just as bad with his woman.

Now that I had Meredith, I knew. I'd become acquainted with the nature of obsession fifteen years ago. Now, it was more like we were on intimate terms.

Oh yeah, obsession and I were good fucking friends.

And I had a feeling, things were only going to get worse.

Or better.

I settled on better.

"What are you thinking about now?" she asked, a mischievous grin on her face as she lifted her head and cupped my balls with her hand.

Fuck. Me.

My dick twitched. I was already getting hard again, and the need to be inside her filled me.

"I'm thinking, you better kiss me, Little Red."

Then I gripped her behind the head and pulled her face to mine so I could claim that sweet fucking mouth.

Goddamn.

She was so hot. So sexy. So primed for me. Always so goddamn wet for me, I moaned as I pulled her astride my ready body.

Her wetness soaked my shaft as she slid up and down, flexing her hips. I grabbed her ass, sliding one hand between her legs and using her own slick to coat her pretty little puckered hole.

"Gonna fuck this ass soon, Baby," I told her.

I sat up, lapping my tongue across her tits before I

moved on to her mouth. Meredith rose to her knees, and I grabbed my dick, putting it at her entrance.

"Sit on me, Baby. Claim me with your wet little cunt," I commanded.

And she did. Fuck, yes. She impaled herself on my dick.

"Now ride me, Little Red. That's it, fuck yourself on my dick. Good Girl."

I watched her obediently swivel her hips, grinding her pussy against me. She gasped, her eyes widening, and something inside me burst with victory.

This woman fit me. She was mine. Sure, I was a fucking monster. The Big Bad Wolf. But she was my Little Red.

And together we were better.

I almost laughed at my moniker. Some Big Bad Wolf I was. One little redheaded woman brought me to my fucking knees.

She made me tremble. She made me ache. She made me dream and desire.

I wanted to tell her how much I loved her. I wanted her to share in this spark of feeling that was growing inside me as each day passed. And I would.

Right after my sexy Wife made me see fucking stars.

"Husband. Josef. My love," she moaned.

Her orgasm rocketed through her, sending me over

the edge, too. And I fell, willingly, willfully, and forevermore.

To think I'd started this thing to seduce Meredith out of vengeance when I was the one who wound up utterly entranced by my wife.

There wasn't one thing I wouldn't do for her. To keep her safe. To make her happy.

"I love you, Wife."

Meredith sighed against me, and I cherished her in that moment. Having her so alive, so soft and warm and in my arms was everything I ever wanted.

She was all I wanted. And so much more.

CHAPTER FORTY-SIX
MEREDITH

Days passed, and Spring turned into Summer since the incident with my stepfather.

The insurance company ruled the fire an accident and with Josef's encouragement I poured that money right back into the shelter.

A few days after the ordeal, I read a news article about the doctor who'd worked on my stepfather, and me that time I'd passed out in the boardroom with Josef.

Apparently, the doctor had been mixed up in some unsavory business dealings with a couple of men you really didn't cross.

Evidence of drug dealing, money laundering, tampering with medical files, and more had been found on his home computer.

The police had him under investigation, but he'd committed suicide before they could arrest him.

The article detailed the doctor's death and injuries, and I wondered how he managed to hang himself with both hands broken.

But when I asked Josef he shrugged it off and I was happy to leave it at that. I didn't want to spend any more of my time thinking about Franklin or anyone connected with him.

I had other things on my mind. Better things. Like my crazy amazing husband who bit by bit was making all of my dreams come true.

I couldn't believe it when Josef explained he'd actually bought out the non-profit and had one set up in my name.

I was now the head of the St. Elizabeth's Shelter for Women and Children. Yes, I kept the name. I figured it was one people knew and trusted.

I'd already started headhunting for the best people to run each shelter, since I was determined to open several more locations across the country, as well as more offsite housing options.

"Okay, here goes," I mumbled, dropping my proofed sourdough inside the preheated Dutch oven, wearing the extra-long silicone oven mitts my husband ordered for me after I burned myself last week.

I'd never seen Josef so mad over nothing. It was a silly little burn mark on my arm.

Not even an inch wide.

But he rushed me to the doctor—*a brand new female one he had thoroughly vetted*—and had me examined like I was made of spun glass or something.

Okay. I kinda liked when he was ridiculously possessive and protective of me.

I mean, he was so caring with me, so loving and attentive, it was hard not to believe how much he loved me.

Which was fine because I loved him just as much.

"Little Red?"

Speaking of the Big Bad Wolf, I mused and turned to face him.

"What are you doing home so early?" I asked.

I was smiling, so it was hard to pretend I wasn't happy to see him. And I kinda sorta had to admit I loved his nickname for me. I mean he had a few, but I loved how he called me Little Red.

It had nothing to do with my hair. And everything to do with him being the Big Bad Wolf, and his insatiable appetite for me.

Josef wandered closer, grabbing my waist and dragging me against his body.

"Adrik mentioned today was the day you three

decided to have your bread party. I came home to help," he said and kissed me quickly.

He looked over my head and frowned, noting the convection wall oven was already on.

"I guess you beat me to it," he said, humming deep in his throat.

It was difficult not to react to that noise. The rumbling was so sexy, it had the most predictable effect on me. I'd scold him for distracting me, but really, why bother?

"I'm sorry, I would have waited, but I didn't know you were coming," I said, my voice breathless.

"I see. So, how long till it's ready to be uncovered?" he asked.

I shouldn't have been surprised that he was already acquainted with the method of baking.

All the vlogs said sourdough should be covered for the first forty-five minutes to an hour, then uncovered for the rest of the baking time to crisp up the crust.

"An hour," I whispered, practically panting.

"I know how we can spend an hour," Josef said, biting on his lower lip as he dragged a hand down my body, cupping my ass.

The shorts I had on were just for the house. Loose and comfortable, they left nothing to the imagination.

Also, I didn't have on any underwear, so when he

slid his hand between my thighs and found only my bare sex, Josef groaned.

"No panties? That's it. You're gonna pay for that, Wife," he grunted, bending down, and hefting me over his shoulder.

"Josef!" I cried out.

I gasped, clinging to him. I was caught between shock and primal need. His big hand came down hard over my ass cheek.

The sting was immediate, but he soothed it with tender caresses from his fingertips as he brought me to our room, dropping me on the mattress with a hard bounce.

I tried to scramble away. I knew he would never hurt me, but it was only natural to run when you were being hunted.

The blazing look in my husband's whiskey colored eyes left no doubt I was being hunted. And by my very own Big Bad Wolf.

Normally, I'd say if he was lucky, I was going to let him catch me. But really, it was the other way around.

When, *not if*, Josef caught me, I'd be the lucky one.

"Naughty Girl, walking around up in here with no panties on when I'm not home," he growled, grabbing my ankle, and flipping me on all fours.

"Sorry, Husband. W-what are you going to do?" I whimpered.

"I'm going to show you the consequences for parading around the house with my pussy practically bare when I'm not home, Wife."

Josef grabbed the material between my legs, pulling it away from my dripping wet heat, and the sound of my shorts tearing echoed in the bedroom.

Fuck.

That was hot.

But not as hot as the feeling of my husband's tongue licking me from slit to asshole.

"So delicious. So fucking good," he growled, kneeling behind me. "But you don't get to come on my tongue yet, Little Red."

"No?"

"No. Teasing me like that. I shouldn't let you come at all," he said, pushing every inch of his glorious dick inside my channel one at a time.

"Please, Josef," I begged, needing more from him.

He grunted, dragging his thick cock out of me, and pushing back in so damn slowly.

"Beg me, Wife. Beg me for more."

He put one hand around the front of my neck, lifting me, so I was kneeling with him. I clutched behind me, grabbing at his pockets for balance.

Holy fuck.

He was still dressed. Just his dick was free, and he was using it to torture me with his long, slow thrusts.

"Please, Husband. Fuck me harder. Make me come, please," I begged.

I had absolutely no shame where he was concerned.

"Good Girl. You asked me so nice, I'll make you come, Baby. I'll make you come all over this dick."

And he did.

Twice.

EPILOGUE ONE
JOSEF

Sourdough Sundays were a regular thing now.

It was already late June, and the sun was shining down on the stone tiled patio behind Marat's new mansion.

The beach sat just beyond the wrought iron gate, accessible by a staircase which was equipped with another gate on the bottom and the best damn security system money could buy.

I should know.

My company designed and installed it. Not to mention the half dozen men that were always on site, circling the grounds and keeping everyone safe.

Sofia, Destiny, Meredith, and even Ellie and her son Sammy sometimes joined in on these weekly get-togethers with Adrik, Marat, me, and even Andres.

The star, of course, was the bread. Ellie was something of an expert and after the first few tries and failures, she'd given a sort of mini demonstration of how to build an effective starter and how to bake actual bread.

I wouldn't tell Meredith, but her first few attempts were like crumbly, flat, dense rocks. As much as I loved her, I ate every fucking bite, of course.

But the bread was much better now. It started right after Elie delivered her tips and pointers, and I was forever fucking grateful to her for helping Meredith, Sofia, and Destiny.

As were Marat and Adrik.

Seriously, we were looking at stock options for the pharmaceutical companies that made antacids with all the damn hard sourdough we were eating.

At least there were other options at these gatherings, too.

I mean, *man could not survive on bread alone* or whatever the fuck that saying was.

Each week, the women baked and tested, complained, and pouted, and sometimes cheered over their varying degrees of success. And each week, one of us—*I was talking about the husbands, the men*—took turns with the cooking.

Adrik grilled. Marat sauteed. As for me, well, I

sucked at cooking, but I could place a catering order like a motherfucking pro.

I got teased a little about not actually making anything, but no one was complaining today, I noticed with pride.

I grinned as I looked at the veritable Italian feast I'd ordered from Fiorino's Deli. Their fresh mozzarella was some of the best I'd ever had.

Platters of cured meats imported from Italy, fresh and aged cheeses, containers of salads, pickled vegetables, sundried tomatoes, hot peppers, olives, and more covered the table.

Next to all that deliciousness was a basket of homemade sourdough bread. And one focaccia that was made by my wife.

It was fucking amazing. The best thing on the table in my not so humble opinion.

She'd drizzled olive oil and sea salt on top and added fresh rosemary sprigs before baking. For someone who claimed instant noodles were the only thing she could make, Meredith was turning into quite the little baker.

Pride oozed from every pore when I thought of my wife.

Amazing woman. My better half in every possible way.

Whoever came up with that saying was a real genius.

Anyway, it was a great lunch. And surprisingly, I was having a great time. Go figure.

Great food. Great people.

My favorite part, of course, was feeding my Wife bite by bite from my plate until she was full. She was digesting now with her friends, and my heart contracted inside my chest as I watched her laughing.

It was all so domestic.

So very Brady Bunch.

Especially for an ex-ops guy who ran a security firm and sometimes still got his hands dirty.

I grinned.

Now that I had Meredith in my life, with my ring on her finger, I had to admit, I didn't mind domestic.

Not one bit.

In fact, I had plans to discuss just how domestic my wife wanted to get. Watching Michaela and Lucy run around Marat's backyard gave me all sorts of ideas about my Little Red, swollen with our baby.

Fuck.

She would be such a wonderful mother. Meredith was the most caring person I knew. She'd look gorgeous pregnant and later nursing a baby.

But I still didn't know how she felt about it.

Maybe it was time I asked.

Meredith was sitting in the corner of the lone, sectional, outdoor sofa with all the other women, just sipping her red wine and lemon-lime soda spritz that Destiny made her, sharing stories, and simply being.

Her happiness was contagious. I needed to be near her, so I stood up and ambled over, ignoring Marat and Adrik.

"You owe me twenty dollars," Adrik told his brother.

"No way. I said he would break first," Marat argued.

"Did not. You said *I* would break first," Adrik growled.

Fuckers, I thought, shaking my head.

"No way. Andres, what was our bet?" Marat called to Andres who was building a racetrack with Sammy.

"Marat pay Adrik," Andres said, shaking his head.

I placed my hands on my wife's shoulders. The pink silk blouse she wore felt cool beneath my palms, and I was glad she was comfortable.

"Hey, Babe," she said, her pretty green eyes smiling at me. "Wanna join us?"

"Would I be interrupting?" I asked, hating to infringe on girl time.

"Not at all," Ellie answered when Meredith seemed frozen in her stare.

I returned her smile and sat beside her, careful to situate myself on the other side of my wife, so I was on the end of the sofa and not near any of the other women. It wasn't that I didn't like them, but I knew how possessive the men were of their wives.

As for Ellie, the younger woman was always a little wary whenever any of us got too close. Knowing her history, I understood, and tried to make myself as still and small as possible.

"You having fun?" I whispered in her ear, wrapping my arm around her shoulders.

Meredith hummed and leaned into me, and I kissed her temple.

"Yeah. I really am. Thank you."

"You never have to thank me, Wife."

"Maybe not. But I will. So just say you're welcome," she chided.

"You are most welcome, Little Red."

My eyes were all on her, but I saw Adrik and Marat snuggle up to their wives in the periphery of my vision.

I never thought I would see the day those two formidable men would find happiness, but they had.

And it dawned on me I was just like them. Or maybe they were like me.

Once upon a time, I had no one and nothing.

No job. No money. No family. No friends. No woman.

But now, I had everything.

And she was right there in my arms.

The sound of a child squealing with laughter filled my ears, and I turned to see Andres tossing Sammy in the air and catching him before falling to the grassy patch of earth where they were playing.

"Sammy!" Ellie called his name, the young mother rushing to make sure her son was unharmed.

Andres' eyes burned as he watched her check the boy over, then nodded as he ran to play on the next thing with Lucy and Michaela, with one of Marat's staff watching over them.

I turned away from where Andres was trying to speak to Ellie, focusing instead on the children. And I snuggled my wife closer.

"Do you want children?" I asked the question.

She was quiet for so long, I didn't think she heard me. Then she turned her head, and I saw her eyes well with tears.

"What is it?"

"I was trying to figure out a way to ask you that question," she confessed.

"I want whatever you want, Little Red. Whatever you need. Whatever you say. I'm yours, Baby."

Her smile was like the sun coming out all over again, and I almost forgot to breathe when faced with her beauty.

"Well? You gonna leave me hanging or what, Wife?"

"Yes. My answer is yes. I want it all. A house. A child. And you. Most of all, you. I want it all with you, Josef."

"You give me so much. And I'm gonna give you

anything you want," I replied, and pressed my forehead to hers.

I was so overcome with emotion it was all I could do not to break down. I just held on to my beautiful wife and let her love and color seep into my soul, anchoring me.

She was too good for me.

But she was mine now.

And that position was permanent.

EPILOGUE TWO
ELLIE

tupid, bossy, know it all, dumb man!

Ugh.

I was so pathetic, I couldn't even curse him out in my own head!

But who did he think he was?

Andres Ramirez. Recently made partner in Volkov Industries. Certifiable genius, according to Meredith, who happened to impart the information after she saw his IQ test results.

So what if he was single? And sexy. And nice to small children.

Oh my God! Stop that!

I tried not to listen when Mer, Sof, and Des chatted about their men and Andres since he was part of their inner circle.

I had my own problems.

One very big, very scary problem to be precise.

My now ex-husband—*the divorce papers came through while I was at the shelter, thank God*—was demanding alimony from me and visitation with Sammy.

My sweet four year old son.

I was so mad I could spit. But I would give him money if it meant keeping him away from Sammy. But he wouldn't back down.

All Gary Peters ever wanted was Maxwell Mining.

He never wanted me.

And he never wanted the child he'd purposely gotten me pregnant with, thinking it would make him the next heir to my father's business.

Little had he known, my father never believed a girl could run his company.

Dad set up procedures to sell the company when he died, which all went into action eighteen months ago when he passed away from a sudden stroke.

That was the first time Gary hit me.

Like an idiot, I stayed.

I didn't really understand what happened. He was angry when they read the will. He called me names. He said I was worthless.

Told me he never wanted a *frigid little bitch* for a wife and that he only knocked me up so he could get his hands on the company.

And that was the first time I tried to leave him.

Afterwards, he begged, he cried, he apologized. I faltered. I gave in.

But he did it again.

Like most abusers, Gary was not really sorry. He blamed me for all his problems.

The last time he hit me, when he broke my arm and bruised my eye, he'd been going towards Sammy's room with his belt in his hand.

I couldn't let that happen. I covered my son's door with my body, and when Gary tried pulling me off, that was when he broke my arm.

The black eye was from his belt. A little bit to the left of that bruise was the scar I would carry forever, just where my hairline met my left cheek.

It was from where the heavy buckle connected with my skin, breaking it, and causing me to bleed.

Here's a fun fact in case you didn't know, head wounds bleed a lot.

Gary saw all that blood, saw me fall to the floor, and he ran, giving me the opening I needed to get me and Sammy away from him.

Thank God.

Knowing he'd tried to hit my son with that belt buckle was all I needed to get out of there.

I was dumb for waiting. But I couldn't be dumb anymore. For Sammy's sake, I had to be smart.

I grabbed everything I could, and I ran straight to the shelter I'd seen on a billboard once when walking Sammy to preschool.

I had to pull him out early. But that was okay. We both needed time to heal. The mental scars were the worst, but with Meredith's help and some serious therapy, I was doing much better.

I was starting to like myself again. To trust myself. But this last bit of news from my ex was too much.

I was never going to allow Gary access to our son.

No, I didn't have the kind of clout necessary to make him go away, but I knew someone who did.

I hadn't told Sof, Des, or Mer about what happened after Andres escorted me and Sammy home after our *Sourdough Sunday* lunch just before Labor Day.

It was almost Halloween now.

I hadn't told anyone how I let Andres carry my sleeping son up the stairs that late afternoon.

Mrs. Stevens had been on an errand, and the rest of the house was empty.

For the first time in a long time, I wasn't scared to be alone with a man. And no, I was not coerced in any way.

In fact, it was me who'd started things.

All me.

I'd cornered Andres in the living room of our little

makeshift apartment where a sofa sat against one wall, and I kissed him.

A lot.

On the mouth. On his biceps. Those sexy pecs. The tattoo he had of a full moon on his side.

I kissed him everywhere. Then, I had sex with him. And it was good.

Really good.

Better than I'd ever had, actually.

And ever since that Sunday when it happened, I just couldn't stop thinking about him and all the things we did.

The feel of his hard body as he took me exactly like I needed him to. The way he seemed to worship me with his sea foam colored eyes. I wasn't sure what color they were. Sometimes they seemed blue, other times gray.

Andres was simply the sexiest damn man I'd ever laid eyes on.

Having intercourse with my ex was, well, it was dull and embarrassing. Sometimes painful. Truth was, I never came with Gary. Not ever.

But with Andres, I didn't even have to touch my clit.

He made me come so hard it was like his body knew exactly where and how to touch mine.

Holy cow, I saw stars that night.

Despite all that, I didn't return any of his calls or his texts. I just couldn't. I mean, what kind of person had sex with a virtual stranger when she was living in a woman's shelter?

My therapist said I shouldn't judge anyone, especially not myself, for my actions.

But it was hard not to.

Sammy was my focus. I needed my son to be safe.

I shouldn't be thinking about sexy men, or how good their dumb big cocks felt inside me.

Oh my God.

He felt so good.

Shut up, Ellie.

Fine.

Ugh.

I was a big, fat coward. And not because of my size sixteen ass. Because the size of my cowardice was even fatter than my ass.

Pfbbbt.

But I needed help.

And he was the only person I could call. It was time to eat crow, even though I had no appetite for it.

Shit.

EPILOGUE THREE
ANDRES

My phone buzzed, and I ignored it.

Weeks had passed, fucking weeks since I'd been inside Ellie Maxwell, and ever since, I felt like I was losing my mind.

I was impatient. Ornery as fuck. Short-tempered. And I couldn't sleep for shit.

Ellie. Ellie Maxwell. Why won't you let me in?

No, I wouldn't use her piece of shit ex's name when I thought about her.

I'd been putting in sixteen hour days, doing everything I could to stop myself from hunting her down.

There was something about her. Something untamed and wild behind her eyes. Something I wasn't sure she even knew about herself.

But I recognized it as something special.

She called to me like a siren's song.

Attracted me like no one else ever had.

I knew where she was. I knew exactly where that fine as fuck woman parked her sweet ass every night.

But what kind of fucking animal would I be if I stalked a woman on the run from her abusive ex?

That motherfucker.

I growled and tried to focus back on work. Ellie was none of my business. Neither was her ex.

She obviously wanted nothing to do with me.

Well, nothing anymore.

Thinking back to the amazing sex we'd had in her living room, against the fucking wall, half-dressed, and panting—*fuck!*

My cock was uncomfortably hard just from the memory, and I wanted her all over again. I wanted more of her soft skin. More of her sweet sighs. More of her fiery passion.

The attraction between us wasn't normal. From the first time I laid eyes on the woman with the pixie cut and the enormous hazel eyes, I was a goner.

She had this sweet persona that I had no doubt was real. But that was only half the story.

When she pinned me to that sofa and fucked me with glorious abandon, I saw a side to Ellie I never suspected existed beneath her snug blue jeans and peasant blouses.

She was dominant. Demanding. Confident. And sexy as hell.

I'd been dreaming about that night ever since.

There wasn't another force on earth that called to me with the same powerful pull as my attraction to Ellie.

Life dealt her a rough hand, but that just made her perseverance even more spectacular.

She was one in a million.

Ellie might have an abusive ex, but she was not a cowed woman.

She just didn't know her own strength. And fuck, I wanted to be the man to see it when she finally understood how powerful she really was.

My phone rang again, and this time I stopped and looked at the screen.

Unknown Caller?

My heart caught in my throat.

Fuck. Ellie. Sammy. Did something happen?

"Hello?" I asked, my heart pounding.

Meredith, Josef's wife, outfitted all the women who came through her shelter with untraceable burner phones, which meant Ellie had one too. And she was the only person with an *Unknown Caller* ID who had my phone number.

I'd made sure of it.

"*Andres? It's me,*" she said, her voice sounding tinny through the cheap phone.

"Ellie, is everything okay?"

I closed my eyes, forcing my pulse to stop racing. If something was wrong and she called me for help, I would give it.

No matter what.

"*Yes. Well, not really,*" she said.

"Which is it? Do you need me to send a security team?"

I already had my other phone in my hand, ready to send a team from Sigma over to make sure she was safe.

"*No, no. Um, I was wondering, would you, that is, if you don't have anything better to do,*" she mumbled.

I could almost picture her cheeks burning red as she tried to work through whatever she was trying to ask me.

Curiosity about why she called warred with pride that she'd come to me with a problem at all. But curiosity won out. I wanted to know what she needed help with, and if it brought me into close proximity with her again, I was all for it.

"Ellie. Spit it out."

"*Would you be willing to marry me?*"

Well. Shit.

Whatever I thought she was going to ask, I wasn't expecting her to say that.

"Oh my God! I'm being dumb. I'm sorry. Um, forget I said—"

But before she could spiral, I cut her off.

"I'm coming over," I said, clicking end call, before jumping out of my seat.

This wasn't the kind of thing you talked to someone about over the phone.

My heart thudded inside my chest, and that wild attraction, the insane pull I felt towards Ellie was stronger than ever.

It seemed to increase with every inch as I moved closer and closer to her.

I'd never considered marriage before. Hell, my mother was always yelling about how the Ramirez line would end with me if I didn't find a girlfriend. I loved my mom. She was awesome.

It was too soon to say if I loved Ellie. But I was attracted to her. I wanted her. And when she asked me to marry her, my instinct was to say yes.

It was always good to follow your instincts, wasn't it?

EPILOGUE FOUR
MEREDITH

The cool fall breeze lifted the fallen leaves and sent them swirling around my legs as I walked across the backyard of the home we recently remodeled in Long Island, closer to Des and Sof, and therefore, closer to Marat and Adrik.

They were Josef's chosen family, and they were mine now, too.

I smiled as I placed my hand on my still soft abdomen. We'd been trying for months, and finally, I had some good news to share with my handsome husband.

I'd wanted to cook something for him. But since the only thing I was getting any better at was sourdough bread, I'd ordered some Szechuan delivery.

It was too early for cravings, but I never met a fried

noodle or rice dish I didn't like. Biting my lip, I tried to imagine what he would say when I told him.

Having a child was such an enormous responsibility, the weight of it came crashing down on me.

I stilled, leaning against the stone fence that surrounded our yard and sucked in a breath.

Panicky moments were normal.

At least, I thought they were.

I mean, I'd never been pregnant before, so how could I really know?

After all the pain and the mistakes of our turbulent past, I was so ready to move on to the next stage of our lives together.

These past few months with Josef were better than I could have ever hoped. He gave me more than I'd dreamed.

He called me his color, his Little Red. He said I brought the sun back into his life. But what he didn't know was he did the same thing for me.

"Hey, didn't you hear me calling your name?" Josef asked gently and wrapped his arms around my shoulders.

He pulled my back flush against his chest. I jumped at first, exhaling when I recognized him.

Then I slumped back, allowing him to bear my weight, but careful of the new ink he was sporting on his chest.

My sexy as fuck husband had tattooed an anatomically correct heart wrapped in pink ribbon right above where his real one beat solidly beneath his breastbone.

God, I loved him.

"Sorry, I was daydreaming," I replied, turning my head for a kiss.

"The food you ordered arrived at the same time I did. Mario brought it inside for us. Come on," he said and took my hand in his much larger one.

I knew he was still pissed at my bodyguard, but I told Josef it wasn't his fault, and he relented, allowing the man to stay.

Although, I admit he looked like he'd had some sort of accident right after the whole incident with Franklin —*the man I no longer called my stepfather.*

It was time we put all the ghosts of our past to rest. Time we looked towards the future.

We walked in silent comfort across the backyard, and I smiled at the red, yellow, and orange splashes of color the leaves made dancing across the dry grass.

"You always remind me of the fall," Josef murmured.

"Do I?"

"It's your gorgeous hair. Those eyes, That smile. My color," he said, kissing my hand.

"But how do you feel about summer?" I asked, biting my lower lip.

"Summer? Why?"

"Around June third, to be more specific," I said, pausing before we went inside.

"The third? What are you—wait," he said, eyes dropping to my softly rounded belly that was not showing any signs of the life we'd created yet.

It was far too soon for that.

"Josef?" I said his name, uncertainty creeping in.

Then he dropped to his knees, his arms around my waist as he cried against my stomach, dropping kisses on it and whispering things I could barely make out.

"Baby, a baby, you're giving me a baby," he said over and over again.

Then he stood up, taking me with him and spinning me around.

"WE'RE HAVING A BABY!!"

"Josef!" I laughed and clung to him, knowing he'd never drop me.

He stopped, allowing me to slide down his body.

"Are you serious? Are we having a baby?"

"Uh huh," I said, nodding and cupping his handsome face with my hands.

I pulled him down for a kiss.

"I love you so much, Little Red."

"I love you, too."

"We're going to be such a good family. Fuck the people who should have been there for us. We're going to be there for each other. Our family. Us. Ours. With the people we choose to let into our lives and our kids' lives."

I openly sobbed then. He was right.

So right.

Any misgivings I had about being a good parent, or a good wife dissolved beneath Josef's steady praise and constant love.

Yeah, we would have ups and downs. Everyone did. But we would get through them because that was what families did.

They supported each other and rallied for one another.

Josef was the family I chose. He was the man I wanted by my side forever. I knew it fifteen years ago, and I knew it now.

"You give me everything, Wife."

"I love you, but you're wrong. You're the one who gives me everything. I love you so much," I said, and he crushed his mouth to mine.

"Come on, Little Red. You're eating for two now, and we've got cartons full of goodness inside."

"Sounds like a date. Hey, does that mean you're going to try to seduce me after dinner?" I asked, allowing him to carry me inside our home.

"Date nights usually end in seduction, Little Red. Don't worry, after you eat, I get to eat, too," he growled, and nipped my earlobe between his teeth.

Shivers ran down my spine, and I hummed my response.

It was a good thing I married the Big Bad Wolf and that he was as insatiable for me as I was for him.

Josef Aziz was my whole heart.

I didn't regret a thing about our lives now. Everything happened the way it was supposed to. It led us right to this point in time.

I was so happy, *so full of happiness*, I hardly had room to breathe in any air.

"Breathe me, Little Red. Just breathe me."

Then he kissed me, and I did. I breathed him in and took him deep into my heart and my soul.

That was where I'd keep him always.

T*he end.*

Did you enjoy this contemporary romance book?
Please consider dropping a line or two in a review so other readers can enjoy it, too.

Look for the next book in the series, His Wild Attraction, featuring the prince of acquisitions, Andres Ramirez, and the wildly beautiful, Ellie Maxwell.

Want more Wild Billionaire Books? Visit my website for

more: https://www.cdgorri.com/series/wild-billionaire-romance
Thank you and happy reading!

del mare alla stella,
C.D. Gorri

P.S. Indie authors like me count on word of mouth to get my books seen, so if you have a blog or a social media account and you want to post about my books, be sure to include #cdgorribooks so I can see it and I will share to too.
THANK YOU.

His Wild ATTRACTION

A WILD BILLIONAIRE ROMANCE 4

USA TODAY BESTSELLING AUTHOR
C.D. GORRI

LOOK FOR JERSEY BAD BOYS COMING SOON!

Merciful Lies by C.D. Gorri

Lies can be merciful. It just depends on the why.

Anna

I knew the second I saw him, my life would change forever. When my brother offers me as payment to Nico Fury, the king of the Vipers, how can I refuse? Tattooed, built, and tall, he was the only man I saw when I walked into the room. It was like he occupied all the available space, sitting on his throne of blood, sweat, and lies.

Nerves assailed me, but I owed my brother too much to let anything happen to him. One night. That was all. But it would leave me wrecked. Actions always had consequences. Six months later, my brother was killed by a rival organization, and now they were after me. There was only one place I could go to keep my unborn baby safe. I just hoped the king would be merciful.

***

Nico

Perfect things didn't exist, at least not in my experience. But she was pretty close. I had her in my bed for one night, and I couldn't shake the memory. No, I wasn't meant to keep soft things like Anna Keller. My life belonged to my crew, and we were a vicious group. Hell, we weren't called Vipers for nothing.

But she was different. She made me want, and I loved and hated her for it. Anna was light in a world of constant darkness. She was all warmth and beauty like no other. And I craved her like a drug.

Six months had passed since I took her in return for clearing her brother's debt to me, but that man attracted trouble like honey did flies. It wasn't long before I learned Sam Keller had gotten himself killed. Less than an hour later, Anna came back to me, on her knees, asking for sanctuary.

I knew the moment I saw the swell of her stomach she was carrying my baby. Anna thought coming here would protect her, but she was walking right into the Viper's nest. Before I was finished, my little runaway would be begging me for mercy.

Merciful Lies is the first in the contemporary romance series of connected standalones, Jersey Bad Boys. This series features familiar tropes such as enemies to lovers, forced proximity, arranged marriages, secret babies, and contains some violence and explicit scenes.

ALSO BY C.D. GORRI

Contemporary Romance Books:

Cherry On Top Tales

Her Yule His Log

His Carrot Her Muffin

Her Chocolate His Bar

Wild Billionaire Romance

His Wild Obsession

His Wild Temptation

His Wild Seduction

Jersey Bad Boys

Merciful Lies

***

Paranormal Romance Books:

Macconwood Pack Novel Series:

Macconwood Pack Tales Series:

The Falk Clan Tales:

The Bear Claw Tales:

The Barvale Clan Tales:

Barvale Holiday Tales:

Purely Paranormal Romance Books:

The Wardens of Terra:

The Maverick Pride Tales:

Dire Wolf Mates:

Wyvern Protection Unit:

Jersey Sure Shifters/EveL Worlds:

The Guardians of Chaos:

Twice Mated Tales

Hearts of Stone Series

Moongate Island Tales

Mated in Hope Falls

Speed Dating with the Denizens of the Underworld

Hungry Fur Love

Island Stripe Pride

NYC Shifter Tales

A Howlin' Good Fairytale Retelling

Witch Shifter Clan

Young Adult/Urban Fantasy Books

The Grazi Kelly Novel Series

The Angela Tanner Files

G'Witches Magical Mysteries Series

Co-written with P. Mattern

Witches of Westwood Academy

with Gina Kincade

<u>Blackthorn Academy For Supernaturals</u>

<u>*Be sure to check out my BUY DIRECT BUNDLES</u> and get 30% off when you buy available only my website.

Click here for The Official C.D. Gorri Reading List - free download

ABOUT THE AUTHOR

USA Today Bestselling author C.D. Gorri writes paranormal and contemporary romance and urban fantasy books with plenty of steam and humor.

Join her mailing list here: https://www.cdgorri.com/newsletter

An avid reader with a profound love for books and literature, she is usually found with a book in hand. C.D. lives in her home state, New Jersey, where many of her characters and stories are based. Her tales are fast-paced yet detailed with satisfying conclusions. If you enjoy powerful heroines and loyal heroes who face relatable problems in supernatural settings, journey into the Grazi Kelly Universe today.

You will find sassy, curvy heroines and sexy, love-driven heroes who find their HEAs between the pages.

Wolves, Bears, Dragons, Tigers, Witches, Vampires, and tons more Shifters and supernatural creatures dwell within her paranormal works. The most important thing is every mate in this universe is fated, loyal, and true lovers always get their happily-ever-afters.

In her contemporary works, you will find fiercely possessive men and the smart, confident, curvy women they are crazy about. As always, the HEA is between the pages.

Thank you and happy reading!
    del mare alla stella,
    C.D. Gorri

http://www.cdgorri.com
    https://www.facebook.com/Cdgorribooks
    https://www.bookbub.com/authors/c-d-gorri
    https://twitter.com/cgor22
    https://instagram.com/cdgorri/
    https://www.goodreads.com/cdgorri
    https://www.tiktok.com/@cdgorriauthor

Milton Keynes UK
Ingram Content Group UK Ltd.
UKHW012001140524
442726UK00003B/30

9 781960 294487